An Engagement with the Enemy

An Engagement with the Enemy

Castles & Courtship Series

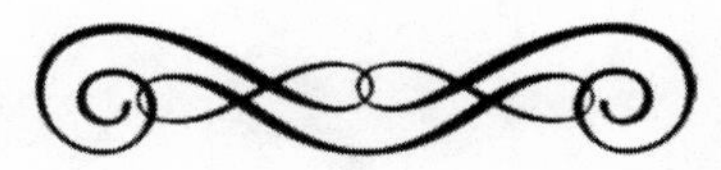

Sally Britton

Edited by Jenny Proctor

Cover Design by Ashtyn Newbold

Created with Vellum

Dedicated to Jenny Proctor:
Thank you for helping me polish the words until they shine.

The rules of fair play do not apply in love and war.

— JOHN LYLY, *EUPHUES: THE ANATOMY OF WIT*

CHAPTER ONE

The morning sun filtered through the stained-glass windows of the library, dappling the floor with colorful shapes that danced across the carpet and the pages of James Aldwick's open book. He lounged in an overstuffed armchair, one leg draped over the armrest as he let his mind wander through the world of a novel by Sir Walter Scott.

Yesterday, a certain lady had caught him reading the book and threatened to tell him the ending, as she had already completed reading it. James momentarily glowered at the page with that memory.

Fortunately, not even his sworn enemy, Miss Westcote, possessed the audacity to ruin the end of a good book. Why his sister's best friend had determined herself to be a thorn in his side since her infancy, he couldn't say.

The sound of someone clearing his throat came from the doorway, and when James swung his gaze that direction, he immediately dropped both feet to the floor. His father stood there, dressed in his customary deep blue frock coat and cravat. The corners of Baron Retford's mouth turned down in disapproval, likely over finding his son in such a lazy pose.

"Must you lounge about like an uncouth vagabond?" His father's clipped tone made James inwardly groan. His father didn't usually begin a conversation with a correction. Unless the rest of his chosen subject matter had to do with one particular matter. An heir's duty and responsibility.

James straightened and set the book aside. "My apologies, Father. How may I be of service?" He kept his tone neutral and his expression respectful.

Baron Retford's frown deepened.

"We have had this conversation before, and it is high time something is done. Your duty is to this family. You must settle down and choose a wife."

James swallowed a sigh. This again. His father had been after him for months to find a suitable bride, though James had no intention of marrying some naive girl barely out of the schoolroom, likely with more pedigree than wit if his father had his way.

"There are many fine ladies who would make a worthy match," his father continued. "What happened with Lady Anne in April, while we were in London? She has a generous dowry, and her family's status would reflect well on our own. We should invite her to the castle this summer."

At this, James could no longer contain a grimace. Lady Anne was as dull as she was vain, caring for nothing but the latest fashions and increasing her collection of admirers.

His father's gaze sharpened. "Do not scowl so. I expect you to treat all ladies of quality with courteous attention."

Courteous attention. James swallowed a biting retort. He had no desire to waste his summer trotting after females in hopes of an alliance. He wanted more than that for himself.

But he held his tongue, offering a stiff nod instead. "As you wish, Father."

If he placated the baron enough, perhaps he would gain a few more weeks before the subject came up again.

"Good." The baron went to the stained glass, looking through a green pane with a somewhat relieved expression. "Because your mother and I have decided it is time you took your future more seriously."

A sense of unease settled in his stomach, hinting at what might be in store. He had an intuition, a sense that he could anticipate what awaited him. And it was unpleasant.

"We do not think it wise to wait until the next Season to begin your hunt in earnest." Baron Retford spoke more to the window than he did his son. "Your duty is to restore the reputation of this family."

James's attention fell away as his father continued a lecture he'd heard many times before.

Their family name didn't actually *need* restoration, to James's way of thinking. Though his father had been born illegitimately, he'd been legally recognized before he'd reached his majority. He carried his father, the fourth baron's, name and had inherited all his lands and wealth.

He'd even successfully petitioned Parliament and the Crown to restore the title that had died when his father, the fourth baron, had passed on. They'd made John Aldwick the First Baron Retford. The title hadn't been continued but remade.

Something that had seemingly caused James's father to feel less than equal to his peers.

"...I will not have you wasting away your days in frivolity—"

James interrupted. "Frivolity? Father. I am reading a book. I do not go about our little village gambling, carousing, or courting actresses. For one thing, none of those activities are available to me here." He tried to keep his tone light. Tried to bring his father back to reason with humor. "Considering I do not take part in such things even in London, and at the height of the Season, I cannot think it just for you to accuse me of frivolity."

His father glowered at him. "You are not taking this conversation seriously."

"I'm only eight and twenty. Many men of our rank do not marry until thirty or older."

"Most men do not have a family scandal to erase from history." His father pinned him with a hard look. "And it is time to move forward with your life. Your mother and I have a plan."

James gritted his teeth. "A plan? For what?"

"For your future. Your marriage." His father came closer and bent at the waist enough to bring him eye-level with James. "What do you think of this: a series of house parties, balls, and outings, all summer long, with invitations sent to every young lady of quality—and her family, of course—to attend? You will meet eligible, unmarried women here, without the pressures of London's social schedule, and have their full attention. You will see how they fit into life at Amoret. One of them is bound to suit you."

James slowly came to his feet, leaving his book in the chair behind him. "You expect me to endure the spectacle of women being paraded through our home, hoping that by some chance I may find a suitable match among them to marry? Everyone invited will see through the ruse of a house party and know precisely what you intend. What lady will agree to such a display? This is a terrible idea."

His father's chest puffed up. "Invitations have already been sent—"

"What?" James stiffened, but his father ignored him.

"—and we have drawn up a schedule, a calendar, of events and plans. Not only for the castle, but for the village. We will host a fair, races, and your mother has plans to bring in actors."

"You did all this without consulting me first?" James asked, pushing a hand through his hair.

His father drew himself up to his full height, still three inches shorter than James's six-foot frame. "Have I need to consult you before planning entertainments at my expense?"

"When the entire goal of said entertainment is to procure a wife for your son, one would think the son worth consulting." James moved away, dropping both hands to his side and trying not to curl them into fists. He'd ignored the lectures too long, it would seem, if his father had moved to the desperate point of planning what would amount to a search for a bride, bringing willing ladies to the castle to act as the quarry to James's reluctant hunt.

"James," his father snapped, and James turned to see the dark frown on his father's lined face. It wasn't anger he saw, though a stranger might mistake the wrinkles in the baron's forehead as impatient furrows and the flat set of his mouth as a warning. James knew better. "The guests are invited. We are doing this for the good of the family. And for you."

No, his father wasn't angry. He was *worried*. And getting older. A grandson and heir would no doubt ease his mind about the future of Castle Amoret and the title.

James's shoulders fell. He didn't have the heart to argue. What was done was done. "I understand." He took in a deep breath. "I will do what I can to ensure our guests enjoy their time at Castle Amoret."

"Thank you, son." Apparently satisfied, and perhaps realizing any further conversation would be detrimental to the already precarious calm, Baron Retford took his leave.

Try as he might, James couldn't escape the truth that his aging father simply wanted to see him settled and secure before he passed. When viewed in that light, the baron's plans seemed almost thoughtful, even in their misguidedness.

James waited until his father's footsteps receded down the corridor before collapsing back into the chair. Marriage and duty. Always his father's refrain.

James yearned to live as he chose, unburdened by the demands of society and family. But as the eldest son, he had obligations he couldn't ignore, no matter how he chafed against them. With a sigh, he picked up his book again, but as he stared at the page, the words blurred together. He could not stop thinking about what this would mean for his summer. The idea of being paraded before a bevy of eligible women left a bitter taste in his mouth.

Glancing at the stained glass again, he studied the shift of light on the carpet. For a moment he allowed himself to picture a different life, one where he chose his own bride and followed his own passions rather than duty. Yet the next instant he thought of his mother's hopes, his sister's dependence on a settled line of inheritance, and the stability his marriage would bring to both. His future wasn't the only one at stake.

He shook his head with a rueful smile.

Daydreams would get him nowhere.

Setting the book aside, James stood and straightened his coat. He would play the part his father required and smile through the coming parade of eligible young ladies, even if he held no hope of finding one he could truly call a match.

He would spout pleasantries, engage in meaningless conversation, and endure the entertainment his mother had arranged. He would smile and play his part, concealing his bitterness behind a mask of cheerful obligation.

With grim resignation, James steeled himself and left the library, along with his personal wishes, behind. What choice did he have but to endure what he could not avoid? This was yet another duty to tick off his list, another thing to suffer in silence. And then, with luck, it would be over.

CHAPTER TWO

As the day unfolded, the countryside came alive with summer's simple pleasures. It was for this reason that Jessica Westcote most enjoyed her afternoon rides with her friend and neighbor, Catherine Aldwick. Everything around them, from birds to the long-stemmed wildflowers, was vibrant and bright. Summer called to a part of her soul in a way no other season could.

Endless meadows, resplendent in deep shades of green, sprawled all around them, creating a tapestry of lushness that stretched as far as the eye could see.

Jessica Westcote's gelding pranced beneath her, his muscles rippling beneath the sunlight. The wind tousled her sun-bronzed curls as she rode alongside Catherine. Their voices carried on the breeze as their horses effortlessly navigated the familiar paths through the rolling hills. The rhythmic clip-clop of hooves echoed in harmony, as if the horses themselves were in tune with the two friends.

Sometimes, Jessica envied her friends' classical beauty,

with delicate features in her softly rounded face. Her skin was quite fair, and as prone to freckle as Jessica's was to darken to brown. Catherine also had the good fortune to have soft brown eyes. Jessica's own eyes were a shade of gray that reminded her of a drizzly rain and did little to compliment her hair which was an indeterminate color between brown and auburn.

"Isn't the sunshine lovely?" She tipped her face upward toward the sky. "I love the summer."

"Spoken like someone who has never had to endure a freckle." Catherine shuddered and adjusted the brim of her riding hat, the very thought of freckles enough to make her concerned.

Jessica tried to reassure her friend. "Perhaps they will one day come into fashion."

"I find that most unlikely."

"Yet you attempt to give me hope that one day my particular oddities will be admired," Jessica reminded her. Her nose was longer than she liked, but she supposed it looked well enough in her oval-face with its too-noticeable cheekbones.

She didn't have the gentle curves that made her friend's gowns drape perfectly at bosom and hip.

No. Jessica had always been stick-straight, with sharp elbows and knees, and a bosom that made the local seamstress sigh with pity before she suggested stays with padding beneath them to *create the illusion of fullness*.

"Stranger things have been popular. Think of that painting in my mother's withdrawing room of the woman with the wig half as tall as she was." Catherine placed a hand to her temple in sympathy with the women of the past. "Can you imagine the headache that would cause?"

"My father blames the French for all fashion atrocities."

Catherine giggled. "Ah, the infamous French!"

Jessica grinned back at her friend before she put her nose in the air. "He cannot resist launching into lengthy tirades about their outlandish fashion choices and their insatiable appetite for conflict. It's as if he believes the French invented both the fashion plate and the battlefield!"

If Catherine didn't adore Jessica's father nearly as much as Jessica herself did, she wouldn't have laughed so much. Even though Mr. Westcote had a few oddities about him, he was well respected by his neighbors.

With a brightness in her voice, Catherine said, "I cannot imagine being forced to wear such a thing. I feel sorry for the poor maids who had to arrange those hairpieces."

"Speaking of maids, I must tell you the most lovely piece of gossip mine told me yesterday." Jessica nudged her horse closer to Catherine's side, a mischievous glint in her gray eyes. "It sounds as though all the servants are whispering the tale."

Catherine's hazel eyes widened with anticipation. "Then you mustn't keep me in suspense. What did you learn?"

Leaning in conspiratorially, Jessica lowered her voice. "It seems our butler, Mr. Riley, has been exchanging secret glances at church with none other than your housekeeper, Mrs. Turner."

Catherine gasped, a hand flying to her chest. "No, you cannot be serious! Mr. Riley and Mrs. Turner?" She giggled. "They have known each other for ages. And they must both be near fifty. Do people of their age even know how to flirt? Is that not a skill lost with time?"

"I doubt it. I think a romance between them a rather sweet idea. Especially since I have seen them together." When her friend gave her no more reaction than raised brows, Jessica continued, "I caught them whispering by the kissing gate yesterday."

The kissing gate was one of two points where their families' properties connected, and Jessica had always loved it. The structure of the gate created a secure passage for people while maintaining a barrier for animals.

The narrow opening, between two sturdy fence posts, accommodated the width of a single person, encouraging one to proceed one at a time. The gate itself required a gentle push, allowing it to move within a restricted range. As the gate swung open, it cleared the way for the individual to pass through, while simultaneously creating a temporary barrier that prevented animals, such as sheep or cattle, from entering.

Catherine's voice dropped to a hushed tone. "Do you think there's a romance blossoming between them?"

A knowing smile played on Jessica's lips. "I do hope so. Mr. Riley is such a kind man. He has looked after our family for decades, and everyone on the staff respects him."

Catherine's expression brightened with excitement. "Imagine, a romance unfolding right under our noses. How thrilling! We must play matchmakers and ensure they have a chance to express their true feelings."

Jessica laughed, shaking with laughter at her friend's ridiculous idea. "That would be terribly meddlesome of us. And if something went wrong? I cannot think of hurting either of them. Your Mrs. Turner is a lovely woman. I think the two of us ought to keep our scheming to the usual things. Planning parties. Confusing our families. Leaving strange gifts in people's homes."

With a put-upon expression, Catherine groaned dramatically. "Do not even speak of parties to me at present. My mother gave me an itinerary for the summer. The *whole* of the summer. Every week we have a new guest coming to the Castle. It is as though my mother decided the country too dull and she is trying to bring all of London Society to us. The guest lists she spoke of sound horrid. Half the people she invited are snobs."

That sounded unusual. And Jessica hadn't heard word of such an invitation reaching her home yet. It was also difficult to imagine their little village being overrun with guests more used to London and its distractions. Though she'd never been to London, she had heard a great deal about it, especially from Catherine. "I know your mother enjoys entertaining, but why go to such extremes?"

"I haven't the slightest idea," her friend admitted, pursing her lips. "But I am most annoyed by her sudden fervor. You will be invited to everything we do, of course. In fact, I quite expect you to spend your every waking moment at my side. How else will I get through it? You will come, will you not? I made a copy of my mother's schedule, and I will send it over directly if you say yes."

"Of course I will come. You are my dearest friend. Not even your dreadful brother keeps me away." Jessica's expression contorted into a subtle grimace, her lips curving downwards involuntarily at the mere mention of James Aldwick. Memories of her childhood flooded back, the vivid recollections of a time when James had delighted in making her life a misery. His mischievous teasing and horrid pranks had been the bane of her existence, causing frustration, irritation, and even moments of anger.

"He isn't nearly so terrible anymore," Catherine reminded her. "I cannot understand why the two of you keep this feud alive."

Jessica resisted the urge to scoff.

"Not so terrible?" Jessica repeated. "Only last week he loudly insulted my favorite novel within my hearing, knowing full well I'd been deeply moved by the story."

While James had stopped his childish tricks by the time Jessica turned eighteen, the frustrations of their younger years still lingered whenever she saw his smug face. Like the time James put a lizard down the back of her dress in the churchyard when they were children, making her yelp in front of everyone while her governess tried to free the poor creature.

His mischief had made her blood boil even then...but it had also lit a competitive fire within her that spurred her to meet his tricks with pranks of her own. Like a skilled duelist, she had honed her ability to return his shots with equal measure, volley for volley. A part of her suspected both of them derived some perverse pleasure from their lifelong feud, like dancers who knew each other's steps so well they couldn't stop performing.

"He was in a foul mood this morning," Catherine said, tone suddenly thoughtful. "When Mama was telling us everything she wished to accomplish before the first guests arrive. They are coming this Tuesday."

"That is less than a week away." Jessica raised her eyebrows. "I haven't heard a whisper of this before."

"I have the feeling Mama meant for it to be a secret until now. Apparently, she has sent orders to York for most of the supplies needed at the Castle." Catherine continued explaining all that her mother had told her about the preparations for a ball, of all things, less than a fortnight away. Jessica listened, feigning mild interest, but her heart raced within her chest as her friend spoke.

All those people, in their little town? Balls, fetes, musicians, and even a theatrical troupe coming later in the summer? She had never been part of such spectacles before. She'd never traveled far from home. Never even to York, their nearest town of note. Her father didn't much like travel. He found comfort in familiar surroundings and familiar people. And she'd never gone away. She'd never had the opportunity.

She often wondered what she'd been missing. Perhaps now, she would finally find out.

As Catherine spoke about her mother's plans, Jessica looked out over the endless meadows spreading out before them. Somehow the lush, green fields seemed to reflect the opportunities awaiting her - if only she dared reach for them.

Jessica turned back to her friend with a smile. "You know, this sounds like this could be quite the adventure for us."

Catherine chuckled. "An adventure indeed! Though I suspect it will require a great deal of patience."

"True." Jessica nodded. "However, adventures are not measured in comfort, but in growth."

She thought of Mr. Riley and Mrs. Turner, and the small romances that could blossom even in familiar places. Turning her gaze skyward, she watched the feathery white clouds drift by overhead—a reminder of how fleeting time could be.

Jessica faced her friend once more. "It seems we have a choice—we can either endure what lies ahead or embrace it for the opportunities it may bring."

Catherine grinned. "You sound quite wise today, and I feel rather childish for being so annoyed. Very well. Whatever my mother has planned, we'll face it together."

"Together." Jessica echoed her friend's smile.

They turned their horses back along the familiar path home. Jessica tried to hold on to this simple joy of the present moment - the freshness of the countryside in summertime, the pleasure of her friend's company.

And yet, she could not help wondering at the possibilities unfolding in the distance, beckoning her forward with the promise of new experiences and growth. The future awaited, ready to reveal itself one day at a time.

CHAPTER THREE

"My goodness. Lady Retford outdid herself," Mr. Westcote murmured into his daughter's ear. They had stepped into the Armory, one of the oldest rooms in Castle Amoret, a room Jessica had known as well as she knew those of her own household.

Yet she barely recognized it.

"It's stunning," she whispered, her gaze sweeping across the room. Her pulse raced at the sight of so many people crowded together, the noise of laughter and conversation filling the room. The heady scents of perfumes from both people and flowers made her chest constrict.

Jessica hadn't attended a gathering this large in years. Because there hadn't been one like it in ages. Which had given Jessica a sense of relief, that these things didn't happen all the time. Yet even with the uncertainty a gathering such as the ball caused in her thoughts, she had looked forward to it. Told herself it would be the highlight of her summer, if not the whole year.

She barely remembered to continue forward when her

father did, her hand tucked through the crook of his arm. They'd arrived late to avoid a crush in the corridors, so the family's reception line had already disbanded, and they mingled now among the guests.

She distracted herself from the sounds and the people by casting her gaze around the room, trying to take in details amid the visual and auditory clamor.

Everything sparkled, from the crystals of the chandelier to the newly installed parquet floor with veins of mica in the marble. White and silver ribbons festooned the walls, making the medieval coats of arms hanging in their usual places look like fruit growing from elegant vines.

The footmen were stationed at regular intervals between windows, and they wore livery with silver buttons. Their shoes were polished enough to reflect light from the flickering candles in nearby wall sconces.

"Perhaps we ought to hold a ball of our own," her father said, his smile teasing. But when she met his gaze she saw the concern in his eyes, the silent question. Was it too much? The crowd, the noise, the press of all her senses at once—was it too much? He covered her hand on his arm, giving it a reassuring squeeze.

He lowered his voice when he asked the question out loud. "Are you well?"

Jessica tried to reassure him. "Of course." She wouldn't tell him that her hands grew damp within her gloves, that her heart had sped faster and faster as she looked about the room. Instead, she would devote herself to counting her breaths. Slowing them. "Merely surprised by the display. Can you imagine the work the servants must have put into this? I wonder if it took days or hours to prepare."

"Weeks to plan, days to set up properly," a bright voice

said from behind them. They both turned to find Catherine Aldwick grinning like an imp. Her brown eyes were dark in the candlelight, and her chestnut hair shimmered with pearls. "I cannot recommend the experience, though the outcome is lovely enough, I'll grant you."

Mr. Westcote nodded his agreement, his gaze reluctantly leaving his daughter's. "Beyond lovely. Will all the festivities held at the castle this summer be similarly elegant?"

"Most likely." Catherine laughed merrily, her cheeks pink and her eyes dancing with amusement. "My mother has never been happier. I think planning such extravagant entertainments has given her more vigor than any tonic ever could."

"It would exhaust me," Mr. Westcote admitted freely. His eyes met Jessica's again. "Shall I leave you to enjoy the evening?"

With Catherine present, Jessica gave a firm nod. "Yes, Papa. Thank you."

He gave Jessica one last squeeze of her hand, then released his daughter's arm. "Two young ladies ought to enjoy every moment of a night such as this. I am off to find old men to speak of politics and our shared dislike of the French. I hope you enjoy the evening, Jessica. Miss Aldwick. If these younger gentlemen do not keep you occupied in dancing all evening, I will be sorely disappointed in them. You are both quite lovely tonight."

"Thank you, Papa."

"Thank you, Mr. Westcote."

"Send for me if you need me, daughter." He reassured her with one last smile before he withdrew.

Catherine tugged Jessica away from the door, guiding them along the wall. Avoiding the knot of people in the center of the room. "Papa had all the old knights moved out of doors, along the garden walk. They have been propped up and made to hold torches."

"That must be a sight." Jessica glanced toward the open doors that led to the outside, a sudden longing for fresh air overtaking her. "Even the one-legged knight?"

They spoke not of real knights, of course, but of empty suits of armor that had stood guard in the room currently filled with guests.

"Even poor old Sir Hop." Catherine led her friend along the wall, the two of them nodding to the other guests for the evening. Most were known to Jessica. They were neighbors and friends, the people she had grown up seeing at village fetes and in the old church pews. As that realization settled in her mind, the tightness in her chest relaxed.

"The Armory Room makes a splendid ballroom," she said, raising her eyes to the thick beams that ran from east to west on the ceiling. How many celebrations had been held here, when it was a hall full of living knights and women with bell-like sleeves and wimples covering their long, loose hair?

Catherine hummed her agreement. "Papa tried to complain of the expense, of course. But Mama reminded him of some sort of bargain they struck when they began all this nonsense." She looked out over the crowd, a small frown marring her enjoyment. "They insist that James spend all his time with Lady Emily. I had thought they would push me to befriend her."

Having spent most of her time with Catherine the past week, Jessica had met the guest in question. "I suppose you see the reason for it as well as I do. They are hoping he shows matrimonial interest in her."

"James?" Catherine issued a snort that somehow managed to sound ladylike. "He has ignored everything they have said about marriage for the better part of two years. Though I suppose you could be right. Dear me. Why didn't I think of that before?"

"You have been quite overturned by the preparations for this event. I should not wonder that the idea didn't take hold until now. They have brought the lady to him since he refuses to find one himself."

"It makes perfect sense. Though why no one tells me of these things beforehand is a mystery."

Jessica's gaze returned to the center of the room, where a tall figure stood, greeting guests with a tight smile. "How is your horrid brother accepting his place as the reluctant Romeo?"

If Catherine was soft and round, her brother was square and stretched. The siblings shared dark hair and eyes, but little else. He was tall. Angular. With a noble nose bent in the middle from a childhood break, a high forehead, and a divot in his chin that he hated. He'd once told Jessica she resembled a stork with her lanky limbs and pointed nose. She'd retaliated by comparing him to an unfortunate scarecrow after a windstorm.

Catherine was staring at her brother, too. "Now that you've mentioned it, he has behaved rather oddly. It's quite the spectacle to witness his struggle to dedicate his time to a lady while resenting such a commitment."

James had outgrown the awkward years of stick-like arms and clumsy movement. Jessica, on the other hand, hadn't changed much. A pity, really. The circumstance left him with all the fodder for tormenting her that he'd had since childhood. Whereas she had to grow more inventive in their verbal battles.

She spotted Lady Emily at James's side. Jessica hadn't

found the youngest daughter of an earl a friendly sort, though she didn't dislike her, either. Lady Emily had a list of accomplishments that included the ability to speak seven languages. Yet from where Jessica stood, Lady Emily appeared reluctant to say a word in any tongue to the man holding his arm out to her, likely to lead her in the first dance of the evening.

"Are you dancing tonight?" Catherine asked abruptly, drawing Jessica's attention back to her friend.

Here, a curl of worry went around her heart again, but Jessica steadfastly ignored it. She loved dancing. So long as she knew her partner. Standing up with a stranger for a quarter of an hour or longer was her very definition of torture.

"As often as I'm asked." She nudged her friend's shoulder gently. "I am surprised you are not already spoken for."

"I am, in fact." Catherine looked away, her eyes searching the room before landing on a gentleman weaving his way through the other guests toward them. "Mr. Hammond has asked for the first set."

Jessica shook her head at her friend's ability to attract gentlemen. That aspect of Catherine's life she did not envy. Not in the least. "He stepped on my toes at the assembly. Mind your own if you hope to dance again this evening," she advised with an exaggerated wince.

Mr. Hammond arrived a moment later and bowed to them. "Miss Aldwick. Miss Westcote. I have come to claim my partner." He was a kind gentleman, only three years their senior at eight-and-twenty. One of James's gentler friends. And he stood to inherit his father's estate someday. Catherine would be content in his company for the quarter hour they spent dancing together.

As they joined the couples forming two rows to dance, Jessica made her way to the open doorway, to peer out at the gardens lit by torches. They were a lovely sight, flickering in the darkness, beckoning her to escape into fresh air and friendly shadows. She pulled in a deep lungful of air, quieting the rising agitation in her mind.

"Jessica, my dear. Why are you not dancing?" Lady Retford had found her, and Jessica embraced the woman after performing a respectful curtsy. The baroness returned the affectionate greeting. "And you look so lovely, too. Have I seen you in that dress before?"

"Yes." Jessica turned in a circle to show the gown off. "Last Christmas. It is one of my favorites." It was an ice-blue gown that almost persuaded Jessica's eyes to turn the same shade, in the right lighting.

"Beautiful, as always." The baroness gestured to the room full of people. "You ought to be out there, letting everyone admire it as you dance." The concern Jessica had seen in her father's eyes appeared now in the baroness's. Few people were privy to the way such events could play with Jessica's peace of mind. The baroness was one of them.

Jessica laughed, pretending she didn't see the gentle worry in the lady's eyes. "Everyone here is quite familiar with the sight of me, I assure you." She moved the conversation toward complimenting the room, the music, and the baroness's own excellent taste in fashion. They spoke together throughout the course of the first dance, and then the vicar's son engaged Jessica for the length of a single *Galop*.

With eager anticipation, she stepped onto the polished floor, feeling the rhythm of the music glide through her veins. The world around her faded into a blur as she gave the whole of her attention to the movement of the dance.

The vicar's son was safe and young. She knew him well.

Dancing near Catherine, Jessica sent her friend more than

one knowing grin as they wove themselves through the formations and steps required of them. The vicar's son, only twenty years of age, managed not to step on her feet, but concentrated too closely on the steps to make conversation. She didn't mind.

The music wrapped around her like a warm embrace, its melodies guiding her movements, which she executed with an instinctive grace. For her, dancing wasn't about finding a suitor or fulfilling societal expectations; it was a celebration of life, vibrancy, and joy. With each skip and spin, she felt a surge of exhilaration, a rush of pure bliss her everyday life didn't often bring her.

When Catherine came close again, she spoke barely loud enough for Jessica to hear her, saying, "At least we're having a good time. Look at poor Romeo."

A mischievous glint sparked in Catherine's eyes as she nodded down the line. Jessica turned in that direction, curious. There he was, as artful a dancer as ever. She knew him to be quite skilled, having been forced into practice with him several times over the years.

His steps were precise, his movements fluid, but there was a certain stiffness to his demeanor that couldn't be ignored.

Across from him, Lady Emily appeared bored. Their gazes rarely met, and their smiles were quite stiff. It was clear to Jessica that their dance was lacking in anything more than politeness. As she watched them navigate the steps with a distinct lack of genuine connection, a smirk played at the corners of her lips.

It wouldn't do, of course. It wasn't kind. But she couldn't quite help herself. Seeing James look miserable with Lady Emily made her feel a trickle of amusement. It seemed her childhood enemy was reluctant to engage the woman in a reel, let alone a dance of courtship.

The thought brought Jessica immense satisfaction.

As the music carried on, James couldn't shake the overwhelming sense that this ball, with its grandeur and forced festivities, was nothing more than a charade. A waste of time and energy that left him feeling trapped within the suffocating confines of his parents' expectations.

Lady Emily and her parents wouldn't extend their stay at the castle. James had spent the last several days in the woman's company, nodding as she spoke to him of flowers and furnishings, politics and pleasantries, without finding himself with much to say in response. It wasn't that he couldn't converse on such things. Or that he didn't enjoy a lively discussion on matters inconsequential or important. Only that...well.

He felt she weighed every word he said, performed some sort of mental calculation on their value, and found him wanting. And he hadn't the least idea why.

"You do not wish for another set this evening, do you?" she asked while they were yet going through the figures of their second dance.

"No," he said, forcing a polite smile. "I think I will allow the other gentlemen the pleasure of your company."

At least the discomfort was mutual.

She was undeniably beautiful, with her copper-brown curls and dazzling gown, but the connection he sought eluded him. He yearned for something more, something beyond the superficiality of the ball. And he doubted he would find it at any point soon, so why go through all the bother?

His mind wandered, yearning for an escape from this orchestrated spectacle. He longed for genuine conversation, for connection, for a spark that could set his heart ablaze. Amidst the sea of polite acquaintances and childhood friends, he couldn't find that elusive connection he sought.

He hadn't met the woman for him. Of this he was quite certain.

A deep sigh escaped his lips, betraying his restlessness. This ball, this parade of empty gestures and hollow conversations, held no allure for him. He yearned for something more meaningful, more substantial than what his parents wished for him to content himself with.

After he completed his second obligatory dance with Lady Emily, he guided her back to her father and mother and left her in their care. Paying the expected compliments first, of course.

Her father, the earl, appeared disappointed and strained when he smiled his acceptance of the compliments. The countess's expression was more difficult to read, but at least he sensed no hostility from her. From any of them.

They had tried an experiment, it had failed, and no one was to blame.

In his mind's eye, he drew up a list titled *Bridal Candidates*. And he imagined a thin-inked line crossing Lady Emily from off the top. Perhaps he really ought to make a list, somewhere, to better track his parents' scheme.

Leonard Harrington, his cousin and closest friend, met James at the punch bowl. "You haven't the look of a man besotted by a lady's charms." Leo ladled lemonade into two cups, handing James the first. "Will they go home then?"

"Most likely." James drank the lemonade and wished for something stronger. "There is no reason for them to linger when Lady Emily has made her opinion clear. As I concur with her, it is no great loss."

"A shame. She liked speaking Swedish with me."

"You don't speak Swedish."

"I know. But that's the only language she would address me in when we were in the same room together." Leo drained the rest of his cup in a gulp. "I pretended I understood every word, which likely entertained her sense of the ridiculous."

James's shoulders sank. "She got on better with you than me, then. I doubt I said a single thing that she liked."

"Cheer up, James. It could be worse. She could be the twentieth fair maiden to reject you as a possible husband rather than the first."

"Are you certain you must go to Northumbria?" he asked his friend. "You have barely returned home from Scotland. You must be exhausted by the travel."

"Quite the opposite. I enjoy it, immensely. At least this time I'm not on my way to a party, only visiting relatives." Leo put his empty cup on a footman's tray as the servant passed. "You ought to get out more. I told you to come to Scotland with me."

"It was your friend's engagement party, and I hadn't been invited."

"Lord Lismore wouldn't have minded. I think he needed all the friends he could get."

"I heard it was a somewhat mercenary arrangement." James raised both hands when Leo shot him an annoyed look. "Gossip makes its way through Amoret village as well as it does anywhere else."

"Lismore and Miss Godfrey seemed well-suited. Granted, I

am not especially close to Lismore. Haven't been in years. But still." He shrugged. "An engagement party may have put you in a better mood."

"I'd rather go with you to Northumbria." James glowered at his friend. "You will leave me in desperate circumstances, you know. I haven't any other allies in this part of the world."

"Familial obligations are what they are." Leo didn't spare James even a moment's pity. "Cheer up, old fellow. I will only be away a month. You will get through this summer in one piece, I have no doubt, and maybe even end it with a pretty bride."

With each passing hour, James doubted it. The bridal search his parents had arranged was the last thing he wanted.

"You shouldn't look so glum." Leo slapped James on the shoulder. "Your mother is watching us with that look of hers. The one that asks, 'Why are you not dancing? I specifically commanded it!'" He put his cup down. "As I wish to stay in her good graces, I say we both find partners for the next set. Are you ready?"

James glanced to where his mother stood, near the open doorway leading to the gardens. Indeed, she had her chin tilted at an angle and her eyebrows raised, staring directly at him. He released a sigh and put his cup down next to his cousin's. The dishes were immediately swept away by a footman in the ridiculous powdered wig and livery his father insisted they wear during social events.

James searched out a partner from among the unmarried ladies and invited her to cavort with him in a Scottish Reel. His mother knew he was doing his best. But his father would certainly express his displeasure over the evening's failure.

An hour passed, with James taking the hand of one lady after another, each of them declared unsuitable brides due to their lack of connection to nobility. Friends of his sister, women he had played games with as a child at summer picnics, each of them quite aware his family hadn't any intention of his courting them.

They didn't seem to mind. Most were happy enough to enjoy the evening and the conversation. Perhaps he would have felt better if a few had set their cap at him. But no. Everyone seemed to know he had to find a woman at least his equal in rank.

Though it grew cooler outside, the interior of the ballroom remained summer-warm. Despite the open doors and the high windows above the beams. The scent of flowers adorning every surface and hanging from the beams mingled with the scent of bottled perfumes and the fumes of dozens of candles.

He needed air.

As soon as he could, he slipped away into the gardens. And he had no intention of coming back. Not until the end of the evening, when people were too tired, too tipsy, and too wrapped up in their evening to ask him questions about Lady Emily. There wasn't any use in pretending to enjoy himself when most of his friends knew he'd been rejected. Or at least that there'd been a mutual lack of interest, if he were less dramatic and more honest about it.

He slowed his walk as he passed a suit of armor holding a torch. It was quite clever, really, the way things had been arranged with wires and a narrow pole to make it look as though the suited knight held the flame. "Sir Hop," he said, nodding respectfully to the only incomplete suit of armor his family displayed.

One leg of the armor and its accompanying boot cover had disappeared, perhaps fifteen years previous. No one claimed to know where it had gone. Not a single family member, servant, or troublesome neighbor would admit to removing the knight's pieces. Nor could James even think why it had gone missing. But the distinction had earned the suit of armor its own name and a place in the family's affection.

"Come to commiserate with Sir Hop?" a cheerful voice asked, and James winced. It was his sister who spoke. But at events such as these, nine times of ten, his sister had her dearest friend by her side. Chances were excellent that when he turned around, he'd come face to face with his sworn enemy.

"If he cannot dance, why should I?" James asked, putting a note of defiance in his voice that he didn't feel. He turned on his heel and met Jessica's dark-gray gaze. "Ah. Miss Westcote. I sensed a chill in the air."

"Mr. Aldwick, you are as charming as ever." She had her fan out and waved it beneath her chin, smiling languidly at him. "Are those the sweet words that won Lady Emily's heart? Surely, I must owe you my felicitations. Yours would be quite a match. If you managed to make it." The triumphant gleam in her eyes was evidence enough she knew the truth.

"Catherine, are you spilling all the family secrets to your friends again?" he asked, turning a disapproving frown to his sister. No one was supposed to know about the bridal hunt. At least, no one was supposed to speak of it so openly. He hadn't thought Catherine even knew what was happening, beyond their mother's desire to host as many guests as possible over the course of the summer.

His sister didn't seem the least upset. "Oh, come now, James. Everyone in the neighborhood surely guessed why Lady Emily was invited. It's hardly a secret with how often our parents throw the two of you together."

Knowing that his future, a future he didn't even decide for

himself, was freely talked about in the neighborhood nettled him. Gossips would discuss each guest his family invited to stay, debating the merits of one family and their bridal representative against another. They would dissect his intentions and interactions with each other, whispering about him behind fans, snickering at his situation in their parlors. And he could do nothing about any of it.

Except pretend he wasn't miserable. That none of it mattered to him. Which he did, at that moment, wearing a smile that felt completely unnatural on his face. "I suppose we cannot expect to get the thing right the first time. Perhaps the next one will work out better."

"The next *one?*" Jessica repeated, her eyes narrowing rather dangerously. "You mean the next lady? Are there to be other guests invited for the singular purpose of wedding you?"

"That sounds rather unlikely," Catherine said lightly.

She didn't know, then. Not really. But she would catch on soon enough. Everyone would. James gritted his teeth. "What does it matter why they are invited?"

Jessica's chin lifted. "You speak of people as though they are of no consequence. As if one lady is as interchangeable as a wagon wheel."

James hid his grin behind a lazy shrug. He'd hit upon one of Jessica Westcote's most passionate views. She believed all men looked down upon women as a whole, and she never failed to engage in verbal battles with anyone who voiced an opinion that came close to confirming that belief.

"You mustn't mind a word he says." Catherine put a hand on her friend's arm, as though ready to physically restrain her if necessary. "James is obviously in a poor temper. I think he means to drag you into it with him."

"Drag her?" James scoffed. "I would never dream of forcing Miss Westcote to occupy the same space with me. Indeed, I would prefer the opposite." He tucked his hands behind his back and changed the subject. "Why are you not dancing, Catherine? We cannot both abandon the ball. Our parents will notice and come searching."

"As I am not the one they are trying to marry off—"

"Yet," he inserted.

She glowered at him. "—I doubt they will mind my absence the way they will yours." She snapped her fan open. "You didn't even like Lady Emily. I cannot understand why you are out here sulking as though her rejection wounded you."

He bristled. "I would have had to make an offer for there to be a rejection."

A sudden, short laugh escaped Jessica. "That is why you are here, then. Your pride is wounded because you did not even come close to that point."

"Must you really interject yourself where you are not wanted?" he asked, giving Jessica a meaningful stare, full of the weariness she caused him on a near regular basis. "Haven't you anyone else you can annoy at present? Some gentleman to lecture or matron to befriend?"

Jessica pulled back at the same moment she drew herself up into a defiant posture. "There are a dozen people, nay, a hundred, I would rather speak to than stand here and trade unpleasant words with *you*. I am here to support Catherine; it is merely an unfortunate circumstance that links my favorite person in the kingdom to someone I loathe."

"The unfortunate circumstance being my existence?"

"Quite."

Catherine sighed and rubbed at her forehead. "That is

enough from both of you. Jessica, let us return to the ball. James, stop trying to hide. You will only make things worse for yourself." She turned on her heel and walked back the way they had come, but Jessica remained a second longer to glower at James before she followed.

James smirked as they withdrew, his gaze involuntarily lingering on Jessica's gown and the captivating figure she possessed. He couldn't deny the allure she exuded, her tall and slender form reminiscent of a graceful Grecian column. It was a shame, he mused inwardly, that such an enchanting exterior was accompanied by a frigid demeanor, as if her heart were carved from unyielding marble. Though, he couldn't help but wonder if there was a flicker of warmth hidden beneath that icy façade, especially given the friendship shared by Jessica and his sister.

He let his eyes follow their path up to the Armory doors, where he found his mother standing and looking out into the night, searching for him. He gave Sir Hop one last commiserating look. "My apologies, old chap. It seems I am wanted elsewhere."

He patted the suit of armor on the shoulder, then made his way back to the ball. Where he would receive sympathetic glances, and Lady Emily would maneuver to keep to the opposite side of the room from him the rest of the evening.

CHAPTER FOUR

The Honorable Thomas Westcote, Jessica's father, had kept a lease on property that belonged to his brother, the Earl of Wyndham, since the first year of his marriage. This meant the house, gardens, and farmland of Fairbrook Lodge were all part of Jessica's home, and well-beloved by her.

When she awoke the day after the ball, she stood at the same window as she had every morning. The window that had been hers since she left the nursery. Facing southward, her gaze traveled over the gardens, stretching down a hill, across a small wood, and then up again to the top of Amoret Castle's tallest chimney.

She unlatched the window and opened it inward, then took in a deep breath of the late-morning air.

"Good morning, miss." Her maid, Bessie Albright, came into the room with a freshly pressed gown draped over her arm. "It's nearly noon. But I sp'ose you were that tired, dancing all night at the castle."

"Can one ever be weary from dancing?" Jessica left the

open window with a small twirl, then curtsied elegantly to her maid. "If we must blame something for my fatigue, let us pick something less enjoyable. Such as the less than stimulating conversation I had to make with other guests."

Bessie laid the dress on the bed, then approached with hands out. "Are you saying you didn't enjoy gossiping with your neighbors and friends?"

"Of course I don't mean anyone we know." Jessica raised her arms as her maid assisted her in removing her nightgown. Left in a thin chemise, she went behind the screen that hid a basin and pitcher for her use in washing away the last particles of sleep. She kept speaking from behind the screen as she used a cloth to scrub herself over with the cold water. "I meant Lady Emily's party of snobs. Did you hear how many servants they brought? Ten. Who travels with so many servants? And those were the governess, maids, and a hairdresser, expected to stay in the house. There were also five servants to keep their coaches and horses. Six horses, mind you, and two coaches. Then the lady, her parents, her younger brother, and two dogs. Sweet little things, the dogs. The rest of the party hardly made a favorable impression."

Bessie's voice carried through the room with amusement. "I heard from the Amoret folk that the dogs had their own servant, and they hand-fed the creatures minced duck and quail eggs."

Jessica finished her morning ablutions and came out again to put on her stays. She kept her posture straight and her hands on her hips as Bessie laced up the back.

"They were not the worst people I have ever met," Jessica conceded. "For an earl's daughter, especially." Jessica had five female cousins, all daughters of the same earl who owned the land on which she lived. This made her rather intimately acquainted with the behavior one could expect from the female offspring of an earl.

For Bessie's part, Jessica's maid possessed a wisdom that belied her youth, though she was two years Jessica's junior. Perhaps it was a result of her mother's nurturing who had always imparted invaluable wisdom.

In stark contrast, Jessica's own upbringing had been marked by absence. The untimely passing of her mother when she was a mere four years old had left a void in her life, a void that had not been filled by conventional teachers.

Sometimes, that hadn't seemed fair at all. Other times, Jessica counted herself fortunate that she had retained one parent and a younger brother. Things could have been worse.

What had they been speaking of before her mind wandered?

Oh. "Lady Emily seemed bored rather than cruel," she observed with a shrug.

"Does the lady's boredom extend to Mr. James?" Bessie asked, finishing the stays. The maid went to the bed and retrieved stockings she had laid out while Jessica washed.

"It must. Catherine expects Lady Emily to leave this morning. I wouldn't be surprised if they have already climbed into their carriages with all their baggage, servants, and little dogs."

"A pity, that." A sigh of disappointment left Bessie's lungs with a heaviness that made Jessica raise her eyebrows.

"Did you have high hopes for James Aldwick's courtship?" she asked, not bothering to hide her incredulous tone. Over the years, Bessie had listened to every word Jessica had said about James. Every complaint, censure, and criticism, usually uttered in a moment of dressing or undressing, about her dearest friend's brother had always been met with sympathy from the maid. That she expressed pity for the man didn't make any sense.

Bessie helped Jessica put on her gown. "Not hopes, miss. Not precisely. I know he vexes you something awful, and I wouldn't want you to think I've put that aside. I just thought that if he married fast, there'd be less reason for you to see him this summer. He'd be too busy courting to offer the usual torments when you and he go to the same parties, or when Miss Aldwick invites you to her home. A man wooing a lady doesn't have time to tease anyone else."

Jessica stood perfectly still, now in front of her mirror as Bessie made final gentle tugs to the shoulders of the dress, ensuring everything was in its correct position.

She hadn't given much thought to what James's wife hunt would mean for her interactions with him.

"I suppose that makes sense," she said softly, studying her own expression in the mirror. She frowned at herself. "Perhaps I ought to hope that the next lady he meets will capture his fancy. Or she will find herself enamored with him —though heaven only knows what lady *would*."

Bessie turned her attention to Jessica's hair, and the conversation to who else had attended the ball. After recounting all the news she had heard, and ensuring that Bessie knew Jessica appreciated her work, Jessica left her bedroom for the family dining room.

Her father sat in his usual place at the head of the table. He had tea before him, but nothing else, and he held a book in his hand which he lowered the instant he saw Jessica come into the room. His eyes darted from her to the long case clock near the door, then back again. He smiled with an indulgent fondness that Jessica never failed to return.

"Eleven of the clock, my dear. I broke my fast an hour ago."

"And you waited for me this long when you could have been tucked up in your study to read?" She came to his side and placed a kiss on his cheek, then took her chair nearest his left. "Are you so anxious for news of last evening's entertainment?"

"Not in the least, so long as you enjoyed yourself. I take it you must have, since you remained for the whole evening." He had left two hours after their arrival.

"I did. Catherine and I danced until we wore our slippers through." A warming pan kept a small selection of meats and pastries at the ready for her, though the textures were not as enjoyable as they would have been if she'd been at breakfast an hour earlier. "The esteemed Lady Emily is expected to leave today."

"Oh? I suppose she wasn't impressed by our rather rustic charm?" Father chuckled and put his book on the table. "Lord Retford isn't likely to be in a cheerful mood today, then. Perhaps I will pay him a call." Mr. Westcote, the second son of an earl and now brother to one, had always been on excellent terms with his neighbors and never acted as though he were of any more importance than anyone else.

It often made Jessica wonder how her cousins, also children of an earl, had turned out with such marvelously high opinions of themselves.

"He will appreciate a friendly face," she agreed, somewhat deflated. Here she had taken some glee in James's predicament, but her father had immediately felt concern for his neighbor.

She twirled a silver spoon in her hand, absentmindedly stirring her tea, lost in a sea of conflicting emotions.

"Jessica, my dear," her father said, his voice laced with a mixture of concern and determination. She glanced up, finding a serious expression etched on his usually jovial face. "I believe it is time we have a serious conversation about your future."

She blinked, her spoon clattering against the porcelain cup. The sudden shift in tone caught her off guard, and she searched his face for any hint of jest. But the lines etched on his brow and the unwavering gaze in his eyes told her he was anything but lighthearted.

Her mind leaped to several possible explanations for his sudden shift in temperament. Was someone ill? Her uncle, the earl, perhaps? Or Tom—her younger brother?

"I don't understand, Father," she stammered, her voice barely above a whisper. "Why is there a need to discuss my future? Has something happened?"

Mr. Westcote's gaze softened, and he reached across the table, gently placing his hand over hers. "No, my dear. All is well. You see, last night at the ball, I had a conversation with Baron Retford. He made me realize that perhaps I haven't been as mindful of your future as I should have been."

"What do you mean? What has the baron to do with my future?"

"He is hoping his son will find a wife."

Jessica momentarily squeezed her eyes shut. Must *all* her conversations revolve around her sworn enemy? "Yes, that is what Catherine and I suspected was behind Lady Emily's invitation."

"He hasn't given up at Lady Emily," her father informed her. "There will be others."

Again, she shook her head. "I am confused, Papa. What

does James Aldwick's matrimonial prospects have to do with me? With my future?"

Her father shifted and appeared somewhat reluctant to say his next words. "I think it time that *you* find a husband. This summer, perhaps, will be your best opportunity without having to travel all the way to London."

Jessica struggled to find her voice. This was not a conversation she had expected to have with her father. He always doted on her and her younger brother, never pressuring them into anything they weren't ready for. The idea of marriage had never been a topic of concern between them, and she had taken it for granted that he wouldn't rush her into such a decision.

Yet now, with her heart beating faster and her palms growing damp, she realized how naive she had been. She swallowed, trying to speak around the sudden dryness of her tongue.

"I appreciate your concern, Father," she said, her voice tinged with a touch of disbelief. "However, I assure you, I have no present intention to marry. I am content with my life as it is."

Heat built in her chest, moving slowly outward and upward. The steady thrum of her pulse filled her ears and made itself felt in her fingertips. It took a swallow, a few calming breaths, to soothe away the trepidation her father's words had caused. And he watched her, all the while. Aware of her reaction to his words. Of what it could lead to.

"Jessica?" She knew what he would ask. She was so tired of answering. Yes, she was well. So long as things remained steady and certain, she would always be well.

The more familiar her routine, her neighbors, her surroundings, the easier it was for her to pretend everything was well. Leaving what she knew behind had always been out of the question.

The words of the physicians her father had hired echoed in her mind, drowning out her father's gentle tone.

Her episodes are a result of weak character. A stricter hand is needed.

She is overly sensitive. Hot and cold baths will fix her addled mind.

Nervous fatigue. A regular sedative will fix everything. A tincture of opium is all that's needed.

These are only the first signs of madness. A hospital isn't out of the question.

Her father's grip tightened on her hand, and she pulled in a gasp of air like one drowning. Her eyes filled with tears as she looked into his worried eyes. "Papa. I can't."

Mr. Westcote's expression remained earnest, his grip on her hand tightening ever so slightly. "My dear, I understand your desire for things to stay the same. For the comfort of the familiar. Yet you have only a modest inheritance coming to you, and I want to see you taken care of. You should make the most of the guests coming to visit the baron this summer. Among them, you might find a gentleman who captures your heart. As your mother captured mine."

Her eyes widened in disbelief. He didn't understand. Though he tried. Too many doctors had assured him that she would one day overcome her difficulty. Perhaps when she had a child, several had suggested. A motherly instinct might well cure her of an unsound mind.

She had expected her father to dismiss the idea of marriage, to join her in the knowledge that she was better off without a husband, but his earnestness was undeniable.

Her father was right that she had only a modest inheritance—but the idea of giving herself to a man less compassionate than her father filled her with dread. It always had. And she wouldn't—couldn't—marry.

"Who will want me?" she whispered, daring to ask of her father the thing that might make him see reason. "Who would want such a burdensome wife?"

"My darling little girl," he said, touching her hand. "You are so much more than the trials of your mind."

The weight of his words settled heavily on her chest and suffocated the lightness of the breakfast room. Her stomach turned unpleasantly, and the food on her plate was no more appealing than bricks of mud.

"Besides," her father continued, tone gentle, "you will not be alone in your endeavors. I've written to my brother, and he agrees he will help find you a husband if there isn't one to be had among the baron's guests."

Jessica's eyes widened. "You asked Uncle to find a husband for me?"

"Not precisely," he admitted. "I wrote to him of some general concerns regarding your future, and in his answering letter he said he could find someone for you. There are men enough who would be content to let you stay at their country house, surrounded by green hills and gardens as you are here. I'd rather you not worry of such a thing, though. It would be better if you found someone on your own. Someone you can devote yourself to, wholly and without reserve."

"What if I cannot find a man to inspire the same devotion in me that you had toward Mama?" she whispered, appealing to the love he'd held for her mother. Marrying someone who would put her in a country house and leave her there, all alone, wasn't her idea of happiness.

"I cannot tell you what will inspire devotion in your heart, my girl. But I do know that kindness, patience, honesty, and compassion are likely ingredients. Look for a gentleman who treats you with those virtues, and the rest may follow in due time."

What if she couldn't find such a man? A man who wouldn't mind the frailties of her spirit, a man who would treat her gently.

"You must try, my girl. Please. If you find someone on your own, someone you love, everything else will fall into place."

Jessica squeezed her father's hand, offering him a small nod. It was a silent acknowledgment that she understood his intentions, even if she wasn't ready to embrace them fully.

Nothing short of the deepest love would tempt her into matrimony. Even then, could she trust anyone with her future? Trust that they wouldn't see her as broken?

Her father cleared his throat and changed the topic of conversation, injecting cheer into his next words. "I have had word from Tom."

Jessica usually brightened at the mere mention of her brother's name. This time, she barely managed a smile. "How go his studies? His apprenticeship?"

"Well enough, though you know how impatient he is." Her father's fond smile held no real disapproval. "He doesn't want to wait another three years to be called to the bar for his examination, even though he has much yet to learn. But here is the real news, my dear. Tom is coming home, mid-July."

With a gasp of delight, Jessica put her utensils down. "Truly? How long will he be allowed to stay?"

"Possibly through the whole of August. Mr. Cassidy's wife persuaded him to take their family to the seaside." Her father tapped the table. "That is why I waited for you at the table. I knew you would want this good news as soon as possible."

The barrister who had taken on Tom's training and support during his education was a younger son of a noble family, and he'd turned to law to make his own way in the world. He'd been an excellent mentor to Tom, or so it seemed from what Tom had shared with his family. The generous leave granted her brother made Jessica even more disposed to like the man of law.

"I am delighted. Tom is always excellent company, and he livens up every event he attends." Tom's presence in their home might *also* distract their father from his sudden desire for Jessica to find a husband.

"Undoubtedly." Mr. Westcote rose from the table. "Will you accompany me to Amoret? I think I will walk. The day promises fine weather. You may visit with Miss Aldwick while I do what I can to cheer up her father." His eyes, a lovely blue Jessica very much wished she'd inherited, sparkled with amusement.

"Yes, please. After I finish breakfast, I will change my shoes and find you." The castle was less than a mile when they took the path across the properties rather than the road. "Perhaps we will find the household cheerful rather than disappointed," she added thoughtfully. "They may be glad to be rid of Lady Emily. I don't think anyone will miss her company, in truth. I cannot imagine them wishing her to stay longer, let alone become a member of the family."

Mr. Westcote tucked his book beneath his arm and kissed his daughter on her forehead. "Let us hope they view the situation in a positive light."

He left the room with a thoughtful expression, and Jessica gave her full attention to the breakfast that had turned completely cold. She winced and gave a pleading glance to one of the footmen in attendance.

"Would you bring me a fresh pot of tea?"

Cold pastries were not the end of the world. Nor was room-temperature bacon. But Jessica couldn't abide tepid tea. She shuddered and moved her cup away. Tea ought to be warm and strong, especially when needed to calm her rapidly beating heart.

When the tea at last steamed from her cup, Jessica held the little vessel by both handles directly beneath her nose. She loved the two-handled teacups that had belonged to her mother. She'd seen cups with no handles, and some with as many as four, but two seemed the perfect amount. It let one hold the soothing concoction in both hands, dedicating their full attention to a drink that soothed as often as it sharpened the mind.

She took a deep breath in and sighed happily. Jessica frequently found that the ritual of savoring her tea calmed her thoughts and helped her achieve mental clarity and focus.

Especially when her heart and mind were filled with anxiety.

The vise around her heart loosened somewhat, as did the ache in her temples, as she let her breathing slow. She didn't feel fully prepared to take upon herself the tasks and decisions that awaited her. Pleasant and unpleasant alike.

The prospect of marriage most certainly fell into the latter category. She didn't want to marry. Because she didn't want to burden anyone with the parts of her she tried to keep hidden. She wouldn't suffer herself to be a lifelong companion to someone who viewed her as excess baggage or some fragile, breakable thing kept behind glass.

This was all James Alwick's fault.

A new reason to loathe James, even though she well knew it was not *precisely* his doing that her father had brought up the idea of marriage. Because *he* was expected to marry, *she* was expected to look for her own suitor. Why did he have to ruin everything merely by his presence?

She finished her tea.

"This will not do," she muttered, narrowing her eyes at the dregs left in her cup. She had heard of people who read fortunes in tea leaves. Sadly, she was not possessed of such a skill. Nor were there any leaves in her cup for her to try.

The tea had still done its job. Even though she hadn't any clear answers, her heart and breathing had calmed. She could consider the problem rationally. If she found a way to prove to her father that no one wanted her for a wife, or that she could survive without the protection of a husband, everything could return to normal.

CHAPTER FIVE

The gardens at Amoret Castle stretched northward in a long rectangle with high walls between the garden and a public road. Trees on both sides of that wall had grown to such a height as to have branches both escaping from and intruding upon the grounds. As a boy of eight, James had spent a prodigious amount of time one summer discovering which trees were best for climbing and which branches were best used for making a sneaky exit from his family's lands.

Today, he hadn't fled the grounds entirely. Merely climbed up one of his favorite trees on the castle's side of the wall and tucked himself into the safety of the branches as though he wasn't a man of eight-and-twenty. Yet he felt no shame as he settled his shoulders against the trunk and let his legs fall to either side of the branch.

Though his position wasn't the least bit dignified, James relaxed for the first time in days. Closing his eyes, he breathed deeply, enjoying the rich scent of the tree, its leaves, the earth below, and the unique scent of a summer's day drenched in sunlight and softened by the occasional breeze from the direction of the lake.

That boy of eight had imagined that this tree in particular was the most special, the best of them all, not merely due to its ease of climbing. No, this tree was more than that. It was the ancient guardian of them all, looking after the land as a shepherd looked after its flock. Or so the boy James had pretended.

James let out a soft sigh, finally allowing his thoughts to form words. He spoke in hushed tones, as if confiding in a trusted friend.

"You know, old friend," he began, his voice carrying a touch of wistfulness, "there are moments when I long for the simplicity of childhood. The days when climbing trees and riding imaginary creatures were the grandest adventures of my world."

He'd once pretended the branches were the long necks of dragons, or the backs of sea serpents, and he was the only person alive capable of riding them as one rode a horse.

He paused, as if waiting for the tree to respond, and then continued with a smile playing at the corners of his lips. "No responsibilities, no expectations. Just the freedom to explore, to imagine, and to be entirely lost in the moment."

A gentle breeze rustled the leaves above him, as if the tree was offering its silent understanding. James leaned back against the trunk, staring up into the lush green canopy, lost in a world of memories.

He chuckled softly, the sound mingling with the rustling leaves. "But here I am now, a grown man burdened with the weight of my family's expectations. And yet, as I sit here, talking to you, I can't help but feel a glimmer of that carefree spirit returning."

James closed his eyes, letting the warmth of the sun and the whispered rustle of the leaves wash over him. His escape from the complexities of his adult life would be fleeting, he well knew.

James stayed perched in the branches, relishing the connection between past and present, between man and nature.

He swung his gaze eastward, to the tops of the shops and buildings in the village.

The village of Amoret, tiny as it was, had been that close to the castle since the 1400's. Thus the family and villagers had always been rather used to one another, and absolutely nothing that happened in the castle remained private for long.

James's failure with Lady Emily was doubtless old news by this point in the day.

His father had already called James to his study. The baron hadn't expressed disappointment in the situation, or in his son. Instead, he'd given James the name of the next invited guest who was expected to arrive in five days.

This time, the potential bride was the sister of a marquess. Lady Isabelle Declan. And she was three-and-thirty years of age, yet never married.

"She thinks marriage an unnecessary business. It is up to you to change her mind," Lord Retford informed his son. "Though if she has held out against the idea this long, I am not certain how you will plead your case. I have already sent an invitation for Lord Richland to join us with his family in a fortnight."

James didn't oppose the idea of matrimony in general, of course. Several of his friends had married and seemed happy, or at least content, with their lot in life. But they had all chosen their brides on their own terms, so far as he knew. And none of them had a father with his mind bent on only one sort of daughter-in-law: a woman with a perfect noble heritage.

"There will be no peace until I'm wed," James muttered to the leaves.

"It is all a lot of rot," a familiar voice said with vehemence.

James jolted with surprise, hitting the back of his head against the rough bark of the old oak tree, then looked through the branches and down the walking path. Jessica Westcote walked alongside his sister, coming toward his tree without any idea he sat within its leafy confines.

So it didn't surprise him when Jessica continued her diatribe, apparently with him as the subject. "Why can James not find a bride during the Season? Then you needn't have all these strangers traipse through your house and our village, nor go to all the expense of balls and house parties. Will you not have a moment's peace?"

Though initially shocked to hear her speaking of his predicament, her near echo of his own words made him smirk. They finally agreed on something.

"It is most unlikely," Catherine answered with a sigh. "Though I wish you would not speak as though I am a victim of some great tragedy. It is an inconvenience, of course, but one that will pass either when James has married or when my parents tire of trying to force a bride upon him."

His body stiffened. He'd known Catherine kept none of her own secrets from her friend, but he'd never supposed she'd shared the family's business—*his* business—so freely. His stomach twisted and an unpleasant flush of heat went up his neck and into his ears. What else had Catherine said about him over the years? And why did the possible answers to that question unsettle him?

"I truly do not understand this sudden mania for a daughter-in-law." Jessica, to her credit, did not sound as though she expected a full explanation. Though the two had never kept secrets from one another. They were as sisters, though perhaps with a stronger bond because they chose one another rather than being forced together by accident of birth.

He didn't begrudge Catherine her friendship, though he occasionally wished she had formed a connection with someone who didn't possess a sharp tongue and the annoying habit of winning most arguments she entered.

They were almost beneath his tree when Catherine spoke, voluntarily giving up more information than James liked.

"It is all Papa's doing, though Mama went along with the scheme the moment she realized it could mean having grandchildren to dote upon." She stopped beside the tree, and James caught sight of his sister's frown. "I hope they are less dictatorial when it is my turn to find a suitable husband."

"Dictatorial? That is an excellent word. Latin?"

"Indeed." Catherine's expression momentarily brightened. "Had you heard it before?"

"Never," Jessica admitted, then waved her hand dismissively. "Are their requirements for their future daughter-in-law severe?" Jessica had stopped directly below James.

In his youth, that moment would have been the perfect opportunity to drop something damp or messy atop her head, like a sack of feathers or the contents of a jar of preserves. It made his fingers itch, to be in a perfect position for some prank or other and unable to do a thing about it.

Engrossed as he was in imagining all the things he could have done to take advantage of a vulnerable moment, he didn't hear the whole of his sister's answer or comprehend what she was saying until the last of it.

"...if not exactly requirements. I think it stems from Papa's insecurities. Legitimizing the barony is something he has cared about all my life. The business with that horrid Lady Joana Tisdale last Season made him cross."

James blinked. He knew the name, but not whatever circumstance his sister alluded to. Jessica didn't seem to suffer the same lack of knowledge, given her instant and vehement response.

"That spiteful woman's complete lack of propriety and manners ought never be forgotten by anyone. It is a good thing you told your parents, as she deserved the set-down your mother gave her. If I had been anywhere near when Lady Joana said what she did to you, I'd have called her out."

Catherine's dry tone still betrayed some amusement as she responded. "Dueling is illegal. Even for women. Though I thank you for wishing to defend my honor."

What the blazes had happened between Lady Joana and his sister? And why hadn't he been told something serious enough for her to take it to their parents? He frowned down at both of them, willing them to say less about his business and more of that event. He'd hardly paid attention to social engagements in London last Season; he'd been far too busy with friends needing him one place or another to give notice to his family's invitations or comings and goings. Had he missed something of importance?

"Still, I'm not sure I understand what Lady Joana's misapplied criticisms have to do with your brother finding a bride." Jessica snorted, and he knew precisely how she looked when she made that unfortunate sound. Her nostrils flared. Her eyes narrowed. And her lips pinched tightly together in disapproval. He'd been the recipient of the look enough times in his life to picture it quite clearly, even though the bonnet she wore shielded her from view.

"Father has worked tirelessly to prove his legitimacy." Catherine's voice grew soft. She bent to pluck a cowslip from the ground, the bright buds having somehow escaped the gardener's spade. They would not escape *her* enjoyment of all things yellow. "Receiving his title by royal appointment, not to mention his father recognizing his *illegitimate* son as his heir, isn't enough for some people."

Though his seat grew more uncomfortable with each passing moment, James didn't shift about. He had no wish to give away his presence. Yet Catherine's mention of the specter that had shadowed their entire family for as long as James remembered made him grasp the branch tighter.

Illegitimacy.

Their lineage wasn't a secret. It was published in *Debrett's Peerage*, for anyone to read the details. James had read them himself when a boy at school had shoved the book in his face to ask what it felt like to descend from a bastard. It was a word James had only heard used to shame and anger others, but it turned out it was the legal definition of his father's parentage.

That didn't stop him from giving the smug little brute a facer, though.

He'd also memorized the entry.

Title: Baron Retford

Current Holder: John Aldwick, 1st Baron Retford

Heir Apparent: The Honorable James Aldwick

Status: Extant

Seat: Amoret Castle, Yorkshire

Family Motto: Rosa Prima, Gladii Postrema (Roses First, Swords Last)

Family History: John Aldwick, 1st Baron Retford, received his title by Royal Appointment, though it previously existed and went extinct when his father, John Aldwick, 4th Baron Amoret, died without legitimate issue. Prior to the 4th Baron's death, he recognized John Aldwick as his illegitimate son and named him as his sole heir, allowing the current baron to inherit lands and wealth.

Eight years after inheriting the estate, John Aldwick married Catherine Ripley, the daughter and heir of Sir Charles Ripley. Subsequently, Lord Retford was created a Baron on June 8, 17__. The issue of Lord and Lady Retford are as follows...

"Your father has held the title for nearly thirty years," Jessica said with a fierceness that surprised him. "And likely half the peerage has brothers and sisters they know nothing about, living in all the nooks and crannies of England."

"You are telling me things I already know and have often contemplated." Catherine laughed and paced beneath the tree, twirling the flowers in her fingers. "Facts rarely change feelings. Father feels looked down upon, and he worries his children will face the same sneers he had to ignore the first time he entered London's finest drawing rooms. Putting a woman on my brother's arm, a woman whose family has roots in the oldest houses of England, will solidify James's place in Society."

He swallowed, his unease continuing to build as his stomach writhed. His sister had clearly told her friend too much of the situation and the burdens such a thing placed on James's shoulders. The humiliation of what his family expected of him, and why, sank like a stone within his heart. Jessica Westcote knew the whole of it. All the better to sharpen her knives and barb her tongue with the truth when next they met.

What she said out loud bothered him less than what she thought of him in private. He'd seen it in her eyes, from time to time. Passionate thoughts she'd never given voice to, whether out of propriety or respect for his sister. And it ate at him, knowing she held back. Knowing there were things she didn't say.

He hated that he cared what she thought. And he didn't want to hear her give voice to any of it at that moment.

James dropped from the tree, less than a foot behind Jessica's back.

The woman released a shouted protest and whirled about, both her hands raised and her slim fingers curled into fists, as though ready to box whatever assassin had descended upon them. In her shock, she swung one of those delicate fists, and James had to jerk backward to avoid the connection of her knuckles to his chin.

"James!" his sister shouted, tone full of relief. "Where did you come from?"

Jessica kept her hands raised and her eyes full of gray ice. "You horrible interloper. Why are you spying on us like a sneak thief instead of announcing yourself at once? You are the most uncouth, ungentlemanly person of my acquaintance."

James regained his composure and his footing enough to smirk at his pretty neighbor. "At first, I hoped the two of you would wander away so I could stay put," he confessed. "Then your conversation became far too interesting when I found myself the subject of it."

"Vanity," Jessica said, her hands finally dropping to her sides where they remained clenched. "Arrogance."

Catherine approached, her cowslips still in hand and a stern frown on her face. "Eavesdroppers never hear anything good about themselves, James. Our conversation was private."

"If you mean it concerned my private business, I agree

with you." He cast his sister a look he hoped she read aright, filling his gaze with disappointment. "Must you persist in confiding everything to Miss Westcote? I suppose her relentless efforts to worm her way into our family ought to be expected, as she has nothing of interest in her own life," James said, casting a disdainful glance at the now mute Jessica.

"James—" His sister's tone held warning, but he kept going, his humiliation and frustration coming together to turn him into a beast.

His voiced dripped with contempt, "It's truly remarkable how she manages to ingratiate herself with everyone around her, pretending to be a cherished member of our family. But let's not forget, Catherine, she is nothing more than an outsider, trapped in this small corner of the world, seeking to infiltrate our private matters because her own are dull and meaningless." James's words carried a cruel edge, meant to wound and humiliate, as he had been humiliated. He observed a pained flicker in Jessica's eyes, yet he couldn't stop himself. "She may be good at playing the part, but let's not mistake her inappropriate curiosity for genuine care."

As the last words hung in the air, James saw the hurt etched on Jessica's face, her spirit shattered. It was an ugly sight, one that made his stomach turn over. Regret washed over him, mingling with a pang of guilt. He had gone too far, allowing his bitterness to consume him, and in the process, he had wounded a woman respected and cared for by his family.

Jessica stepped backward, her chin rising sharply, but he detected an unfamiliar twist to her lips. He'd never attacked Jessica's relationship with his family in their bouts before. Mostly due to sympathy, misguided as he sometimes thought it, because Jessica had lost her mother.

"James," his sister shouted, then stepped between him

and Jessica as though to act as a human shield. For which of them, he could not tell. But she addressed him first. "Everyone was bound to learn the reason behind our father's plans for you sooner or later, and Jessica *is* family to me. Apologize at once."

"I do not want an apology from him," Jessica said, and both James and Catherine turned to look at her. Her face had turned pale, and her gray eyes darkened to the shade of a thunderhead. Every word she spoke shook with emotion. "He never means them, and he usually says something awful within the same breath. Let him say what he will, in fact. I can ignore the buzzing of a gnat, whose existence is insignificant to me even if it is a nuisance from time to time."

The well-delivered words made James wonder for a moment if she had practiced saying them at some point in the past and had merely waited for the perfect moment to use them. Whatever their intended effect, his soul cringed away from what she said. The impression she had of him could not be so bleak, could it? Yet it was quite deserved, this time.

Most of their sparring ended with smiles or smirks. This occasion had gone too far for that.

Catherine glanced from him to her friend with an uneasy grimace. "Then allow me to apologize. You know Mama and I love you, dear. You must ignore anyone"—she cast a glare at James—"who says otherwise."

"Thank you. If you will excuse me." She dropped her gaze to the ground, and a stuttered breath escape her lips. "I have remembered an appointment, and I must be on my way home. If my father is yet with yours, will you please let him know I have returned ahead of him?" She briefly clasped Catherine's hands in farewell. "We will speak again soon, of course. Good afternoon, Cate."

The sudden formality she took on didn't mask the tremble in her voice.

"Jess." Catherine kept hold of her friend. "You should sit. You don't appear well."

A strangled laugh parted Jessica's lips, as pale as the rest of her. "A brisk walk will set me to rights, I assure you." Her voice lowered as she said, "Please, Cate. Just let me go."

He sensed she hadn't meant him to hear those words, and a wave of remorse threatened to drown him. Only a coward would speak to a woman as he had, with intent to wound her heart. And for what? His own stung pride?

Jessica pulled away from Catherine's grasp. She ignored James, marching around him and not making eye contact as she made her way across the grounds to the footpath that led from his family's property to hers. But he caught a strange gleam in her eyes as she rushed by him.

A bruising thump on his arm made him yelp and move away from his sister, who had landed her punch with strength as well as accuracy. "You horrid *child*. How could you give us such a fright and then insult Jessica, my dearest friend in the world, and her place in my life?"

He rubbed where she had struck him. "It is as I said. I didn't mean to overhear anything. I was in the tree first, and there never seemed an appropriate moment to inform you both that I heard every word said." His defense was weak in his ears.

"So you leaped upon Jessica like some sort of villain?" she asked, her voice rising with indignation. "I don't care what she says, you owe her an apology. A sincere, humble, thorough apology. You ought to kneel in the dust at her feet as you give it for how horrible you were." She shook her finger at him. "I've tolerated your dislike of her my entire life. Your teasing and tormenting of her seemed of little consequence given how well she turned your unflattering words back upon you. But this wasn't amusing, James. It was cruel. You would never have said such a thing to anyone else of our acquaintance."

James winced at the vehemence behind his sister's words, yet he tried to justify himself. "I spoke truly enough. She puts herself into our business as though she belongs there."

"Because I have invited her there," Catherine corrected. "Because Mama adores her. Because she is a wonderful, kind, thoughtful woman who has never done a thing to hurt me, nor has she ever betrayed a confidence. Jessica is one of the best people I know, and I cannot understand why you must be at odds with her now that you are both grown. The fighting is childish, James." She shook the cowslip at him next. "If you do not apologize within the day, I will tell our father and mother about every word you have ever spoken against Jessica and let *them* teach you the manners you obviously never learnt in the nursery." She stormed by him, making for the castle.

Hands curled into fists, James glared after his sister, as indignant as a spoiled child. Precisely as she'd said. But the memory of Jessica's wounded eyes, the tremble in her voice, drained the remaining fire from his temper. Without the heat of his emotions to spur him on, the truth and horror of what he had done settled on his heart. Regret weighed more than pride.

Catherine was right. And he knew it.

He had to make amends, to apologize for the hurtful words he had spoken. His behavior was petty and immature, unbecoming of a gentleman.

Her eyes had gleamed, and he realized they'd been brimming with tears. He'd made Jessica cry. Or come near enough to it. The sudden comprehension hit him like a punch to his gut, sickening him.

Jessica had always been a true friend to his sister, and she deserved better. Even if she often played havoc with his sanity and left him provoked to the point of madness.

James tried not to think about what he would say. He would apologize. Profusely, sincerely, and on his knees if need be. And if by some miracle she accepted, he knew their bitter rivalry had the potential to change. Perhaps it was past time for such a thing. All they needed was a chance to move past their painful history toward a more positive relationship, built on mutual understanding and respect.

Or, at minimum, common politeness.

Though without hat or gloves, James didn't dare return to the castle before fulfilling his sister's demand. He hadn't seen Catherine in such a state in years. Not since he'd accidentally beheaded one of her dolls with the blade of an ice skate.

That incident hadn't ended well for him.

Yet it wasn't fear of his sister that drove him. He could weather that storm if he chose. But the raging winds and wash of guilt in his heart? They churned within, urging him to move. And quickly.

Jessica came first. Above propriety, discomfort, and especially his pride.

With a swallow, he turned to the direction Jessica had gone.

She couldn't have gained much ground yet. If he hastened his pace, he'd likely catch up to her without breaking into a run. Hopefully before she arrived at her home.

CHAPTER SIX

Jessica kept the tears at bay until she came to the kissing gate that lay at the exact midpoint between her house and Amoret Castle. She leaned against the fence rather than step through the hinged gate, staring at nothing as her vision blurred.

At least she had hurried away before James could see the worst of her reaction to his words.

The air grew heavy, and her surroundings closed in around her. Unease took hold of her mind while her heart raced faster and faster, pounding in her chest like a bird trying to escape a snare. Each breath felt like a struggle against an invisible force and would soon leave her gasping for air if she did not get herself under control.

Though she and James had exchanged barbed words for years, they'd always skirted any actual cruelty. She'd never felt threatened by him or what he said. Frequently vexed, but not wounded. Even today's excessive sharpness she could have brushed aside, knowing what she did of his current situation.

However, Jessica's state of anxiety due to her father's

sudden push for her to marry and her own conflicted feelings on the matter had weakened her defenses. Thus, she keenly felt the sting of James's judgment, the weight of his disapproval penetrating her deeply.

Her chest tightened, as though a band of iron wrapped around her ribs. If only she had made it onto her father's property. If only she could remain hidden, unseen by anyone, as the world closed in around her.

James couldn't possibly know how much she feared that others in Catherine's family felt as he did about her relationship with them. She had often been the lone little girl, longing for a playmate, in search of a mother who would never return, visiting the houses of others and trying her best to belong, to please the ladies who invited her to play with their little darlings. She had spent years waiting to step into a wider world, only to find herself too broken to find what she needed there, too.

Catherine's family had always been a refuge—a place where she felt safe and accepted and loved. Was she wrong to have felt that way?

"No, *he* is wrong," she whispered to herself, her hands trembling.

Lady Retford had always been attentive to Jessica and her brother. She'd invited them to her home often enough that the need to have an invitation vanished altogether. She'd included Jessica in everything that involved Catherine's upbringing, especially the sorts of things a mother would oversee.

Other mothers in the neighborhood had been gracious on occasion. But they kept Jessica at arm's length, especially as the end of her years in the schoolroom approached. Some actively compared Jessica to their daughters, never favorably, in front of the little girls. Putting Jessica in her place as a motherless child, whose father leased land from his more worthy, titled brother.

Dashing those thoughts from her mind, she used a trick taught to her by one of her governesses, years and years before.

The governess, Mrs. Winbourne, had witnessed one of Jessica's fits. Though she hadn't called it that. Through the years, doctors, nursery maids, and governesses had noted Jessica's problem using different words to describe it.

Hysterics. The vapors. A nervous disorder. Lack of character. Weakness of mind. Mental fatigue. Swoons—even though she never fainted. Fainting would have at least been an escape.

"Compose yourself, Jessica," she reminded herself aloud. "Think only on the present." That was the trick. To stop thinking. Stop feeling all the emotions and focus instead on physical presence and sensation.

It usually worked.

As her gloved hands clenched around the weathered stones of the wall, Jessica willed herself out of her gloomy thoughts. She focused on the sensation of the coarse texture of the ancient stone pressing against her fingertips, grounding her in the reality of the world around her. Her gown, a delicate cascade of fabric, whispered against her legs with every slight movement. The gentle breeze caressed her face, teasing strands of her hair, while a chorus of birdsong enveloped her, filling the air with nature's melodies. Solace would come from the tangible, giving her respite from the tumultuous thoughts and emotions swirling within her.

Her pulse slowed. The vice around her chest stopped squeezing. The chill on her skin warmed beneath the sun.

"Miss Westcote?" a hesitant male voice called from behind

her, as though it was not the first time he'd tried to gain her attention. "Jessica?" Footfalls on the grass thumped closer, and a rock scraped against another.

Releasing the wall, Jessica hurried to loosen the strings of her reticule and retrieve her handkerchief. She kept her back to James as he approached.

"What do you want, James?" she asked, hating the tremulous sound of her voice. How much had he seen?

"Catherine was right. I owe you an apology."

Irritation sparked in her chest. "I told you that I am uninterested in such a thing from you." She found the scrap of lace and linen and hastily wiped at her cheeks, removing all evidence of tears, then blew her nose as daintily as she could.

"Nevertheless, you shall have one."

She whirled around, evidence of her shame crumpled in one hand, and a tart word on her tongue. How dare he seek to humiliate her only to then demand her forgiveness?

She blinked when he wasn't standing behind her, and immediately dropped her gaze lower.

James Aldwick, the future Baron Retford, was on his knees before her. Both knees. In the grass. His arms were spread, his hands open and palms up, as though he kneeled before a queen to beg for a boon. His usually mocking eyes brimmed with genuine regret. It was such an unfamiliar sight, it caused all her words to dry up, though her mouth remained open in surprise.

"Miss Jessica Westcote," he began in earnest, his tone catching her off guard. This wasn't their usual sparring; his words were laced with a sincerity that was unfamiliar to their bickering relationship.

"I kneel before you a repentant fool, unworthy of your acknowledgment, let alone your forgiveness." The weight of his words hung heavy in the air, leaving her stunned. James had always been an antagonist, his jibes and scoffs a constant annoyance, but there was something different in his voice now. The 'gentleman' inside him, whom she sometimes doubted existed, seemed to be making an appearance.

"The words I spoke were an abomination, and I was dishonorable to say them."

Was this some sort of new trick?

"I promise to make amends for my actions as soon as I am capable of such a thing," he vowed, both hands going to cover his heart. The overly dramatic gesture warred with the sincerity she heard in his voice. Which did she believe?

He couldn't actually want to make peace?

"And that's not all, Jessica," he added, a familiar spark of mischief twinkling in his eyes. Yet, it was softer, humbler this time, completely void of the arrogance she was used to. "I am at your mercy and fully willing to accept any punishment you deem suitable for my transgressions."

For a moment, the implications of his offer held her silent. This was no jest. He was sincere, offering her an olive branch with a touch of his characteristic humor, adding a slightly lighter tone to the profound apology. James, the eternal pest, was showing he could be a gentleman.

"You cannot be serious," she said aloud, skepticism dripping from each syllable. "You have *never* apologized to me."

He tilted his head to one side, the grin he usually reserved for charming others upon his face. "I have. Once," he reminded her.

Immediately, she remembered that circumstance. James had discovered that Catherine and Jessica, four and three years younger than his fourteen years, had hidden a rotten egg in his favorite pair of boots.

In retaliation, he had held a bucket over their heads when they sat beneath a tree for a planned picnic, informing them it was filled with slop meant for the pigs and he would dump it upon their heads unless they promised to leave him be.

Jessica had wanted to call his bluff, Catherine had burst into tears, and Lady Retford had appeared from nowhere at the exact moment the contents of the bucket splattered all over the girls' dresses and picnic.

Though James had professed he had never meant to follow through with his threat, that the bucket had slipped, his mother had chastised him and forced him to apologize. Then she'd taken his pocket money for the month and given it to the girls to replace their bonnets.

"Do you accept my apology?" he asked in the present, still on his knees, his eyebrows raised and his smile faltering. A reluctant respect for James bloomed within her, coupled with a surprising urge to laugh. She suppressed that feeling and crossed her arms over her waist instead.

"I ought to make you kneel there all day."

"If you wish it. Though I would ask that you inform my mother I will not be present at the dinner table." That infuriatingly charming smile appeared again.

A mixture of emotions welled up inside Jessica. Part of her still didn't quite trust this new, thoughtful side of James. But another part—the part that had longed for a kindred spirit all these years—wanted desperately to believe his words.

Surely, that person couldn't be James. Yet knowing they both faced the same unwanted future, the same pressure to wed, united them in a strange way.

James hesitated, then said softly. "I meant to hurt you. A thing I've never wanted before and swear to never attempt again. My own feelings of frustration and humiliation fueled my temper and my words. Yet my situation, vexing as it may be, shouldn't have any bearing on how I speak to others. I am sorry, Jessica. Truly."

Jessica swallowed and nodded. "I…thank you. That means a great deal." She gave him a small, tremulous smile. "And I do forgive you."

James returned her smile, his own expression tinged with relief. An undercurrent of warmth seemed to pass between them in that moment, though she couldn't quite think why.

"Your graciousness knows no bounds." He rose from his knees, looming over her by a head. "I am most sincere about this. I will regret what I said every time I remember it."

Jessica dropped her eyes from his, busying herself with returning her handkerchief to her reticule. "While your sincerity is somewhat perplexing, I do not doubt it. Not this time."

"I know you have always been a true friend to Catherine, and my mother dotes on you with sincere affection," he added while she kept her gaze averted.

"It is strange," she said, raising her gaze to the sky above them. "That they should like me so much while you detest me."

The man shrugged, not denying her words. That caused a prick, like the sting of an insect, in her chest. The emotional and mental strains of the day pressed against her mind and heart, and Jessica's weariness overcame her.

James gestured to the path behind him. "Will you return with me? Catherine will worry. I would like her to see that her brother isn't a complete monster."

"No, thank you. I am quite exhausted. Though you may assure your sister that I found your apology thorough, if somewhat strange, and granted my forgiveness. This time." She stepped toward the gate.

His hand gently closed over her elbow, staying her. "Are you unwell? Would you like me to escort you home? You seemed rather...fragile. A moment ago."

When she looked up at him, shocked by his thoughtfulness, she noted a look of concern in his eyes. Concern—but not pity. She'd seen him look at her with pity before. Once when she'd dared admit in his presence how much she wanted to see London one day. That was before she understood the extent of her strange, panic-laden fits. And her father's determination to protect her from ridicule.

"No. That isn't necessary. Though I thank you for the offer." She curtsied, as a civilized woman would, and as he bowed, she turned away. She moved to the gate, swinging it from one side to the other to open the narrow passage between their estates.

"Jessica?"

She stopped again but didn't turn. Why must he keep delaying her escape? What could he possibly have left to say? She wanted tea and a cool cloth for her forehead. The darkness of her room to hide in, pretending she didn't possess this blasted weakness of spirit.

"Something is wrong, isn't it? Beyond my idiocy, you are troubled. I hope you will tell someone. Perhaps Catherine? It cannot be a good thing to keep your troubles to yourself. Not when it means my stupid mouth can cause such harm."

Shocked again, she turned around, already within the confines of the curved gateway.

"What makes you think you are not entirely to blame for my distress?" She hadn't meant for the words to sound sharp, and yet they had come out with a bite that made him wince.

He shrugged and scratched at the back of his neck, his expression changing to one of confusion. "Intuition?"

For sworn enemies, they knew each other entirely too well.

Despite her sudden exhaustion, Jessica didn't leave, instead yielding to the impulse to simply tell James how she was feeling. In truth, no one would understand her sudden turmoil as he would. "Papa wants me to find a husband. A thing he has never said I need trouble myself about before."

He folded his arms and rocked back on his heels. "Is that so?" She saw the gleam of interest in his eyes. "Surely you knew you must marry eventually."

"Marriage holds no interest for me at present." She could admit that much to him. Though she had no intention of confiding the reason why. James didn't know of her difficulties, and she wouldn't reveal them to him for anything. Especially since his stare so fixed upon her made her stomach feel odd. "After the war, it is not as though there is a surplus of men. There will yet be many maiden aunts and spinsters in England. Why should I not be one of them?"

"You have a dowry of some substance," he said.

Jessica's shoulders stiffened. "I beg your pardon. How do you know that?"

"Everyone knows it." He smirked when she continued to gape at him. "Did you think you and Catherine the only two in Amoret Village who gossip?" He had the audacity to wink at her. "I have always wondered why your father didn't send you to London with us, though I know he doesn't like Town. I thought he'd want you to have a Season or two, find someone willing to marry you."

"Willing to—?" She cut herself off with a gasp. "As though

I am so horrible, that a man must be *willing* to overlook my character. For my dowry I suppose."

His words prodded her bruised heart, even if James didn't know it was less her character and more her brokenness that would make a husband unwilling to take her for less than a large fortune.

"I didn't say anything about your character," he said hastily, his eyes widening with alarm.

She turned and went through the gate. Whatever had passed between them to cause their temporary ceasefire had ended. He had apologized. She forgave him. Things could return to normal.

If only she hadn't confided her trouble to him.

He obviously thought her foolish. Though she ought to have expected her father's pronouncement and accept it. *Fine.* Let him think what he wanted.

Jessica harbored the fervent wish that the next wifely candidate would prove resistant enough to prick James's pride. The man needed to be taken down a peg. She would take no pleasure in any embarrassment of his spirit, only in the hope that he might emerge from this courtship season with a little humility. Still, a part of her looked forward to seeing James thwarted, if only to remind him that he was not irresistible.

Yet in the midst of his apology, ridiculous as it began, a new thought had struck her.

She looked back one more time, and saw that James remained where she had left him. Watching her, concern etched on his brow. A flicker of surprise lit her heart, sparking an odd thought. For the first time, Jessica allowed herself to imagine what it might be like to call James an ally rather than an adversary. She turned away, purposefully.

For now, she left him at the gate, content to let rivalry stand a while longer.

James stood alone in the armory, the room now devoid of its garlands. His gaze settled on the suit of armor affectionately named Sir Hop. The last notes of the music had faded two days previous, the clinking of glasses and murmurs of the departing guests long since gone. Only the echo of his strange conversation with Jessica lingered.

He sighed, running a hand through his disheveled hair. Jessica, his trusted sparring partner, was in distress. Faced with the looming specter of an unwanted husband hunt. A pang of empathy stirred within him as he thought of her tear-streaked face. She had tried to hide it, but evidence of her tears had remained. The glistening gray eyes, the pink nose, and the slight shudder to her breathing had given everything away. Which was why he'd acted like a jester, trying to distract her from the hurt and make her smile.

She'd only thought him a fool.

He shook his head and approached Sir Hop, thinking still of Jessica's confession. Their situations mirrored each other's, both on the brink of an unwanted marital commitment.

"Strange times, eh Sir Hop?" he remarked to the silent suit of armor, his tone a mix of amusement and contemplation. The suit, with its lifeless stare and perpetually clenched fists, offered no comment.

James paced away several steps, then back again, his mind whirling. Surely there must be a way for them both to escape their parents' machinations. But how? Jessica had always struck him as clever. How many pranks had she orchestrated against him?

She'd once replaced all his black ink with purple and convinced his tutor to pretend he saw nothing wrong with the color. She'd shortened the legs on his trousers one summer, and a jacket, making him think he'd grown several inches overnight. She'd even convinced the grooms to shorten his stirrups to enforce the ruse. Once, she'd released a flock of chickens into his chambers. Another time she'd brought Leo and Catherine into a scheme to convince him he'd lost his hearing while they carried on a conversation by doing nothing but moving their mouths without sound.

He'd retaliated every time, of course, but he'd always felt her plans were somehow better than his own. More creative.

Could they perhaps devise a strategy together? After all, who better to conspire with than the woman who matched—he wouldn't admit that she exceeded it—his wit at every turn?

"Are we doomed to the shackles of matrimony, Sir Hop? Or can we find a way to outsmart our parents?" he queried, casting a sidelong glance at the armor. Again, Sir Hop provided no answers, the cold steel faceplate remaining inscrutable, its metallic form illuminated by the dying light of sunset.

James rubbed his temples, his mind teeming with half-formed plans and strategies that went nowhere. There had to be a solution, a way out. He only needed time to think, to unravel this tangled web.

"Perhaps it's time for a strategic retreat, to gather our thoughts," he mused aloud, his gaze returning to the suit of armor.

It was late. He needed to prepare for dinner.

With a final sigh, James turned on his heel, casting one

last glance over his shoulder. "I'll figure this out, Sir Hop. For Jessica's sake, and mine."

Before James reached the large, double doors of the armory, the soft rustle of silk made him pause. Catherine stepped onto the threshold, her brows knitted in confusion.

"Who were you speaking to, James?" she asked, glancing around the empty room.

James blinked in surprise, quickly replying, "No one. Just...musing aloud."

His sister's skeptical gaze lingered on him a moment longer before she shrugged and entered the room. Her vibrant yellow gown, a stark contrast to the fading grandeur of the room, swished around her as she moved closer. "I thought I heard you talking to someone."

James glanced at Sir Hop from the corner of his eye. He chose to redirect the conversation. "Tell me, have you noticed anything odd about Jessica recently? Perhaps some lingering sort of worry? Or distress?"

Catherine's face scrunched in confusion. "Jessica? Distressed? Not that I know of. Other than what your sudden attack provoked. Why? Has something else happened between the two of you?"

James frowned. He had assumed Jessica would have confided in Catherine, her closest friend, before anyone else. The fact that she hadn't was intriguing.

"Nothing in particular," he hedged, not willing to betray Jessica's trust. "Merely a feeling."

His sister gave him a suspicious look but didn't press further. She merely shrugged. "I'll speak with her, but you likely imagined it. You *did* hurt her feelings, James."

He winced at the reminder. "She forgave me."

"Hm." She appeared unimpressed. "Don't be late for dinner."

As Catherine walked away, James found himself wrestling with a new curiosity. Why would Jessica tell him about her father's intentions before she told Catherine? What made her trust him with that information, despite their antagonistic relationship?

It was a puzzle; one he was determined to solve. After all, he and Jessica had always been entangled in each other's lives. And with the specters of unwanted marriages looming over both of them, they had more in common than ever before.

Perhaps, James thought, watching his sister disappear from the room, the answer to their predicament lay in that commonality. And with that, he exited the armory, leaving Sir Hop standing in silent vigil, the only witness to James's frustration.

CHAPTER SEVEN

Under a cloudy afternoon sky, Jessica found solace in the tranquility of her family's garden. The overcast conditions had allowed her some much-needed solitude, the ominous clouds warning off most visitors. The threat of an impending downpour seemed a small price to pay for a few moments of peace.

Engrossed in the delicate fragrance of the blooming roses, she was taken aback when James appeared at the garden entrance. Her brows furrowed as suspicion surged. He'd never visited her unless as an escort for his sister—who was nowhere in sight.

"James?" she questioned, trying to mask her surprise. "What brings you here? Is Catherine well?"

His eyes flicked toward her before shifting awkwardly to the flowers, the man appearing oddly out of place in the lush serenity of the garden.

"Yes, yes. She's perfectly well. I needed a walk, though, and thought I'd see the famed Westcote roses," he offered, his voice holding a touch of nervousness that was rather unlike him.

Jessica raised an eyebrow but said nothing. Instead, she watched as James fumbled with his next words, mumbling something about the unique hue of the petals. It was clear that he was out of his element, and her suspicion only grew.

"Are you certain you wished to speak to me about roses?" she asked, and his deep brown gaze snapped up to meet hers.

Thunder rumbled above them.

"There was one other thing." He straightened to his full height and winced. "I thought we might—"

The skies chose that moment to open, the anticipated rain falling in fat, heavy drops at a speed that would soon soak them both. Jessica reacted quickly, ducking under a nearby ivy-covered archway for shelter. James followed suit, a sense of urgency replacing his previous awkwardness. Once under the relatively little protection of the stone arch, James glared up at the sky.

They stood quite close. Both of them avoiding the droplets falling from the greenery. Jessica looked down the pathway to the house. If the storm moved along quickly, she wouldn't mind being stuck under the ivy. Alone. But with James there, taking up more than half the dry area, she'd happily risk catching a cold by making a run for it. She glanced at him as he removed his hat to keep it from butting up against the stone above them.

Would it be rude to leave him behind in the inadequate shelter? Most likely.

James's eyes found hers. They spoke at the same time, both shouting to be heard over the drumming rain.

"We should run for the house."

"I've had an idea."

Jessica blinked at him. "To get out of the rain?" she asked, then pointed. "As I said, we can run for the house."

He shook his head. "Not about the rain. About our situation. The marriage problem." His gaze held a determined glint that piqued her curiosity despite her wariness.

"An idea?" she shouted back, trying to keep her voice steady over the rain's tumultuous rhythm.

"What do you think of working together?" he proposed, his voice rising above the rain and echoing around the garden. "We could help each other by sabotaging potential suitors."

His words hung in the air, their implication lingering even as the rain attempted to drown out everything else. Jessica felt a rush of surprise and, she had to admit, a spark of intrigue. James, wanting to work *with* her? It was as unexpected as the summer downpour.

Generally, even when the two of them agreed on something, they batted the subject back and forth as though they didn't. It had always been their way, to mildly harass if they couldn't outright challenge and debate one another.

"How would that help either of us?" she asked, raising her eyebrows and keeping her gaze trained on his. "How would such a thing even work?"

"Simple." James grinned down at her. "My father will not tolerate the idea of *me* rejecting every female who comes my way, but if the ladies themselves are not interested, he can hardly object. Lady Emily is the perfect example of that. She found my conversation boring. Tedious, was the word she used, though she said it in German."

Jessica smirked. "I cannot say I blame her for the comment or the language in which she delivered it." She shook her head. "What would you have me do? And do you truly need my help? I think any lady who comes to know you as well as I do will immediately turn and flee the county even without my influence."

Rather than glower at her, as he usually would when she delivered such an insult, his eyes gleamed with approval. "That is precisely what I want. You will tell each of the eligible guests exactly what *you* think of me. Lay my every fault and failing bare before them, as though you wish to drop a helpful hint rather than dissuade them. You are clever enough to bring up such things in conversation, are you not?"

"Of course I am," she said with some irritation. "I best you in most of our conversations, do I not?"

"I haven't the faintest idea. It is not as though I keep score on such things."

"Perhaps you should. Noting your failures is one certain path toward finding ways to improve."

"Would that comment be a point in your favor?"

"Most of my comments would be, of course." She waved her hands between them, trying to dismiss the absurd line of conversation in favor of returning to the point. "The matter at hand is what concerns me. You want me to tell women of standing, the daughters of influential and titled men, everything I think is wrong with you?"

A wicked excitement pulsed through her, and Jessica didn't immediately push it aside. It was as though Christmas had come early.

Perhaps something of her feelings showed in her expression because James finally narrowed his eyes at her. "Nothing scandalous, of course, or untrue. My family's reputation must remain intact, and if I find someone I actually wish to marry—someday, in the far distant future—I would not have her warned away because I am a Bluebeard or some such thing."

His reference to the old French fairy tales they'd read in

the nursery to frighten one another made her smile. Bluebeard had been one of their favorite villains, but James had later used the tale to frighten Catherine and Jessica terribly, claiming Bluebeard's ghost haunted their castle. She'd been terrified of the cellar for weeks.

"You aren't charismatic enough to be a Bluebeard," she said with a toss of her head. "And Bluebeard only took wives, not suitors, to their deaths."

The gleam in his eyes made her wonder if he remembered the summer they tried to frighten one another with the darker stories from the French collection of tales. Bluebeard had been one among several of the villains they invoked to make each other shudder. Catherine had been the best at making the stories truly terrifying.

"If you do this for me," he said, his expression changing to a rather serious frown, "I'll do the same for you. I will tell the gentleman guests who show an interest in you the things that would most likely make them withdraw. Nothing that would harm your reputation, of course. Just something unpleasant enough that no offers of betrothal are made."

She stared at him, studying his dark brown gaze and trying to find any hint at all that this was part of another prank. "We would have to trust one another completely to agree to something like this."

"You would never do anything to harm Catherine," he said without hesitation. "Hurting my reputation, or me, would be a detriment to her. I trust you, for that reason alone."

The mention of Catherine made Jessica hesitate again, but slowly, she nodded. "And you love your sister. You wouldn't cause her harm through damaging me. And I know you to be a man of your word."

He blinked, surprise showing before he squared his shoulders. "Of course I am. So? Have we a deal?"

"There are particulars we may have to discuss from time to time," she said, still reluctant to fully tie herself to James. They had never done anything like this before. Always, they pitted their wits and jests against one another. Never had they worked as allies. "If anything goes wrong, or too far, we can call the whole thing off?"

He'd given her a way out, at least temporarily. If she had time to make her father see reason, to understand that no one would want a wife whose body betrayed her when surrounded by crowds and strangers, perhaps she could secure permanent freedom from the pursuit of a husband.

"Yes. Either of us may dissolve the agreement at any time." His gaze darkened and he leaned nearer, bringing their faces within inches of each other. Despite being out of doors, beneath an open archway, the rain falling on all sides made her feel as though the area they occupied was much smaller. His next words were hushed, barely carrying to her ears. "You have my word that I am trying to help you, Jessica. Help us both."

"I don't doubt it." She swallowed. Why were they whispering? "Very well. I agree. We will help one another avoid unwanted entanglements by sabotaging such things before they can even begin."

His grin broke out, as bright as the sun that the current cloud cover hid from view. He stood straight again and held his gloved hand out to her. Having been wandering in her gardens, her own hand was bare. Yet she put it inside his, the clasp sealing their pact. She felt the warmth of his palm through the material of his glove and realized, with some dismay, how much larger his hand was than her own.

It really wasn't fair he'd grown so tall and fashionably sized while she remained as she had since her seventeenth year, narrow and straight as a stick.

"The next guest arrives the day after tomorrow," he said, still holding her hand in his. "And she has an older brother."

"A perfect chance for both of us to try our hand at this." She removed her fingers from his grasp. "Make certain I am invited to the first dinner with them both."

"Done."

The rain still fell, but an agitated twist to her stomach made Jessica eager to end their conversation. She looked at the house again. "I am making a run for the house. You are welcome to return the way you came."

"What?" He raised his eyebrows at her, and his smirk returned. "You won't invite me inside?"

"A little rain never hurt anyone. And your home is not all that distant. Or you can stay here." She glanced upward. "Perhaps it will stop soon. Good day, Mr. Aldwick."

"Good day, Miss Westcote." He bowed, but she didn't return the courtesy. She was already running away, avoiding puddles and ignoring the feel of his gaze on her back. Once she reached the house, she looked back, and there James stood. He waved, then turned and walked into the rain on the other side of the arch, looking as if he wasn't in a hurry and didn't mind the damp at all.

CHAPTER EIGHT

The first evening of the Marquess Londonderry's visit arrived, with a formal dinner prepared to welcome them. James's mother was beside herself with enthusiasm. Truly, she delighted in the arrangement of parties, menus, and all the things James found socially tedious.

After greeting his family's guests, James took himself to a corner of the room near the doors. He stood with perfect posture, surveying the opulent sitting room. A grand, gilded mirror adorned the wall above the mantel, reflecting the soft glow of the chandeliers. Seated on stiff, embroidered cushions of the two sofas were their guests of honor: Lord Londonderry, his wife, Lady Londonderry, and their unmarried siblings, Lady Isabelle and Lord Frederick Declan.

Catherine wandered to his side, wafting herself with an elegant lace fan. She spoke to him in a low tone. "I trust you shall be on your best behavior this evening, brother."

James bowed his head. "You need hardly remind me. I am always on my best behavior."

"Always?" She arched her eyebrows at him. "I seem to recall more than one occasion in our youth when that was not the case."

He smirked and heaved a put-upon sigh. "You speak truly. I shall endeavor to conduct myself with the utmost propriety this evening."

"Good. Because more than your reputation is at stake," she reminded him. Then Catherine's expression turned less teasing and more earnest. "Please treat Jessica with kindness this evening and show her you meant your apology."

"I did mean it," he protested quietly. "Though if she begins a debate, you know I will counter. That is the nature of our relationship."

"Relationship? Do you mean the nature of your hostilities?" Catherine gave him a significant look. "Nevertheless, a woman's feelings must always be honored. So perhaps a cease-fire is in order this evening."

James inclined his head. "As you are my top advisor in matters of war, I shall heed your counsel."

That elicited a snort from her, which she quickly covered by clearing her throat. "A wise decision indeed." She snapped her fan open again. "Now, if you will excuse me, I had better make certain our mother and the marchioness are getting along."

Though spoken in a lighter tone, her words remained with James. He had plans for that evening, and none of them involved battling Jessica. Not tonight. Perhaps not for some time in the future.

One didn't start skirmishes with potential allies.

He studied their guests again, mentally sorting through what he knew of them.

The Marquess Londonderry was a man of distinguished

bearing in his late thirties. His wife, Lady Londonderry, was a woman of elegance, her dark hair adorned with sparkling gems. Her emerald-green jewels worn to match her gown hinted at her wealth and status.

The Declan siblings, Lady Isabelle and Lord Frederick, were not as genial as their elder brother and his wife. Lady Isabelle wore a more modest gown of blue, her curly black hair complimenting her soft features. Her expression was inscrutable. James couldn't decide if she was bored or annoyed. Lord Frederick, on the other hand, was a robust figure, his hair the same shade as his siblings's, but his eyes held a glint of amusement to them.

The room buzzed with the hum of polite conversation when the door opened, causing James to glance over. In walked Jessica on the arm of her father, and James immediately glanced to Lord Frederick. The man had caught her entrance, too. And he appeared interested.

Mr. Westcote had already met the noble family. He'd been present for their arrival. But his daughter still needed introductions. And James would be the one to make them.

He left his place along the wall with speed, and as he came to stand before Jessica, he tried to see her as a stranger would. As Lord Frederick would.

The soft glow of the chandeliers illuminated her coppery-brown hair, and the soft pink gown she wore accentuated her willowy figure and matched the blush in her cheeks. Her gray eyes were dark in the evening light, like the shade of the sky when it faded from purple twilight to black.

A hint of surprise made him tilt his head to the side; it wasn't often he saw Jessica so formal, so ladylike. He'd found her pretty enough in the past, when he tried to be objective.

Tonight, however, he could easily call her appearance attractive. Charming, even.

Clearing his throat, he bowed to Mr. and Miss Westcote. The room quieted as he extended his hand toward her, a small grin playing on his lips. "Miss Westcote, good evening," he said with a bow, his voice loud enough for the room to hear. "Mr. Westcote. May I have the honor of introducing your daughter to our esteemed guests?"

Her father stared at James as though he'd never seen the younger man before. "I suppose. If Jessica does not mind?"

Jessica reacted without hesitation, stepping away from her father's escort as though it was quite normal to do so. "Not at all, Papa. If Mr. Aldwick wishes to take his duties as host seriously, we must allow him that privilege, mustn't we?"

The moment she was on his arm, James lowered his voice. "You look radiant this evening."

Jessica raised her eyebrows at him. "Mr. Aldwick, you flatter me. Though I'm sure you pay the compliment with some ulterior motive."

James feigned offense. "You wound me, Miss Westcote. I speak only the truth. You are quite lovely. One would almost think you wish to attract a certain lordling."

A smirk played on Jessica's lips. "I dress for my own enjoyment, Mr. Aldwick. And no one else's."

He didn't doubt it. And he admired her the more for it as he led her to the guests of honor, who rose from their seats at their approach.

"Lord Londonderry, Lady Londonderry," James said, stepping away enough to allow Jessica room to curtsy. "May I present Miss Jessica Westcote. Lady Isabelle Declan, and Lord Frederick Declan. Miss Westcote."

Lord Londonderry rose from his seat, bowing slightly

toward Jessica. "A pleasure to make your acquaintance, Miss Westcote," he said, his voice deep and smooth.

Lady Londonderry, on the other hand, examined Jessica with a curious gaze before offering a small smile. "Delighted to meet you, my dear."

As Jessica curtsied, James glanced toward his family. He caught them exchanging surprised glances from where they stood near the hearth. No one had the slightest idea what he was up to, he thought, a bit smug.

This was a game his parents and Jessica's father had started. A game he would win, because for once he and Jessica were on the same side.

Jessica stepped into the vast dining room on Lord Frederick's arm, trying to hide her nervousness. The mahogany table stretched the length of the polished marble floors, lights from the chandelier casting glittering reflections. Every place setting was laid with the finest flatware and silverware.

Jessica glanced at James as he settled in the seat across from her, giving him the subtle hint of a smile. Though her stomach flipped at this new game they were playing, she wouldn't back down now. James gave an imperceptible nod in return, his eyes dark in the candlelight.

Lord Frederick's expression remained neutral as he settled into the seat to Jessica's left, politely offering to fill her plate.

As Jessica asked for the dishes nearest them, she caught Lady Londonderry watching her closely. The woman's gaze seemed kind yet searching. It seemed the marchioness was as interested in her brother-in-law's prospects as she was her sister-in-law's possible match with James.

Why were they surrounded by people determined to make matches?

Jessica looked away, unsettled.

Throughout the meal, Lord Frederick attempted to engage Jessica in conversation. To his credit, he seemed content to speak on subjects that she showed an interest in.

"Miss Westcote, you must let me know your favorite way to pass the time. Especially when in the country, of course. What passions or interests inspire you?"

She delicately speared a carrot on her fork as she answered, "Riding brings me much happiness, my lord. As do books and music. Simple pleasures, really."

"Riding? How marvelous. That is one of my favorite pastimes as well. I could spend an entire day in the saddle and think it a good use of time." His smile appeared at last, wide and genuine. A pang of unease hit Jessica. She hadn't wanted to actually stimulate the conversation. "There are some splendid trails on my family's estate. Perhaps we could go riding while my family is here. You could show me your favorite paths. I'm quite an accomplished equestrian myself."

This wasn't good at all. She didn't want more time with the man. She glanced at James to see him busy in his conversation with Lady Isabelle. He wouldn't be of much help yet. "I would be delighted to ride with you and your sister, Lord Frederick." An idea hit upon her, and she put her hand to her heart, lowering her voice as she said, "Though I am no expert rider. Merely someone who finds the freedom and solitude in the countryside rejuvenating."

For a moment, disappointment flashed in his eyes. Yet he gave her a cheerful enough smile in return. "Skill is sometimes less important than enjoyment, Miss Westcote. Perhaps I might even offer you some advice. I enjoy sharing my knowledge of horsemanship. We shall have you jumping hedgerows in no time."

She had been jumping hedgerows since her fourteenth birthday. But no use in letting him know that, given his obvious enjoyment of the sport. She feigned a polite laugh. "I cannot imagine a novice rider's skill growing in so short a time."

He lowered his gaze to his plate, wincing. "You must think me rather presumptuous, Miss Westcote. I assure you that was not my intent. Though I hope we will have an opportunity to ride together." He cleared his throat. "Perhaps we should discuss reading. You did say that was one of your preferred activities. Have you read any of the latest novels? Personally, I find Walter Scott quite diverting."

Had she not been glancing at James in that moment, she would have missed the way his attention turned toward them, his eyebrows raised. He made brief eye contact with her, then quickly turned his attention back to Lady Isabelle. Strange.

"I've read some of Walter Scott's works." She had enjoyed them, too. But his obvious enthusiasm made it impossible to say as much.

Lord Frederick's eyes lit up. "*Rob Roy* is a personal favorite of mine. I have read it twice through. Scott's characters are vividly drawn."

Jessica's lips curved into a small smile. James had devoured that book. Twice, if she wasn't mistaken. And she'd debated the story with him merrily for weeks. But she couldn't let Lord Frederick know that. "The characters are well represented, indeed. Though I found the plot wandered at times."

A faint line appeared between Lord Frederick's brows.

"Wandered? But the tale of Rob Roy's adventures, defying the London authorities—"

Jessica interrupted, softly but firmly. "The adventures themselves were riveting. However, Scott allowed several unrelated subplots to distract from the central story."

A flash of annoyance crossed Lord Frederick's face, though he tried to hide it with a chuckle. "I suppose a woman may find the political machinations of the story less engaging."

Heat rose in Jessica's cheeks at the subtle condescension in his words. At last, a clear reason to dislike the man seated next to her. Though her experience in the world couldn't be called vast, her father had been her tutor on the subject of politics. She leaned forward.

"On the contrary, my lord, the political elements themselves were trite and one-dimensional. Scott focused on surface issues over meaningful commentary on matters that could have led his readers to think differently about their own closely-held political affiliations."

Lord Frederick opened his mouth, but no retort came. After a moment he gave a strained smile. "You have given me much to consider, Miss Westcote. Scott is surely a master with words, yet perhaps no author is above reproach."

Jessica inclined her head, satisfied. "We must appreciate popular authors with a critical eye, my lord, lest we be slave to fashion over reason." It was a load of rot, and she hated saying it. Jessica could analyze a work of literature critically, of course, and she regularly debated such things as theme and social commentary with James and Catherine. But in her heart, she believed a story that made someone *feel* things, like joy or sorrow, was every bit as important as the highest forms of literature.

Stories were meant to be enjoyed, savored, and lived again

and again in the heart and mind. Not examined and pinned to a wall like a moth in an entomologist's collection.

The lordling nodded slowly, though she caught a slight narrowing of his eyes as he studied her. "You are wiser than I on this subject, it seems. I appreciate the enlightening conversation."

Jessica smiled. "As do I, Lord Frederick."

They spoke of less important matters and when dinner ended the ladies withdrew to the baroness's favored sitting room. A pianoforte held a place of honor along the center of one wall, and Lady Isabelle went there with a lightness in her step. The baroness and Lady Londonderry settled on a couch to converse in hushed tones, while Catherine sidled up to Jessica near the window.

"Your father is a delightful dinner companion," she said with true warmth in her voice. "I thought it would be a dreadfully dull evening, seated between him and the marquess, but they proved solicitous all evening. How did you enjoy your conversation with Lord Frederick? It seemed every time I glanced over, the two of you were engaged in a serious conversation."

"Serious?" Jessica shook her head. "Not at all. I think I contradicted him at every turn." At least, that was what she had attempted to do. "Your mother will be most distressed if she ever learns of what a poor showing I made."

"Doubtful. Mother couldn't ever be distressed or disappointed with anything you do," Catherine pointed out, tapping Jessica's arm with her fan. "She sees you as another daughter."

Lady Isabelle finished a short piece, and the other ladies in the room politely applauded while the baroness praised the woman's talents.

"How old is Lady Isabelle?" Jessica asked, lowering her voice. "Not that it matters, really, but I thought most unmarried ladies of rank were as young as us. Or younger."

"Three and thirty," Catherine answered from behind her now-open fan. "The woman is wealthy as Midas, too, from what I have heard. She has said she has no desire to marry. With the power she has from her family's title and her fortune, why should she? Giving all of that up for a man to take control of her life would be a rather horrid decision."

Jessica's admiration of the woman grew. She'd felt the same, and it was one of the few comforts she'd taken when she decided she couldn't risk marriage. Perhaps, she had reasoned with herself, keeping her independence would make up for the lack of husband.

When the gentlemen arrived in the room, Jessica and Catherine parted briefly. Catherine fussed over helping her father with his pipe, a thing she had done since her youth, while the baroness served cakes and coffee to the others. The evening was meant to be one of conversation from this point forward. Lord Frederick went to his sister at the pianoforte, speaking in low tones with her.

James took the opportunity to sidle up next to Jessica. "Lady Isabelle has a fondness for cats we might exploit, though she mentioned it only in passing. She abhors all insects, though I am uncertain how to use that to our advantage. I found her engaging. I would like her if I was not expected to court her."

"I could say the same of Lord Frederick," Jessica confessed. "Up until the moment he implied women haven't any understanding of politics."

He chuckled. "I made that mistake with you once. You set him aright?"

"Of course. But I doubt it cooled his interest. He thinks himself an expert horseman and has a fondness for romantic adventures in novels. I insulted his favorite book and author."

"An excellent first step, and innocent enough. Very well. I think we all ought to go riding tomorrow to see how we can use this information to our advantage." James's eyes glowed in a way she recognized at once. It was the same light that appeared there, a gleam of impishness, when one of his pranks were underway.

Unable to help it, Jessica leaned toward him with narrowed eyes. "Remember, nothing that harms a person or our reputations."

"Of course not." He offered her his arm. "You will abide by the same, I trust?"

A nod was her answer as she laid her hand on his forearm. "My only desire is to remain unattached at the end of summer."

Then there would be fewer men coming and going from their part of the county, and she could find a way to prove to her father that marriage simply wasn't in her future.

"We are agreed." He nodded to their guests. "Come. We have more information to mine and a duty to uphold."

She wore her friendliest expression as they approached the siblings at the instrument. Though trusting James was a new sensation, Jessica found she didn't chafe beneath it. The unfamiliar situation ought to have made her uncomfortable. Yet somehow, all she felt was excitement for what was to come. This was turning out to be a truly marvelous little plot between the two of them, one bound to be both amusing and, she hoped, successful.

CHAPTER NINE

The early afternoon sun bathed the castle's gray stones in a warm glow, making them bright despite their age, as the group gathered in the courtyard, preparing for their horseback ride. James had arranged the ride as promised, much to his father's surprise.

James and Catherine took the lead, their horses stepping briskly along the well-worn path. Lady Isabelle came next, her horse trotting gracefully as she appeared to observe the picturesque countryside that unfolded before her. Jessica and Lord Frederick followed closely behind, enjoying the lively conversation that flowed between them.

The rolling hills of the English countryside were a tapestry of vibrant greens, adorned with wildflowers that swayed in the gentle breeze. The summer light cast a warm glow on the landscape, accentuating the beauty of the sprawling meadows and farmer's fields beyond the village.

They rode with purpose toward one of Catherine's favorite picnicking spots, a small grove of trees on the bank of the River Nidd. It wasn't a far distance, which made it suitable for their group, one that, overall, seemed more enthusiastic about a picnic than a bracing exercise.

As they rode, James couldn't help but steal glances at Jessica every time he turned in the saddle to address Lady Isabelle, wondering if she'd already found occasion to speak of him with the lady. The marquess's sister gave him short answers and tight smiles but responded with more warmth to anything Catherine said to her. Though, his father *had* said the woman was determined not to marry and he would have to change her mind. Perhaps her behavior wasn't so out of the ordinary if she was as much against the idea of a match as he was.

Regardless, her curtness was fine with him. After a time, he let Catherine and Lady Isabelle take the lead while he dropped back to the middle of their party. He stole another glance at Jessica to find that her eyes sparkled with what he assumed was enjoyment, though she barely cast him a glance.

Lord Frederick matched her enthusiasm, but his gaze upon her struck James as somewhat calculating.

James gently guided his horse to slow his pace, straining to catch the pair's words over the clop of hooves and the rustle of wind through the tall grass.

Lord Frederick had taken up the subject of books again, it would seem. "Miss Westcote, your insight into Walter Scott's novel is fascinating. Most ladies—pardon me, most people—fail to consider the subtleties of narrative structure."

Jessica's reply was somewhat dry in tone. "You flatter me, my lord. Though I suspect your passions run deeper for such subtleties than most."

The lordling laughed, though it sounded somewhat forced to James. "You have seen through me at once. I do enjoy analyzing literature. The nuances of language and storytelling are endlessly fascinating."

"They are indeed," Jessica agreed. "But we must tread lightly upon the subject, lest we exhaust it completely and leave no room for deeper conversation." She glanced at James, a touch of humor to the quirk of her lips.

"There is no danger of that," Lord Frederick assured her. "We speak only of art and the life of the mind. Such things elevate the spirit and couldn't possibly be exhausted by an afternoon's ride."

"Perhaps," Jessica replied. "Yet I find the subject of literature may not be lively enough, considering we are out in nature rather than indoors. And Mr. Aldwick has heard my thoughts on Scott's work more times than he would like."

James tried to hide his amusement behind a thoughtful smile. "Indeed. We have worn that subject out, between the two of us." And though he suspected Jessica enjoyed *Rob Roy* as much as he had, he'd enjoyed the way she challenged all the points the book made. And how often she'd lamented Rob Roy's wife having little more than a mention in the novel.

She sent him a glance of understanding. "Perhaps we could discuss something else?"

Lord Frederick hesitated before giving his overly cheerful agreement. "Of course, Miss Westcote. Forgive me. I hope I have not bored you?"

"Not at all." Jessica's polite expression gave away little. "Our discussion has been most enlightening." Only someone who knew her well would see the slight furrow of her brow as indication she meant the opposite of what she'd said. How long had Lord Frederick been speaking to her of books with such a condescending tone?

The lord smiled. "Then perhaps we might—"

James brought his horse to a stop, effectively interrupting the conversation of the people behind him as they had to do the same. "Lord Frederick, I have neglected you terribly. Are you certain my father's hunter will do while you are at the castle? It can be quite uncomfortable to ride a strange horse."

Lord Frederick replied amiably, "Thank you, Mr. Aldwick. The beast suits me well. But we were in the midst of—"

"I'm sure Miss Westcote can spare you while we have a proper test of the animal's suitability," James cut in. "A quick canter ahead of the group, I think, will prove him. Shall we?"

Jessica shot James an amused look but held her tongue.

"That may be wise. If you will excuse me, Miss Westcote?" Lord Frederick moved his horse to ride beside James.

"I wouldn't dream of delaying such an important examination of man and beast," Jessica said, and James caught the barest relief in her smile. Ah, so he *had* sensed gratitude beneath her annoyance at his interruption.

He would have Lord Frederick's ear the moment they were ahead of the rest of the group, which meant starting the plan in earnest. A few well-placed words about some of Jessica's least-attractive qualities, accompanied by a display of horsemanship he intended for her to handily conquer, and Lord Frederick would be even less interested in matrimony than his sister. At least in regard to Jessica.

After they'd put several horse-lengths' distance between themselves and the ladies, James heaved a dramatic sigh, catching the other man's attention. "I must tell you, Lord Frederick, after even our short acquaintance, I have come to respect you. Truly. And as one gentleman to another, I feel I must warn you of something. Though this is perhaps a delicate topic to speak upon. I have seen you pay particular attention to my sister's friend, Miss Westcote."

"Indeed? I hope you do not think any such attention inappropriate or too forward—"

"No, your lordship. Not at all." James tried to sound reassuring, even as his mind spun a tale that might give Lord Frederick pause. "In truth, that is why I thought it best to have a conversation with you in private. I respect the Westcote family, of course. My family's intimacy with theirs is of long-standing. So I hope you will excuse me if this conversation is too forthright, but I feel it only fair to you that you know something of what you are getting into."

Lord Frederick's eyes narrowed, and he slowly shook his head. "I am afraid I do not follow, my friend."

"Putting it delicately, you ought to know that Miss Westcote has some—well. Some peculiarities."

Lord Frederick turned to him in surprise. "Oh? She seems a lively, intelligent lady. I have seen nothing odd about her behavior."

James nodded. "Indeed, she has a bright mind. There is nothing to fear about that. But you ought to know that her health is rather...delicate."

The other man frowned. "How so?"

Glancing over his shoulder, as though concerned he might be overheard, James said in a low voice, "She is often beset by headaches and other ailments that confine her to bed for days. It is why you have never seen her during the London Season—the travel does not agree with her, they say."

Comprehension dawned on Lord Frederick's face. "Now that you mention it, I had wondered why I never met Miss Westcote before now. Do you mean to say she has never been to London?"

"Never." A thing James couldn't explain. Nor had he ever heard a reason behind it. Yet that fact suited the fabrication he had invented. "The attention and exertion required of a wife in Town would likely exacerbate her condition."

Lord Frederick sighed. "A fragile wife would require a husband's constant attention." He glanced over his shoulder, his lips pursed in thought. "She seems healthy enough at the moment."

"Yes. She does." James made a show of thoughtful reluctance before adding, "Though in truth, I suspect some of her 'illnesses' are merely excuses to avoid obligations."

The other man eyed Jessica, who rode cheerfully behind them, then turned forward and spoke to James. "A penchant for dishonesty to shirk duty is just as troubling a trait in a wife. I appreciate the warning."

"I thought it right to tell you, though I beg you not to spread word of such a thing. My family views Miss Westcote as one of their own." James smiled, somewhat grimly. "I merely wished to share my honest opinion. You must decide what path is best for you."

"You've given me much to consider."

It wouldn't take much more to dissuade the man. James smiled. "Glad to be of service." He then raised his voice for those behind them to hear, pointing to the grove of trees where they would picnic. "We are nearly there, ladies. Do stop dawdling."

His sister raised her voice. "Dawdling? You were the one who raced ahead." He heard her say in a lower voice, "He is forever impatient, isn't he?"

Lord Frederick waited with James until the ladies caught up to them, though his expression remained closed, the man lost in thought.

If James managed to chase off this suitor, Jessica might actually begin to trust him. And then work with him to ensure that he remained a bachelor at the end of summer, too.

After dismounting at the picnic spot, Catherine took command of the situation. Like a general giving marching orders, she had all of them contributing to setting up an outdoor repast that would serve as their afternoon tea.

As Catherine supervised the gentlemen in laying out the picnic blanket, James went in search of a rock to hold down one corner of the large square of fabric. He searched near where Jessica secured the horses beneath the shade of the trees.

Glancing over his shoulder, ensuring no one else was nearby, he whispered to Jessica, "I told Lord Frederick you pretend to have headaches to avoid doing unpleasant things."

"You told him what?" Jessica's eyes widened. "I have never pretended to have a headache in my life. For any reason."

"That isn't the point, though, is it?" He winked at her, and Jessica's cheeks turned pink. Then she narrowed them, glaring at him in a manner he'd seen quite often.

"You're quite horrid, you know." She opened and closed her fingers, as though wishing to grasp at something out of reach. She settled for folding her arms across her chest, tucking her hands tightly beneath her elbows. "Did you really need to invent such a story?"

James simply shrugged. "He is far more interested in you than I believed possible, given such a short acquaintance. I thought it best to head him off, so to speak."

"Dear me," she said, her voice lowered as she peered over the back of her gelding at him. "It sounds as though you think someone's opinion of me would improve upon greater acquaintance. How strange we are not the best of friends, if that is true."

He smirked. “Perhaps I am merely immune to your charms. Whatever they may be.”

“That you think I have any is a marked improvement to your view of me. Should I be grateful?”

“Gratitude is a virtue, I’m told.”

She batted her eyelashes at him and put one hand to her chest, feigning a gasp. “Now you think I am charming as well as virtuous? And after a single day of our truce? We ought to be careful, or you’ll be the next gentleman I’ll have to rid myself of.”

He choked back a laugh. “You have nothing to fear on that account. Charming and virtuous you may be, but I’m well acquainted with your razor-sharp tongue. What man would wish a companionship with that for the whole of his life?”

“What woman would want to be stuck with someone who didn’t value her sharp wit?” she returned with a confident lift of her chin.

“Touche.” James scooped his rock up from the ground at last. “Don’t forget. You get headaches when you find things unpleasant.” He walked away, smirking to himself.

Their meal was small, but perfectly suited to the day. Slices of bread, cheeses, dried meat, and fruits sprinkled with sugar kept them from needing utensils. Lady Isabelle remarked that it felt quite wild, eating with her fingers out of doors.

“It is one of my favorite things about summer,” Catherine said with a happy sigh. “Slipping away like this, ignoring the conventions usually forced upon us. Even eating is fraught with rules and expectations.”

“Oh, I quite agree,” Lady Isabelle said, plucking a fig from her plate. “Especially if you have ever eaten at the table of someone like the Prince Regent, or a duke. Despite a lifetime of training, I always worry I will use the wrong fork or drink from the wrong cup, and everyone will notice."

The two of them giggled, but James's attention remained on the other young nobleman. The man had been quiet, and he'd spent most of his meal frowning at his food or sneaking curious glances at Jessica.

It seemed he'd finally found a way to approach the topic that bothered him, thanks to the conversation of his sister.

"Miss Westcote, do forgive me if I am wrong, but I cannot think that I have ever seen you at such a formal evening before. I cannot remember meeting you in London during the Season. I know I would have remembered catching a glimpse of one so stately as you." His smile would have charmed a lesser woman, but James saw Jessica's posture grow rigid. She wasn't about to be soothed by the compliment amidst the implied question.

Still, she replied tactfully. "The air in Town doesn't agree with me. I much prefer the countryside and its tranquility." She tapped at her lips with her napkin. "London causes the most fearful headaches."

James gave an apologetic shrug when Frederick glanced his way.

Catherine's expression changed to one of confusion, and for a moment James's lungs seized up. She could give away everything by one comment. Instead, his sister gave an indifferent shake of her head and spoke as if she'd known Jessica's aversion to town all along.

"I certainly cannot blame anyone for such a thing. London is terribly sooty, is it not, Lady Isabelle? Not at all like the country. One has only to look about on a day like today and prefer this to the other."

"Of course. The country is likely much better for one's health," Lady Isabelle agreed.

Catherine and Lady Isabelle thankfully turned the discussion to how lovely the countryside was, and Lord Frederick applied himself to their comments rather than risk another with Jessica.

James tried to catch Jessica's eye with a triumphant smile, but she kept her gaze lowered. She fiddled with the napkin in her lap, not joining in the conversation. Soon, her eyes grew rather dull and as distant as a faraway thundercloud.

Had telling a single falsehood bothered her that much?

He doubted it. But what had discomfited her? The remarks about Town, perhaps, and her avoidance of it. He'd always found it strange that she looked quite wistful when she spoke of London, yet hardly ever said a word about her lack of travel. He'd assumed at some point that her father didn't wish her to leave their home. Hadn't that been something a father had decreed in one of those books Catherine made him read last summer? What had that book been called? A woman's first name. *Ellen* or *Emma* or some such thing.

Jessica had never acted upset. Yet here, studying her, he saw a hint of something akin to sadness.

Puzzling.

Once the picnic ended, they prepared to ride back to the way they had come, packing everything away well enough that the servants wouldn't be troubled with broken dishes or squished fruits.

As they mounted their horses, Frederick approached Jessica and said in an annoyingly patronizing tone, "Mounting without a block can be tricky for ladies. You must allow me to assist you."

Jessica had been prepared to use the same stump as the

other two women, but she forced a smile and used Lord Frederick's offered knee and hand. The man smugly smiled up at her, and James knew at once that Frederick had misstepped.

The stiff hold of Jessica's chin said everything politeness wouldn't allow to be spoken out loud. And poor Lord Frederick hadn't the skills needed to read Jessica's expression the way James could.

Jessica had experienced enough of his condescension.

As soon as the five of them were on the road once more, she raised her hand and pointed to a wide hedge near the road.

"What a marvelous opportunity that shrubbery presents. Mr. Aldwick, do you think your horse equal to taking it in a jump?"

Without thought, James knew how she wished him to respond. "My horse is equal to the task, I would wager, but his rider is not."

"I cannot imagine there are many who would take such a risk," Lord Frederick said, studying the hedge as well. "Even with intimate knowledge of my steed, I would not try it."

"You wouldn't, my lord?" She blinked at him, quite innocently. "And I suppose you would never try it if you rode sidesaddle, as I do?"

He chuckled. "Of course not. What folly. It would be a certain route to disaster to attempt such a thing."

She joined him in his laughter, and James tightened his grip on the reins in his hands.

"Oh, no," Catherine muttered from behind them.

James knew what was coming as well as his sister did.

And Jessica did not disappoint them.

Without hesitation, she spurred her horse into a gallop.

off the road, into the meadow, and made straight for the hedge. A hedge she had jumped successfully every year since her thirteenth birthday.

"Merciful heavens," Lady Isabelle gasped. "Someone should stop her! Freddie!"

Freddie had frozen in place. All of them had. Watching as Jessica guided her horse across the bright green grass, then took a perfectly executed jump over the large hedge, landing smoothly on the other side. Her laughter floated back to them on the breeze.

Lord Frederick fell silent, and James had to bite his lip to keep from joining Jessica's whole-hearted mirth. She returned to the road ahead of them, and when their party met up with her, it was Lady Isabelle and Catherine who praised her. Catherine with reluctance, Lady Isabelle with true admiration.

James kept silent, riding alongside Lord Frederick.

They went first to Jessica's home, Fairbrook Lodge. Lady Isabelle and Catherine waited at the bottom of the drive while Lord Frederick and James escorted Jessica all the way to the lodge's door.

When she dismounted at the steps of her house, a groom appearing to take the reins from her, she turned around with a wide smile.

"That was a lovely afternoon. Thank you for inviting me along."

"Are you joining us for dinner tonight?" Lord Frederick asked, glancing at James. The man appeared quite beaten already. "At Castle Amoret?"

It took all of James's willpower not to laugh, or fall off his horse, as Jessica politely placed her hand to her forehead and said, "I fear I have the beginnings of a headache coming on. I couldn't possibly participate this evening."

Lord Frederick seemed to shrink as he murmured a reply that was likely as polite as it was inaudible, then turned his horse about to rejoin his sister and Catherine.

Jessica glanced once more at James, and he tipped his head in a subtle salute.

She narrowed her eyes at him, then whispered quietly, "Kissing gate. We need to talk."

He raised his eyebrows and glanced over his shoulder to ensure no one else was within hearing distance. "Tomorrow. At ten?"

Jessica nodded, satisfied, and went into the house.

They had done it. Her first summer suitor wouldn't linger, nor take a request of courtship to her father. A flutter of guilt stirred as he realized he had deliberately misled the other gentleman, who seemed a good sort, all things considered. But the end justified the means, he told himself.

He and Jessica were both quite safe from courtship and matrimony for at least another week.

CHAPTER TEN

With a gloved finger, Jessica tapped the stone wall separating her father's property from the baron's grounds, where James would soon appear. Staying on her side of the boundary wall seemed best. Jessica's irritation at James simmered just below the surface, held in check only by years of practice. Jessica wanted nothing more than to throttle him at that moment.

Even after spending hours in Lord Frederick's company, the best thing he could think of to make Jessica a less than ideal marital candidate was to say she pretended to have *headaches*?

Perhaps she could tell the next unmarried lady that James belched uncontrollably whenever he found a conversation dull. It would serve him right to have to perform such a rude action in front of others.

Though, she supposed, it would be somewhat of an escalation on her part. At least headaches produced no shameful sights or sounds. Still. He needed to know there were better ways to chase off men as patronizing to ladies as someone like Lord Frederick.

A dog yipped, and Jessica looked across the stone wall to find a little white terrier with black spots charging toward her. The animal barked happily again, then pranced on his side of the wall.

"If it isn't Ottis." She leaned over the wall and grinned at him as he sat, like the very best of dogs, grinning up at her with his tongue lolling outside his mouth. "What are you doing all the way out here?"

"I thought he would appreciate a change of scenery," James's voice called as he appeared, jogging and grinning at her. "The old boy hasn't had his run of the place since he was granted retirement in the kitchens."

Ottis, a handsome terrier nearing fourteen years of age, yipped again. Directly at Jessica. She sighed and went to the gate, making her way through it with cares to avoid catching her skirt. The dog met her the instant she was on his side, both front paws tapping happily on the ground until she crouched down to rub him behind the ears. She crooned to him, as one must to such a delightful animal, then looked up at James.

He'd leaned against the wall, crossing his boots at the ankles, and appeared quite smug.

"You brought him because you knew he would weaken my irritation with you. Didn't you?"

His eyes gleamed with laughter, but he shrugged. "I haven't any notion what you could mean. Ottis caught an especially terrifying mouse yesterday, according to the kitchen maids, so I thought a jaunt through the trees a suitable reward. Given that he's a pensioner, and the cat ought to have been on mouse patrol, he went above and beyond his duty."

"He likely misses all the rabbit hunts from his youth." Jessica removed her gloves the better to lavish affection on the dog, who promptly rolled onto his back and wriggled happily beneath her attention.

"You mean the actual hunts, or the pretended ones you sent him on?" James's smile softened as he shook his head. "I still haven't determined how you made him, made *my* dog, run about the house like a beast possessed, barking at shadows and driving everyone mad. And who took the blame?"

Arranging her features into those of a wide-eyed innocent, she glanced up at him to ask, "Who?"

He glowered at her. "Me. I did, Jessica. And the lectures I received—yes, plural. There was more than one. They were long and awful. How did you recruit Ottis into your service so handily?"

She bit her lip and avoided looking at him. "I haven't any idea what you could mean. Everyone thought you'd trained him to cause a ruckus anytime you felt the least bit bored."

"Like you. With your headaches."

Her gaze came up and she gasped. "Is *that* how you came up with the idea? Instead of a barking dog to save me from tedium, I have headaches?"

He narrowed his eyes at her. "How did you turn Ottis against me, Jess?"

A little thrill went through her, from the top of her spine all the way to her toes. Not because he called her Jess, of course. That would be silly. But because he'd finally acknowledged a time when she'd bested him.

That had been a marvelous autumn for her, nearly ten years previous. James had been home, taking time away from his studies at Cambridge. Jessica, fifteen years of age, had found herself uncertain how to treat him. Surely, they were both too old for pranks. And she'd caught herself glancing at him rather too often. Every time she visited Catherine, her gaze would linger on James.

She'd almost found him charming.

Then he'd put an alarming amount of cayenne pepper in her teacup. And anyone who knew Jessica knew that ruining her tea would incur her ire. Tea was soothing, and quite sacred.

That had put them back on familiar ground. And Jessica, having developed a rapport with Ottis, had struck back with a plan as clever as it was creative.

Despite knowing James's intention, Jessica had to admit to herself he knew her far too well. Ottis's cheerful presence *had* diminished her irritation with his owner.

She stood up again and brushed her hands along the front of her gown, then tugged her glove back into place.

"How do you think I managed it?" she challenged. "You have had years to puzzle it out. If I was the one to make Ottis go on the hunt, how could I have done it?"

Slowly, James shook his head. "I've only seen him in such a frenzy of barking and dashing about when there was a rabbit or a weasel to run to ground. Squirrels, sometimes. I doubt you released live game in my mother's withdrawing room the night my great-aunt Mary came to visit."

A laugh nearly escaped, and Jessica covered her lips with her gloved fingers, pressing the laughter backward before she spoke. "I remember that."

He would never guess how clever she had been. And that she'd managed her prank without Catherine's help, for once. It helped that she was on good terms with the castle's kennel master. Since childhood, she'd dragged Catherine with her to visit the kennels every time puppies were whelped. At first, Mr. Forrester had disapproved. He'd hurried her along or told her she asked too many questions about the dogs.

But then he'd let her watch his training sessions with them.

She'd seen how Ottis was trained, along with several of his brothers and sisters, to hunt rabbits.

"Tell me," James said, bringing her attention back to him. They were both leaning against the wall now. He moved closer, so that when he bent forward their faces were no more than two feet apart. He lowered his voice, his tone almost beseeching. "Please? I have always wondered."

The satisfaction that admission brought couldn't be overstated. Years had gone by, and he'd never figured it out. A delightful moment of triumph made her heart race, and she looked down at Ottis, now rolling in the grass near their feet. The dog saw her state and froze, opening his jaw and panting at her.

"Ought we to tell him our secrets?"

The dog yipped at her, and she giggled.

James laughed too. "That sounds like he wants to confess his part in it, at least."

"I suppose if my co-conspirator wishes it, I must tell all." She lowered her voice, as though there was a chance someone spied upon them. "I hid training lures made of rabbit fur around the castle and on my person."

His mouth fell open. "You did *what*?"

She grinned at him. "Mr. Forrester let me watch when he trained Ottis's litter. The dogs were taught to recognize and follow the scent of rabbits when he would expose them to fur and droppings." She wrinkled her nose. "Then he would make trails in a field, using those scents, and leave a false rabbit for them to bring back to him. Made of rabbit skin. They always had a reward after, so they were quite eager to play such games."

"You put rabbit droppings in your reticule?" he asked, eyes gleaming.

That made her snort. "Never. Only the lures made from fur." She wrinkled her nose at him. "And when Ottis was about, and I knew you would benefit from his causing a scene, I would fetch the fur from where I had put it and dangle it within his view, then hide it. No one else noticed a thing."

James's brow furrowed and he stared at her with such a fierce expression that, for a long moment, she thought he was upset. But then his frown melted into a smile, which grew to a grin, and he finally threw his head back and laughed. Long and loud, the rich sound coaxing back the warmth of delight she'd felt at besting him.

"I never imagined," he said at last, his voice still choked with amusement, "that prim and proper Jessica Westcote would sneak about my castle with rabbit-scented lures, *knowing* I would eventually be reprimanded for it."

"There were several layers to my plans," she admitted with a shrug. "I thought you would either be embarrassed, eventually, or caught out by your parents."

"Oh, indeed. I was." He sobered and a gleam of trouble appeared in his lovely blue eyes. "You are too clever by half."

"I did feel guilty about one thing," she admitted, casting her gaze downward.

"Really? You? My arch nemesis cannot have felt any remorse for my sake." Yet he didn't sound entirely disbelieving. In fact, he seemed curious.

Best to disabuse him of that notion at once, lest he think

she'd softened toward him. Because she certainly hadn't. Even if she had agreed to help him through the summer.

"I did feel remorse," she said, stepping a little closer. She sighed, looked directly into his dark eyes, and said, "Poor Ottis always had to wait hours before I could reward him for his efforts."

The dog yipped at hearing his name and rolled about in the grass again.

James groaned and put both hands to his heart. "I knew it. You've never had a care for my wretched self." Yet his expression was as merry as ever, and almost...admiring? No. If he admired anything, it was having a worthy opponent.

With an unrepentant grin, she assured him and herself, "Never a moment's pity, either."

"Then I suppose we had better get on with things, lest your patience with me run out as well." He gestured to the path along the wall, worn into the grass by man and beast over the years. "Shall we walk? You can tell me whatever it was that made you scowl at me yesterday."

Jessica fell into step beside him, and Ottis trotted along in front of them, lifting his head to look about for any sign of threat from squirrels.

"You told Lord Frederick that I'm dishonest."

"Not exactly."

"But that is the crux of what you told him," she insisted, and that twist of discomfort in her stomach made her swallow. "Even in all our battles with each other, I've never been accused of dishonesty, or telling falsehoods. It isn't something I wish people to associate with my character, either."

"It was a believable way to express your disinterest in him and in London. Women feign headaches and illness all the time," he said, looking at her askance. "I cannot tell you how often I have heard a woman beg not to dance because her feet hurt, even if she has just arrived to a ball. It had more to do with who was asking than her well-being. I have even heard a woman claim an aversion to flowers rather than agree to a walk in the park."

Her stomach clenched unpleasantly. She had a view to such things that James had never seen. Even though his travels and movements in Society made him more worldly, it didn't sound as though he understood this thinnest level of defense that women had been taught to hold between themselves and unwanted attention.

"I will not say such a thing is right." How could Jessica make him understand? "And I cannot say this is true in every circumstance. Yet how often, in your experience, can a woman simply decline a man's attention without being perceived poorly? Or as giving an insult?"

His eyebrows drew together. "What do you mean?"

"Let us say I am at a ball. A man I have been introduced to in the past comes toward me to ask me to dance. The thing is, I know this man is terribly unkind in the way he speaks of others. He is most unpleasant to spend a moment with, let alone a quarter of an hour through a dance. Or longer, if what I hear of London Balls is true."

"Horribly true," James muttered, then raised his hand. "Pardon me. You were saying? This odious man has asked you to dance?"

"Yes. I have three options in such a circumstance. The first is to politely decline with honesty. 'Thank you for asking, sir, but I would rather not dance with you.' What might the reaction be?"

"He would feel insulted," James acknowledged. "Perhaps even tell others you slighted him."

"Even though he is the one with the poor behavior, I will be the one to suffer damage to my character," she pointed out. "A second option would be to accept his offer and spend a quarter of an hour to half an hour listening to his cruel criticism of others."

"Untenable," James muttered, looking away as his lips formed a flat line.

"The last option, the one that many a young lady will choose, is to decline with a reason that has nothing to do with the man's character. 'I thank you for asking, sir, but I am afraid I have torn my hem and must search out a maid.' Or perhaps, 'I promised my friend I would find her.' And so she has told a falsehood purely to protect herself."

His jaw tightened somewhat. "I hadn't given a circumstance like that much thought. When the excuse is made in such a way, the man cannot possibly defame the lady without sounding like a brute for insisting she dance despite a headache, sore feet, or so forth."

"It is a lesson women learn early. Even women like me, who never venture far from their home." She tried to smile, despite the sudden weightiness in the air. "So when you told Lord Frederick that I lie to avoid unpleasant things, that was untrue about me, and quite a harsh criticism on ladies who must tell polite falsehoods to protect themselves from the attentions of men they would much rather avoid."

"I think I understand." James paused and took in a deep breath. "It seems I owe you another apology."

"Not at all." She clasped her hands behind her back and examined his expression, tilting her head to one side. "That you listened is enough. There are other ways to make someone like me unappealing to a man like Lord Frederick, you know."

"You ought to have heard what I did." James came back to himself with a playful swoon, bringing his shoulders back against the stone wall behind him. "'Can you believe that woman? Jumping a hedge that she'd no right to! She could have broken her neck. What a thoughtless thing to do, to display herself in that way.'"

When Jessica only stared at him, James opened one eye at her.

"That is a near-direct quote from the man himself, speaking to his sister-in-law, about your skills with a horse."

"Ah. I thought you'd lost your senses for a moment." She laughed. "But you *do* see what I mean about him?"

He stayed leaning against the wall and crossed his arms over his chest, making himself the picture of masculine smugness. "He's a feather-brained fop. He genuinely believes that a woman is less inclined to grow in skill or intelligence than a man, even if presented with the same opportunities. I asked him last night—and I wish you had been there—if he thought a woman schooled in mathematics would be as likely to pass an exam as a man. Do you know what he said?"

"No," she answered with some amusement. "I wasn't there. Remember?" Yet he'd wished she had been there. Why? For her company or for the pleasure of exchanging their usual barbed conversation?

"He said any man possessed of rational thought would know it impossible for a woman to make the calculations of which a man is capable."

"A ludicrous presumption," Jessica agreed with a slight smile. "Why did you make that particular argument?"

"Catherine found out that Lady Isabelle is a mathematical expert." He grinned at her. "And when he said his opinion on the matter, the marquess stepped in and came as close to reprimanding Lord Frederick as he could, in public anyway, for saying such a thing."

Jessica shook her head and retrieved a stick from the ground. "I find myself in agreement with you about one thing."

"What is that?" James sounded surprised.

She tossed the stick for Ottis to chase. "I wish I had been there last night, too, if only to see that moment."

CHAPTER ELEVEN

Though Catherine expressed sorrow at Lady Isabelle's departure, as the two had become fast friends, the baron wasn't surprised when the marquess and his siblings left without any word of courtship between James and the unwed lady. At breakfast the next day, the baron merely announced that their next guests would arrive in two days' time.

James managed to suggest Catherine invite her dearest friend to be present when this new family arrived. To "save time later" on introductions. Though she seemed somewhat suspicious of his motives, Catherine had invited Jessica to appear by her side when the coach with Lord Richland and his family arrived.

"Here we are again," Catherine muttered quietly enough that her voice didn't carry beyond James or Jessica, the two of them flanking her. "Trotting the prized ponies out to see if they suit one another."

Jessica cast Catherine a grimace. "At least you aren't part of the herd. This time." Jessica had finally told Catherine about her father's desire to see her wed. Good. James hadn't liked knowing something about Jessica that his sister didn't.

It had felt odd.

"Maybe next year," James said, as though to cheer his sister up. "Perhaps all three of us can go through this exercise again."

"You aren't going to get out of it," Catherine said, caution in her tone. "They *will* see you married off by the end of the year, James."

James glanced over his sister's head to make eye contact with Jessica as he said, "We'll see about that."

The invited earl, his wife, and his daughter descended from the carriage. Riding behind them in a smaller vehicle were the earl's two grown sons, both of them bachelors.

As Lord Retford made the introductions, both eligible sons tried to stand a little taller. Yet no matter how they tried to stretch their necks upward, they still found themselves too short.

Jessica wore half-boots with two-inch heels. At James's suggestion. Footwear she normally reserved for outdoor use when there was a chance of puddles. Her natural height, with the two inches added, put her five or six inches taller than both bachelors. And they looked at her as though she was a giantess.

"Miss Westcote, you say?" the elder of the two, Lord William, the next in line to be earl, simpered up at her. "Any relation to the Earl of Wyndham? I believe his family name is Westcote."

Keeping her posture perfect and her head tilted slightly upward, Jessica gave a succinct nod. "He is my uncle. My father's older brother."

Lord William exchanged a glance with his younger

brother, Lord Henry, their look significant. Neither said anything more on the matter.

"A pleasure, Miss Westcote," was all Lord Henry said as he bowed, then tucked his hands behind his back and glanced impatiently at his father, waiting to be led into the house. Not deigning to have another word with Jessica or anyone else.

Perhaps being tall himself made it difficult to understand why certain men cared about such a thing as their wife's height. What did it matter how tall a woman was when she carried herself, as Jessica did, with grace and confidence? And had a beautiful, Grecian look to her features, too.

The fashionable set was mad for all things Greek and Roman. Why didn't that same fervor apply to a statuesque woman like Jessica?

Dissuading the men from courtship with her would be simple this time. As James bowed to Lady Helen, he took in her soft smile and glowing eyes and realized that he faced greater danger than Jessica.

Fortunately, when the guests went to their rooms to freshen up from their journey, James found Jessica and Catherine in the Rose Room. They were going through the list of activities planned for the week. He pulled a chair closer to where the two of them perched on a sofa then settled himself as casually as he could.

Catherine stared at him as though he had lost his wits. "What do you want, James?"

Jessica bit her lip and said nothing, though her eyes danced in merriment. He rarely sat with them when no one else was in the room. Of course his sister would experience a level of suspicion.

He shrugged. "'Misery acquaints a man with strange bedfellows'?"

Catherine's eyes narrowed. "Do not quote Shakespeare at me."

At that, Jessica's smile slipped free. "Really, James. You cannot be in misery already. They have only just arrived."

He huffed and slumped a little more comfortably into his chair. "I would tell you what Shakespeare said about time, but I have been warned off quoting him." He glowered playfully at his sister.

Catherine looked upward abruptly. Perhaps searching for her patience. "Do you want something, James?"

"Companionship."

"Then do as Papa says and find someone to marry."

Jessica winced. "The right someone, though."

"Ah, there's the rub—"

"No *Hamlet*, either," Catherine cut him off, then sighed. "I'll call for refreshment." She stage-whispered to Jessica. "Maybe once he's fed, he will leave us alone." She rose and went to the door, leaving it open as she stepped into the hall to speak to a footman.

James leaned forward and spoke quickly, in a whisper, "Begin by exaggerating any flaws you think I possess. Start small and work your way up."

A smile spread across Jessica's lips. "An excellent plan. I can certainly think of a few things."

Before he could begin to worry what she meant by that, Catherine returned to the room and assured them tea and biscuits would arrive soon. James settled back in his seat and let his sister and her friend speak as freely as ever, without interrupting them. Enjoying the domestic chatter without feeling the need to do more than take it in.

There was much to be said for enjoying the simple pleasure of a comfortable room and good company. With his eyes closed, he listened to the gentle flow of conversation. Catherine's cheerful chatter with Jessica's calmer tones had nearly lulled him into sleep by the time two footmen reappeared with trays of food and drink.

"I thought we'd lost you to your dreams," Jessica said, putting delicately cut slices of bread on her plate. "Do we bore you that much, James?"

"Not at all." He served himself a large fruit tart. "I found myself content to listen. Contrary to what you may think, a lively conversation between the two of you could never bore me. You're both intelligent ladies with interesting thoughts. Or so I find. I was merely enjoying the moment."

Catherine paused before taking a sip of her tea. "Goodness, James. You needn't waste your flattery on the two of us. We know you too well. But I suppose we appreciate your company. When it is *silent* company. Do we not, Jess?"

"Indeed." Jessica gave him a good-natured grin. "Though I'm surprised you managed to keep your thoughts to yourself for so long."

"There is wisdom in knowing when to speak and when to listen." James settled more comfortably in his chair.

The two ladies shared a surprised glance before turning their stares upon him. He grinned, pleased to have taken them by surprise, and gave his attention to his tea and tart. After listening to the likes of Lord Frederick the week before, noting how often the man felt the need to interrupt women speaking to interject his supposedly superior thoughts, James had determined to avoid acting similarly.

The distaste he'd felt toward the marquess's brother would likely stay with him for some time, with Lord Frederick an excellent example of everything *not* to do. After the first meeting with their new guests, James had a feeling he'd be adding Lord William and Lord Henry's traits to that growing list of qualities he didn't wish to embody.

When he caught Jessica's gaze a moment later, he noted the curiosity in her eyes. She studied him without attempting to hide it. He raised both eyebrows and saluted her with his teacup. Her cheeks pinked slightly as she gave her attention back to Catherine and their discussion of two servants they suspected had a romantic interest in one another.

James let himself enjoy the quiet, and neither lady remarked when he stayed long after they had finished eating their light repast.

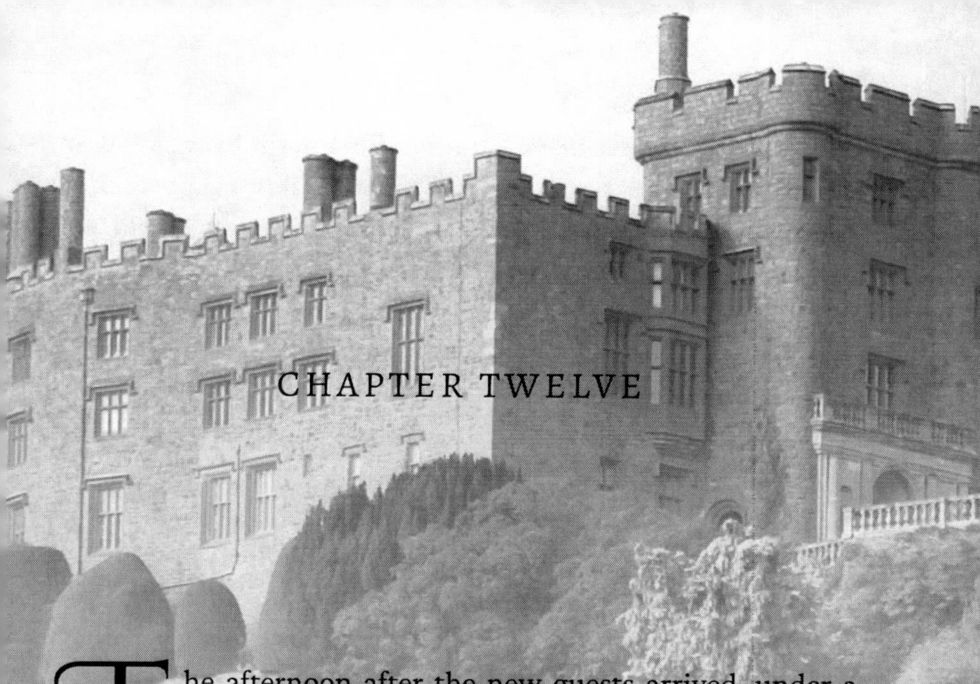

CHAPTER TWELVE

The afternoon after the new guests arrived, under a clear sky decorated with fluffy, wandering clouds, Jessica embarked on the next step of her mission. The gardens of Castle Amoret, with their blooming roses and a small maze of hedges, provided the perfect atmosphere for conversation. She found herself strolling leisurely with Lady Helen and Catherine, navigating the intricacies of garden paths while subtly undermining James's prospects.

"And this is the rose garden," Catherine said as Jessica walked behind her friend and the lovely Lady Helen.

"It's beautiful," Lady Helen replied, her tone soft and awed. "It must be a delight to walk here every day. Do you visit your friends' garden often, Miss Westcote?"

"I do, indeed. And I find it both lovely and peaceful. Although," Jessica made a show of hesitating before lowering her voice to a conspiratorial whisper. "Some might say it's too serene."

"Oh?" Catherine chimed in, slowing her pace and raising her eyebrows. "How so?"

Catherine's presence meant handling her role as saboteur with the greatest of delicacy. Her friend couldn't suspect that James and Jessica had joined forces in their mutual bid for independence. The only time Jessica had expressed her reason for not wanting to marry to her friend, Catherine had lectured her for more than an hour about not letting her short-comings blind her to future happiness.

Easy for Catherine to say, when she didn't have to worry about having a fit in the middle of a ball.

"Well," Jessica said, drawing out the single syllable. "Consider your brother. Mr. Aldwick. He does love a good jest, doesn't he?"

Catherine laughed lightly. "He can be insufferable at times," she admitted to Lady Helen. "And the garden is one of the places he enlivens with his pranks."

Jessica didn't let the story telling end there. She hastened to add, "He once hid live frogs beneath a *cloche* at a garden party. Lady Retford thought she was revealing a particularly elegant arrangement of pastries and didn't immediately see the reason for the guests' sudden shrieks."

Lady Helen turned somewhat pale, though she released a weak giggle. "Oh dear. Was he quite young when he did that?"

"Not at all," Catherine said with a wince, and the look she gave Jessica was full of regret. Jessica knew her friend well enough to guess that Catherine realized they weren't painting her brother in the best light.

"I was twelve, so he must have been fifteen," Jessica said to the wide-eyed lady. "It was the first time Catherine and I were invited to one of Lady Retford's garden parties."

Which had been why James sabotaged it. Because Jessica had put on airs, and he'd likely wanted to get revenge for a similar joke when she'd put a frog in his pocket the first time his father had asked him to make a toast at dinner.

"Was his mother very upset?" Lady Helen asked, lowering her voice.

A movement, or perhaps merely the suggestion of movement, caught Jessica's eye. She turned her gaze toward the tall hedges that made up the border for the maze.

"At first," Catherine said, tone still serious. "But then she laughed and had the frogs removed. Mama is quite skilled at making the best of any situation."

Jessica moved closer to the hedge wall. She knew this maze quite well, though the gardeners changed entrances to walls from time to time. They stood where there had been a break the year before, and the foliage hadn't quite filled in the gap. She narrowed her eyes as she stared through the leaves.

"All of Mr. Aldwick's jests are made in good humor, of course," Jessica assured her friend's guest, turning just enough to keep the hedge in her view. "But his incessant teasing can be a bit... overwhelming."

Catherine sighed. "He enjoys making others laugh. But I suppose not *everyone* appreciates his style of humor." The warning in her gaze was quite clear, so Jessica smiled reassuringly at her friend.

Drawing upon the observations she'd gathered over the years, she tried to speak as though she sincerely found what she said next a positive thing.

Jessica deftly maneuvered the subject to James's literary habits. "Mr. Aldwick has a great love for books. Do you enjoy reading, Lady Helen?"

The earl's daughter relaxed somewhat and nodded. "I do. A few pages of poetry every day is good for one's soul, I believe."

A few pages? Jessica briefly bit her lip to keep from smiling. "I couldn't agree more. Though Mr. Aldwick takes his love of literature to greater heights."

Catherine, accustomed to teasing her brother about his bookish tendencies, fell into the discussion with an easy laugh. "Oh, you mean his habit of disappearing for hours, lost in the library?" She shook her head, "I cannot count the number of times he's been late to dinner, having lost track of time with a book."

Jessica nodded along, adding, "It's charming, of course, to have a man so dedicated to literature, but when it begins to interfere with his social obligations..." Another slight movement on the other side of the hedges affirmed her earlier suspicion.

James was on the other side, listening in.

"Or when he stays up all night to read?" Catherine giggled. "You can always tell," she informed Lady Helen. "He is quite grumpy on those mornings. Late to breakfast. Short-tempered. Until you ask about his book, and then he can speak of how much he enjoyed it, recounting what he read for hours at a time."

Lady Helen, with her youthful curiosity, turned to Jessica. "I have never heard of a gentleman devoting such time to his studies. Are his books of a scholarly nature?"

"Oh, almost never." Jessica met her gaze with a mock-serious expression, shaking her head. "He is a great devotee to novels. And it isn't merely breakfast that suffers for his interest." She couldn't suppress the playful grin that crept onto her face.

With each word, she was aware of their unseen audience. She could feel James's presence behind the hedge, his silence almost louder than the rustling leaves.

"Surely, it's not as bad as you're saying," Lady Helen countered, a tinge of disbelief lacing her voice.

"Oh, it isn't bad," Catherine said quickly, alarm in her tone again.

"Of course not," Jessica agreed with a reassuring smile for Lady Helen. "How could a love for books ever be perceived as a flaw? Even if it means Mr. Aldwick has a strained relationship with punctuality because of it."

"Punctuality?" Lady Helen echoed, sounding confused.

"That is true, though he never means to keep people waiting. And besides, what do a few minutes here and there really matter?" Catherine sounded anxious.

Perhaps Jessica had taken things far enough. Lady Helen appeared less enthusiastic than she had at the beginning of their walk, and Catherine's puckered brow deserved some sympathy from her friend.

Jessica cared a glance through the hedge to find James peering at her through the leaves. His eyes conveyed a silent approval, and she felt a flush of satisfaction. She had done enough.

"But don't let any of what we say put you off," Catherine said, trying to reassure Lady Helen. "James is a good man, with a good heart. Merely a little different."

"Different," Lady Helen echoed, sounding unimpressed.

Jessica smiled through the leaves at her co-conspirator. He winked. Then disappeared. She could only imagine the grin on his face as he withdrew in silence.

She murmured softly, hardly aware she spoke, "I've always been fond of different myself."

Shaking her head, she turned back to the other ladies to find Catherine staring at her with wide-eyed shock.

Oh dear. Perhaps she hadn't been as circumspect as she'd

hoped. But at least James had seemed to approve. Jessica could make amends with her friend later. What mattered at that moment was working in harmony with James.

Bessie met Jessica at the kissing gate at the agreed-upon time to keep her mistress company on the walk home. The baron's family was hosting a card party after dinner.

"Did you have an enjoyable afternoon, miss?"

"I did, thank you. Everything about it was most satisfactory."

What were the chances that James would have a book on hand to keep glancing at throughout the evening, pretending to have more interest in its pages than the company? She felt certain he would match his performance to her words. Knowing him as well as she did, she couldn't imagine anything else.

Bessie raised her eyebrows. "That smile on your face says so well enough. I thought you didn't like the earl's sons?"

"Oh, I didn't see them at all. I spent the afternoon with Catherine and Lady Helen."

"Ah, I see. Do you think Lady Helen will be the one for our Mr. Aldwick?" Bessie asked, facing forward and sounding almost uninterested. Strange. Usually, she adored gossip of this sort.

"No. I doubt it. She's quite young, and I doubt she would want to settle for a man who would rather be home with a book than out at balls. Not at her age."

"I thought Mr. Aldwick enjoys dancing. He certainly seems to at the assembly balls." Again, something about Bessie's tone seemed off. Her disinterest in the matter didn't sound right.

"He does. But Lady Helen doesn't know that." Jessica smiled to herself. "I think I will have all the young people to tea tomorrow. To give Catherine a change of scenery." And watch James smuggle a book to the event.

"I will let Cook know, of course. And Mr. Riley."

At mention of the butler, Jessica turned the conversation that direction, inquiring if there was more yet known about Mrs. Turner, the Amoret housekeeper, and Mr. Riley's budding romance.

At last, Bessie seemed like her usual self, speaking with animation about all the supposition regarding the two upper servants. They had been observed sharing a hymnal at the last evening service they attended, which was nearly as telling as a kiss in Bessie's opinion.

They stayed on that topic as the entire time Bessie helped Jessica dress for dinner and an evening at the castle.

As the sun lowered in the sky, painting it with hues of orange and pink, Jessica wasn't thinking about the placement of pearls in her hair. Instead, she pictured what James would look like that evening, with an elbow propped on a card table and his nose in a book.

Jessica's heart warmed like a cat in a pool of sunbeams. The sensation was quite pleasant. It had to come from her sense of accomplishment. She had fulfilled her promise to James. Lady Helen would be gone within the week. Her brothers with her, thanks to their strange preoccupation with not standing near a woman taller than themselves. They seemed quite content to speak amongst themselves, giving occasional attention to Catherine that she returned with polite disinterest.

What had Lady Helen said of James? That he was unusual? That he was different.

She nearly laughed aloud at that thought.

Yes, that was one way to define him.

He possessed an intelligent mind, but was quick to laugh, forever keeping her on her toes with his unpredictable pranks and unique sense of humor. She couldn't remember now what had started their rivalry. It had been so long ago. Likely, whatever that first jest had been, neither had expected it to begin a lifelong series of battles. A single spark had ignited into a constant blaze of wit and repartee.

As her father assisted her into the carriage that evening, she had only one regret. If James busied himself with pretending complete absorption in a novel, she would lose her most interesting conversation partner for the evening.

James was an ever-present challenge, a provocation that had honed her quick tongue and sharpened her intellect.

"Are you certain neither of the earl's sons are of interest to you?" her father asked.

"None at all. And I assure you, Papa, the feeling is quite mutual. They looked at me as though I was one of those long-necked creatures from Africa. A giraffe."

Her father huffed. "Your mother was tall. Graceful as a queen, too. I cannot understand letting such a thing hinder a chance at coming to know someone as charming as you are, my dear." He patted her hand. "Never fear. There is a man out there who will treasure you. I have no doubt on that account."

She certainly had several of her own. Thanks to years of war, there was a dearth of men in England. Likely in all of Europe. And since she never left home, she was unlikely to find a gentleman on her own. He would have to stumble upon her, somehow. A perfect fit for her, someone who loved her—and she wouldn't waste her life waiting for such a man. It wasn't practical. Even if such a man appeared, prepared to devote his life and heart to her, would he still want her when he witnessed her hysteria firsthand?

She couldn't ask it of a man she loved. So it was better not to worry about such things. Better to convince her father to bequeath her the funds set aside as a dowry for her to set up her own household, when the time came for it.

Jessica shook away the melancholy thought. She had better things to think on. Such as her agreement with James. For the first time in years, she felt excited about what each new day would bring. Most of her days followed an unvarying schedule, which made for a contented life. A predictable one, too.

Sometimes, she missed the years when she worried less about propriety and more about dashing through the kissing gate to visit Catherine and James. Her mind halted, thoughts dashed by a sudden confusion. Visiting Catherine *and* James? She'd never once thought about him when she planned her forays onto their estate!

Except when she made plans of attack.

The carriage jolted over a rut in the road, and the abrupt movement shook loose another surprising thought. Had some of her enthusiasm at visiting Catherine to do with her enjoyment of sparring with James? Even if their every meeting had been fraught with mischief on one side or the other, she had always looked forward to them.

Merciful heavens. Had she truly enjoyed being near him? Even before they'd entered this agreement of theirs?

Yes. The honest answer echoed through her thoughts.

Over the years, their harmless pranks had evolved into something more akin to intellectual fencing matches. Debates that flowed fast and free, glinting with humor and underpinned by a fierce respect for each other's mind. Though she wouldn't admit it out loud, she respected his intellect even when it nearly drove her mad.

"I do hope you will behave yourself tonight," her father said as their carriage rolled through the gates of the castle. As though he'd been privy to her thoughts.

"Papa," she said, hand to her chest as she batted her eyes at him. "I always behave myself."

He chuckled. "I know, my dear. It is that rascal, James, I need to worry about." His smile seemed to freeze a moment, but then he cleared his throat. "Though I am certain he will act the part of a gentleman under his father's eye."

"I wouldn't be surprised if he spends the whole of the evening with perfect behavior," she added as their carriage rolled to a stop. "I doubt he will say more than two words to me."

No one else engaged her quite like James. He was her adversary, her rival, but also her comrade in arms in a world that often didn't understand her need for mental stimulation.

It was all she had, really. Confined as she was to the country, thanks to her strange fits. He would never know how much she relied upon him, either. Not if she could help it. Why tell him about her problem? A condition no visiting physician had an explanation for, nor a cure.

His brown eyes would gleam in challenge, his silence prompting her to justify her viewpoint. Each unspoken question, each subtle raise of his eyebrows, seemed to say, *Are you sure you have thought this through, Jess? You know I can pick that apart, and make you laugh while I do it.*

And he did. As often as he infuriated, she would smirk or cover her mouth to hide a laugh. James always thought he'd won if he stirred her to the point of humor, so she'd often hidden such a reaction with annoyance.

Such interactions stirred a sense of exhilaration within her, their verbal exchanges a dance of the minds that left her eager for the next encounter. He offered her a path for growth, a rare opportunity in their society that often dismissed a woman's intellect.

Her father led her into the castle's entryway, through the corridors to the drawing room where the other guests had gathered. Catherine met them at the door, but after greeting her friend, Jessica's eyes immediately sought out James.

He'd always been so *fun*. Enlivening their interactions with his wit, his humor, his harmless teasing. Even the veiled insults and pranks had been more for amusement than anything, and he'd never minded when she lobbed them right back at him.

James, unusual and challenging as he was, had become an invaluable counterpart in her life. Their competitive camaraderie, their duels of wit, were as intrinsic to her daily existence as the air she breathed.

And if he married—well. She would lose all of it.

The foreign thoughts, the sudden fear they stirred in her breast, alarmed her.

James appeared at her side before she'd recovered, her heart still pounding somewhat painfully. "Here you are. Late." He grinned at her, then held up a slim volume. "Do you approve of my choice this evening?"

She had to blink several times before she could make out the title on the spine of the leather volume. *The Iliad.* An epic poem about a mythological war. Something most people would find dull.

"I do," she said quietly. Her gaze darted up to his, and he grinned at her. Then offered the barest wink of one eye before opening the book and walking away with his nose near its pages, as though completely absorbed by the words on the page.

It was a good thing he wasn't interested in devoting his attention to a lady. But when the day came that he did.... Jessica cut off that thought and focused instead on giving all her attention to Catherine. There was no reason for her to borrow trouble. Or to waste a moment's thought on why the idea of James spending less of his attention on her nettled her heart most unpleasantly.

CHAPTER THIRTEEN

Reclining in the shade of an oak, his eyes watching the border of his property for sight of his neighbor, James tossed a stick for Ottis. The dog dashed off to fetch it and returned again. A simple way to pass the time, James let his thoughts wander as he played the game with the little dog.

Lady Helen and her brothers had left without more than words of friendship spoken between them. And James couldn't tell who was more relieved when she bid him farewell—him or the young lady. It was much easier to say that his father was the most disappointed of everyone.

Until the next guests arrived. And then the next.

The fortnight that followed Lady Helen's visit was a whirlwind of guests and formalities, as a relentless tide of suitors, each with their eyes sparkling with matrimonial intent, descended upon Amoret Castle. From James's perspective, it was a parade of eager faces and hopeful hearts, all vying for his attention. It would have been overwhelming if not for his pact with Jessica.

The future duke and his daughter, who had arrived just

days after Lady Helen's departure, had made their stay *very* short. Then came the brother-in-law to an earl with his eldest daughter and three sons. James had worked diligently to keep all three of them from seeing Jessica as a potential wife.

Today, the seventeenth of July marked the midway point of the month, yet weeks remained of his father's summer scheme.

James counted each day he remained unattached and unengaged as a victory. His father's plans could feasibly stretch across the summer until Michaelmas, at the end of September, if Lord Retford felt desperate enough.

Hopefully, he would give up before then.

If only to spare Jessica from men so blind to her attractive qualities that he could dissuade them with only a few exaggerations of her less attractive habits and features.

"Feather-brained fops and addlepated clodpoles, all of them," he muttered aloud.

Ottis barked, recalling James to his duty as stick-thrower.

He checked his watch. Jessica wasn't late. He'd arrived early. Perhaps too early.

James didn't want her to think him eager for their meeting.

Even if he *was* eager.

Every other morning, they convened at the kissing gate, a landmark which had become their private council chamber.

They discussed their plans, their strategies to put off each new hopeful. They were masterminds of subtle mischief, dropping delicate hints about her aversion to early mornings and his undying commitment to his books, even going so far as to highlight his supposed inability to hold a serious conversation without quoting *Rob Roy*. It was a fine line they walked, maintaining the boundaries of propriety while planting seeds of doubt in the minds of their would-be suitors.

As each suitor came and left, discouraged by their well-spun tales, the success of their strategy only grew. Their mornings at the kissing gate had taken on a strange familiarity, a comfortable rhythm that soothed the discomfort of their social engagements.

In company, they maintained their distance. Though they often sneaked glances at each other, and he at times dared a wink. They communicated their small victories without saying a word where others might hear. A shared smile often said enough on the matter.

An unusual camaraderie settled between them. This was uncharted territory for James, this companionship with a woman who was his equal in wit and resolution.

The days turned into nights and back into days in a loop of banquets and afternoon teas, horse rides and walks in the garden.

With Jessica by his side, it became more of a spectacle, less of a chore. They were a formidable team, their alliance creating a barrier that kept the suitors at bay.

As he waited for her, James found himself oddly at peace. There was an ease in the way he interacted with Jessica now, a peculiar familiarity that came from their shared secret, their mutual goal. It was a strange comfort, but it was comfort, nonetheless.

"I am not late, am I?"

Jessica's voice snapped James out of his thoughts. He looked up to see her coming through the gate, giving more attention to her skirts than to him, ensuring they didn't catch on the gate. Ottis had already darted over to her, prancing on all four paws as he waited for attention.

"Not at all." He slid his watch into his pocket and jumped to his feet. "Ottis merely wanted his exercise to begin earlier."

"He is quite the taskmaster." She bent, gloves already removed, to scratch the little dog behind the ears and give him all the belly rubs he wanted. She was always more relaxed when Ottis was with them, he realized.

"Have you ever thought of getting a dog for yourself?"

She looked up, one corner of her mouth hitching higher than the other. "Me? A dog? My family has never had a pet dog. My uncle doesn't even keep any at this estate, and my father has no interest in them."

She came toward the tree before settling herself on the ground, carefully arranging her skirts around her while Ottis patiently waited for a return of her attention.

"That is why I asked about it for *yourself*, ninny." James lowered himself to the ground again, keeping Ottis between the two of them. "Not hunting dogs for your uncle or father. Merely a small fellow to follow you about, fetch your slippers, and curl up on your feet when you take tea or read. A creature like Ottis, but with better manners."

The dog had flopped down in front of Jessica, and she had resumed lavishing her attention upon him.

She feigned offense with a gasp. "How dare you, sir. Ottis has perfect manners."

Ottis sneezed, then snorted, and squirmed deeper into the grass.

"Yes, I can see that." James raised his eyebrows at her. "My question stands unanswered as of yet, Jess."

She lowered her gaze to the dog again, her brow pinched in a frown. "I asked once, years ago, for a dog. That was when Papa sent me to your kennel master to learn about them. But then, I was with puppies all the time. It seemed unnecessary to have one of my own when I could visit yours whenever I liked." Her smile reappeared, though there was something tight about the corners of her lips. "And I didn't wish to trouble anyone about it, you know. The training, walking, and such."

After a long moment of silence, the only sounds coming from Ottis's happy sniffling of the grass, James gave a firm nod.

"You should have a dog." Before she could protest, he hurried on to the most important point of discussion. "We have a reprieve. The guests invited this week are no longer able to come. Their household has come down with influenza."

"Mr. Arnold, second-cousin and heir-apparent to Lord Raleigh." She relaxed and let her hands fall to her lap. "Will the invitation be reissued after their recovery?"

"Most likely. So we will still have their five children to contend with."

"Three sons, two daughters." She shook her head. "All unmarried. I hadn't any notion there existed so many bachelors and unwed ladies in England."

"Scotland, Wales, and Ireland haven't even been tapped yet," he added with a smirk.

"That isn't an encouraging thought."

He leaned back against the tree again, lacing his fingers behind his head. "Perhaps not. But imagine some Irish baron appears, falls madly in love with you, and takes you away to Ireland with him. Wouldn't that be an adventure?"

The fire came back into her eyes, the familiar flicker of a challenge lighting the gray depths. "It would be more entertaining if you married a Scotswoman who spoke with a brogue so thick you couldn't understand a word she said."

He chuckled and turned his gaze upward. “My father is hosting the fair next week. I think that will provide all the entertainment I could want. Especially given the complexity of the event. And the guest list.”

“Ugh.” It was an unladylike sound, but Jessica rarely bothered to hide behind a polite facade with him. Especially of late. She spoke and expressed herself freely, a thing which gratified him more than she knew. “My cousins will come.”

He winced and sat forward, dropping his hands to the ground beside him. “The Earl of Wyndham and his five daughters. When did they visit last? Five years ago?”

“Four.” She shuddered. “Dare we hope they have improved in manners?”

James shook his head. “I saw them in London last Season and did all I could to avoid an actual conversation. I heard plenty about them, though.”

The Wyndham ladies boasted traditional English looks to go along with their traditional English names. Mary, Jane, Rose, Elizabeth, and Anne. They were beauties, but cold as frost in January.

“My only consolation is that Tom will be home tomorrow.” Jessica fiddled with the ribbons of her bonnet. “He is bringing a friend, too. One of the lawyers who works for the same employer.”

“Your house will be full, it seems.”

She grimaced. “To the very brim. I will not know a moment’s peace.”

“I would invite you to escape to the castle, but we are hosting cousins and another potential bride, along with her family of six.”

“Baron Arnette, your father’s friend.”

“You have a delightful memory.”

"Do I?" She blinked and placed a hand flat against her chest. "Why, James, I believe that is one of the nicest things you have ever said about me. I cannot think of one instance in which you found anything about my person *delightful*. I shall go home and mark the occasion in my diary."

"That cannot be true," he protested. "Are you certain? I think I must have paid you compliments in the past." Had he, though? Of a sudden, he realized he had thought many complimentary things about his foe.

Had he never said any of them aloud?

"You once told me that my sharp tongue might have wounded more Englishmen than a French blade ever did," she reminded him, batting her eyelashes innocently. "I took *that* as a compliment."

James winced. "Is that the nicest thing I have ever said to you?"

Her posture relaxed, and her smile changed from its teasing tilt to something softer. "I haven't exactly showered you with compliments, either. Or said much of anything nice about you. Not directly, anyway."

"I suppose not." But that bothered him less than his own behavior. "I feel like the opposite of a gentleman."

"What would that be?"

"I'm not entirely sure."

"Let me see if I can be of assistance." She tapped her long, tapered finger against her pursed lips. "Perhaps a cad? An imbecile. A bounder. A ruffian, perhaps? Oh, I know. A knave."

He dropped his face in his hands. "There's that sharp tongue again," he said, tone light even though a miserable, pinched feeling had invaded his stomach. He'd never said a kind word to her. The only exception in recent memory was the apology he'd made after wounding her.

"You do find it my best feature, it would seem." She grinned as he peered between his fingers at her. Then stuck that tongue out at him as she had when they were children, seated across the aisle at church from one another. He'd been caught by his mother when he tried to return the gesture and received a sharp elbow in the side for it.

The effect of her sticking out her tongue now was quite different from what it had been then. He'd been annoyed, as a boy of twelve. As a man, staring as her pink lips curved upward in that devious smile, he found himself wanting to lean forward, to attempt to catch those lips in his own.

A shiver coursed through him, and he sat back to try and hide it but forgot the oak behind him. His head slamming against it reminded him quite unpleasantly. He barked a single, sharp word in his pain.

"James!" Jessica leaned forward, her eyes wide and alarmed. Ottis bounded away, startled by her movement. Her bare hand brushed his as she put her fingers to his head. "Let me see."

Too shocked to protest, he allowed her to turn his head and bend it forward while she knelt in the grass, so close he felt her breath stir his hair as she examined him, probing with gentle fingers. His ears had started to buzz, his neck flooded with heat, and he gripped the grass on either side of him with a desperation to keep his hands on the ground. He didn't know what they would do if he let go, but it likely would be very, very bad for him to find out.

James had soft, silky hair that waved just enough to make her wonder about its texture. It wasn't coarse, but thick, and tickled the tips of her fingers as she sought out the lump at the back of his head. The feel of the strands as they slipped through her fingers nearly made her forget her purpose.

An injury. She needed to find the injury. And she shouldn't enjoy the search so much.

He sucked in a sharp breath as her finger grazed a bump. "Sorry," she muttered, gently parting the hair around that area to find where his skin was swelled—and a small cut from the bark. She bit her lip and kept the wound exposed with one hand while she waved the other in front of his face. "Handkerchief, please?"

His movements were stiff as he reached into his coat with one hand and tugged a square of linen free from an inside pocket. She took it from him, then placed it over the blood and withdrew it again to check the severity of the break in skin. The blood returned quickly, so she covered it and held the cloth there.

"It doesn't look terrible, thank goodness, but it will likely bleed for a minute or two. Nothing to worry about."

His head tipped up slightly, and as she still bent over him this brought their faces alarmingly close. She could count his eyelashes, if she wished. They were thick and long, framing his brown eyes in a way that made them quite charming. Attractive, even.

They stared at each other, her hand holding the cloth to his head, her elbow against his shoulder and her body bent over his. Jessica's mouth had gone dry, and she swallowed with an audible gulp that ought to embarrass her.

Though James's right hand remained on the earth between them, the other came up. Slowly. And he reached for her, his fingertips grazing her cheek while her lungs ceased to function. Her mind went completely blank as her whole attention focused on his touch on her skin. Tucking a curl behind her ear, his fingers grazing her skin, his gaze never left hers.

Her heart pounded like a drum behind her ribs, the sound echoing so loudly in her ears she thought James had to hear it too.

Panic ought to have set in. Truly, many of the symptoms of her episodes matched what she felt now. Racing heart. Constricted lungs. Blank mind. Uncertainty.

Yet this was different, too. Because despite her uncertainty, she knew James was safe.

Safe?

James? Her sworn enemy?

A whip cracked within her mind, and Jessica jolted to her feet. She thrust the blood-spotted handkerchief at him. "You ought to find some tea. For your headache."

"Jess—"

"And I had better return home. There is much to do to prepare for Tom's arrival. And our guests. We can speak of our plans another time."

He rose to his feet with a wince, clutching the linen in one fist. "I didn't mean to make you uncomfortable."

She laughed, the sound higher and almost shrill, even to her own ears. "Don't be silly. I am quite well. As you said, we have a reprieve. No matrimonial prospects this week. We can meet again. In a week's time. There won't be a need until then, of course. Look after your injury. And don't forget the tea."

She whirled on her heel, her skirts spinning to catch up with her movement, and walked with determined speed to the gate. She didn't look back until she was safely on her side of the wall, and she found James staring at her, standing exactly where she had left him, his eyebrows pulled together, and his lips turned down in a dark frown.

Saints above, what had she been thinking? A woman never touched a man as she had, even an injured one, unless he was a relative. Or a husband. Certainly not when they were only neighbors. And barely friends.

She hadn't even been wearing gloves! But she hadn't been thinking about propriety. She'd been thinking about playing with Ottis. And she'd told herself it was "only James" who would see her.

Then she lost all reason. All propriety. All *good, common sense*, because he was foolish enough to slam his head into a tree.

Berating herself every step of the way home, Jessica couldn't explain what had happened. All she knew for certain was that she could never create a situation like that again. Not with James.

Everything about that moment, the way her stomach had twisted and heat had filled her cheeks, was far too dangerous.

CHAPTER FOURTEEN

Acknowledging a hard truth ought to be a turning point in a man's life. Perhaps even cause the foundations of his being to quake and shift, changing the geography of his nature and character. Yet, as James stood in the library, the room in the castle that most felt like *home* to him, he stared out of the stained-glass window at a rose-colored world and felt remarkably steady.

It was as though he had stumbled upon an essential truth, one that had been quietly lying in wait, patiently anticipating the moment he would uncover it.

Yes, he realized with a clarity that pierced his soul, he was attracted to Jessica. And it wasn't just a fleeting fascination. It was a deep-rooted, undeniable pull that stirred him in a way that was as frightening as it was surprising.

The door to the library opened and James turned as one of the footmen bowed. "Mr. Leonard Harrington to see you, Mr. Aldwick."

James didn't have a chance to respond before his cousin

strode in, a wide grin on his face and a large parcel tucked under his arm. "I hear you aren't leg-shackled yet?"

Trust Leo to skip over all formalities and dive into the fray of whatever mess James was in.

He was the best of friends in that way.

"Not yet." James relaxed and came forward, meeting Leo at the center of the room with a firm grasp of his forearm. "And you didn't meet your end in Northumbria, I see."

"Not this time. Though my great-uncle certainly gave it his all to make one of us expire before the end of my visit. Yet we both survive." He sighed deeply, with a dramatic heave of his shoulders. "I brought you a gift."

"A gift?" James looked down at the parcel as Leo shifted it to both hands, holding it out between them. "Are we to be those sorts of friends now? Every time I leave home, I'll have to return with some knick-knack for your shelves?"

"I'll pitch you headfirst into the lake if you try to fill my home with clutter," Leo retorted. "My mother does enough of that. We have more statuettes of shepherdesses than there are sheep in England."

James accepted the parcel and took it to the table at the center of the room, where a large globe held a place of honor. He put the package down and untied the twine. "I cannot think what in Northumbria would merit being brought all the way back to Yorkshire."

He pulled away the thick brown paper and found a box with an intricately painted lid featuring a pretty woman with a wedding veil held aloft by tiny creatures with wings, arm-in-arm with a man whose head was shaped like a donkey.

James recognized the scene from *A Midsummer Night's Dream*, and he laughed as he shook his head at the detailed work of a scene that only someone with both talent and an excellent sense of humor could have wanted to depict.

"Titania's devotion to Bottom," his friend said, slapping him on the back. "An avid reader of Shakespeare couldn't fail to appreciate such a find, I should think. And the subject matter seemed appropriate, given your forthcoming nuptials."

It felt good to laugh. "Where did you discover this? It is perfect." He'd put it somewhere prominent at once. The confusion it would cause guests as they tried to sort out where the scene was from, or whether or not to pay it a compliment, would amuse him endlessly.

Leo spoke as though the matter was of no consequence, which made the last several words of his explanation all the more surprising. "My great-uncle introduced me to the most delightful young lady. I think you'd like her, which is why I cannot introduce you to her at present, given your marital obligations. I intend to keep her for myself."

"You what?" James gripped his friend by the shoulder. "You are betrothed? In so short a time?"

With a wry smile, Leo stepped out of his friend's grasp. "Don't be ridiculous. She doesn't even know her days as an unmarried lady are numbered. In truth, if she yet remained in my uncle's neighborhood, I would still be there. But she's coming *here*, James. She's the younger sister to the rector's wife, and they told her all about the fair your family is hosting, so she is coming as their guest."

James crossed his arms over his chest and rocked back on his heels. "I am wounded, cousin. You came back to follow some poor, unsuspecting woman rather than to support me in my time of need? Such betrayal."

His friend snorted and dropped into a chair near the cold hearth, across from where James usually sat to read. "Your time of need? Poor James. Forced to sit at home while women are brought to him, one by one, for his choosing. When the reality none of them know is that you'd rather tuck yourself into a book than into a wedding costume."

Inspecting the box, James opened the lid to find the inside empty. He closed it again, noting the detail the artist had given to the donkey-headed groom's finery. "Your artist must have an excellent sense of the ridiculous."

"She does. And a dry wit to rival even Jessica Westcote's."

James stilled at the mention of Jessica. Leo had been about enough in their childhood to have been party to pranks played against Jessica, and he'd been on the receiving end with James when Jessica and Catherine retaliated. The four of them knew each other quite well.

But Leo had become friends with their former foe several years before. She'd seemingly accepted a truce between them. It hadn't ever bothered James. Not until that moment.

"You compare your romantic interest to Jessica?" James closed the box again. "Interesting. I didn't think you found much about her appealing."

"Jessica?" Leo stretched his legs out and crossed them at the ankle, lazily tucking his arms behind his head. "I think she has many admirable qualities, but as she's your sworn enemy, we've never had reason to discuss them."

"Having a sworn enemy is quite childish. I should think we have grown beyond that."

"Of course we have. Which is why your taunts turned to teasing, and your teasing turned into flirtation. Still, it didn't seem my place to draw your attention to her good qualities when you preferred your relationship with her to remain antagonistic rather than friendly."

James swallowed, then forced a laugh. "Flirtation? I have never flirted with Jessica."

"Oh, please, spare me that denial." Leo chuckled and his head lolled to the side the better to cast a narrow-eyed glare at his cousin. "You flirted like a clumsy boy of fifteen, despite being a decade past that awkward age. But you do flirt with her."

With both hands on the table, James leaned forward and closed his eyes. "I never thought of it that way. It's been a dance of words and wits, challenging each other and pushing to best one another in debates. But it always remained something light and enjoyable. At least for me. It was safe. Familiar."

"Was?" Leo lowered his hands to the arm rests and sat forward. "Has something happened in the weeks I have been away?"

A dry, humorless laugh was the only sound that escaped James's lips. What did he say? How did he explain to his friend what he had barely comprehended himself a scant few hours before? "I may be an idiot."

"I have never presumed otherwise."

James looked fully over his shoulder at his cousin and raised his eyebrows. "Your support in this moment is too kind, Leo."

With a wide grin, Leo gave an unapologetic shrug. "I aim to please. Now. Tell me how you came to the conclusion that you aren't as clever as you thought. And what Jessica Westcote has to do with it. In fact, begin there. Tell me, what is your perception of that lady? I sense she is at the heart of the matter here."

Pushing away from the table, James paced to the edge of the carpet, near the door. Then turned and walked back to the stained glass. "My perception of her? Fine. I can do that." He took a deep breath and began the route again, back to the door, speaking as he went and *not* looking at Leo in an effort to keep his thoughts clear. "Jessica is remarkable. She's a spirited woman with a sharp mind and an even sharper tongue." He winced. "That sounds like a criticism, but it isn't."

"What do you mean?" Leo sounded perfectly at ease. James risked a glance at his closest friend to find the man watching him with a blank expression. Giving away nothing.

What *did* he mean? Sorting through his thoughts, James paced more as he answered.

"In her company, I've never been bored. Quite the contrary. She makes every conversation lively, every debate engaging, and every moment vibrant."

"Vibrant?" Leo sounded skeptical. "That isn't a word I've heard you use to describe her in the past. Loud. Sharp. Discerning." He ticked each of those descriptive words off on one hand as James continued his march across the carpet. "Abrupt. Cutting. Challenging."

"She is all those things, too." James stopped in the middle of the room. "Her ability to challenge me and make me reconsider my own viewpoints is a trait I've admired. But there is more to her than that. Her strength, her resilience, her courage to stand her ground when other ladies demure or stay on safer topics of conversation—I admire all of those things. It's the spark in her eyes, her vivacity, her unabashed honesty."

Leo moved forward on his seat as he listened, settling his elbows on his knees and staring at James with that careful expression that gave nothing away. "Compliments indeed. Very well. I accept that you are no longer censuring her as I had supposed. Indeed, you two have always had a unique bond. For lack of a better word."

James chuckled, dropping his gaze to the carpet as he ran a hand through his hair. "Antagonists may have suited us better. Rivals of wit."

"But something has changed?" Leo prompted, and when James glanced at him, he saw a light in his friend's eye that ought to have made him nervous. Leo wasn't the trickster James was, but he had a sharp intellect and an appreciation for strategy that had made him an invaluable partner in all of James's childhood exploits. And beyond.

Leo knew more than he let on. And he was steering James toward an admission James hadn't been ready to make. Not alone, to himself.

"We have called a truce, of sorts." James looked down at the carpet. "Become allies."

The other man scoffed. "Those are words for men at war and children playing soldiers. Not for a gentleman and a lady."

James tightened his jaw in an effort to stop himself from saying more. Saying things that he wouldn't be able to take back. Saying anything to Leo, though his friend would keep their conversation in confidence, would be an admission he'd be incapable of hiding from himself again.

He thought of Jessica, kneeling beside him in the shadows of the tree, her fingers delicately twisted in his hair. She had been so close to him that he had easily taken in the gentle scent of vanilla and sun-warmed linen from her gown. He'd even felt the breath of her words as she'd spoken.

He closed his eyes. "Why do others not see how beautiful she is?"

The silence following his question made James's skin prickle.

"I beg your pardon. I couldn't possibly have heard what I thought I did. *What* did you say?"

"She's beautiful." He opened his eyes and looked at Leo, feeling like an idiot again. "But I've heard her tell Catherine that she isn't. She doesn't believe she is. Because she's tall, or thin, or what-have-you. Yet, I've thought her lovely for years."

Leo's mouth fell open. "You've never given any reason for me, let alone her, to think that."

James winced. "I suppose not."

"You imbecile." Leo rose from his chair. "You absolute clod-head! You *like* her."

James looked at the closed door and then returned a sharp glare to his friend. "Can you not shout that last part again, please? We aren't the only two in the castle, you know."

Leo placed a hand over his heart. "Forgive me for being *shocked* by this turn of events. I was waiting for something like this to happen, but I never fully believed you would reach this point of self-discovery."

"You speak as if you already knew I felt this way. That can't be possible, given I only discovered it myself mere hours ago."

"I cannot allow you to speak in vague terms like this." Leo came forward and put both hands on James's shoulders, looking him in the eye. "What way do you feel? Be precise. You find her wit and conversation vibrant. You've spoken of her vivacity. Your rivalry. Now, you admit you find her beautiful. These are yet half measures, James. Say the whole of it."

"I'm not certain I want to," James admitted, his heart constricting.

"I don't care." Leo squeezed his shoulders. "I know you better than anyone, and I know if you don't admit this thing aloud that you will do your best to bury it. Speak plainly."

"To what purpose?" James stepped back and turned away.

"As you said, I'm an idiot. No one knows that fact better than Jessica."

"Debatable. I think we're all quite aware of your shortcomings."

"You are most unhelpful."

"And yet I am your closest friend. Who else can you talk to?"

"Perhaps you're right. I should keep this to myself."

Leo groaned and went back to his chair, collapsing into it with a melodramatic huff. "Go on, then. Don't admit you have feelings for your neighbor. See how far that gets you. I intend to be the author of my own happiness, though. I have no hesitation in saying that I am enamored with the woman who painted that box with a donkey-headed lover and a fairy queen. In fact, I have the greatest hope in deepening our acquaintance and following that to its natural consequence."

James raised his eyebrows in question.

"I hope to court her and wed her, if she will have me."

"You do?" James straightened his posture. "Leo, that's marvelous. Congratulations."

"It's too early for that." Leo's smile was slight. "But I thank you. I hope I can count on you to tell her of all my best qualities when you meet her."

James laughed and went to his own seat, falling into it. "Of course." He couldn't hide his grin. "You know, I asked Jessica to do the opposite for me. Every woman who has entered the castle's gate thus far has been gifted with Jessica's worst facts about me. Most of them exaggerated. I hope." He winced again.

"You're only fooling yourself at this point, James." Leo's slight smile kept the words from sounding harsh, and the concern in his eyes gave James the last push he needed to confide in his friend.

"I'm falling in love with Jessica." The world didn't end when he admitted it out loud, though James's heart pounded as though that risk remained.

His cousin leaned forward in his chair. "Good. Now. What do you intend to do about it?"

As James took in the familiar sights of the library, the stained-glass window casting its warm, colored light over his favorite books, he felt a calm conviction.

Nothing would ever be the same again.

The admission made, James's mind began to do what it did best. Plotting and planning.

"I need to determine if she feels the same way. I must tread carefully," he said, giving Leo a warning glance. "I don't want to ruin the friendship she and I are building. I intend to show her what I feel, and that I can be more than her sparring partner, without alarming her or making her uncomfortable. She's said she has no wish to marry, strangely enough. It's a delicate situation, but I must try. She's worth it."

Leo's grin returned, larger than before. "I will help in any way I can. You have my word."

The gravity of what James admitted weighed heavily on him, yet there was a sense of freedom, too. He'd acknowledged the truth that he'd been tiptoeing around for too long. His heart sped in his chest at the thought of what came next.

How would Jessica react when she came to know? The unknown pricked at his fears, but there was a certain thrill to what he felt, too. He'd ridden dragons in his boyhood dreams, and now faced a real challenge.

Winning Jessica's heart.

CHAPTER FIFTEEN

Tom Westcote's return to his family's home was a most welcome distraction. Jessica gave her full attention to her younger brother, pushing all thoughts of her agreement with James to the darkest corners of her mind. She hoped they would collect enough cobwebs in a week's time that she'd forget the way her heart had pounded when she and James had come so perilously close to—to something she wasn't willing to think about.

No, she would heap all her focus on her brother.

For as long as she could remember, Jessica had adored Tom. She'd devoted hours to his entertainment when he'd yet been in the nursery. When he stepped out of the carriage that brought him home, she didn't wait for him to come toward her where she stood beside their father. Instead, she nearly leaped into his arms to give him a welcome embrace.

At eighteen, Tom had matched her in height. Now, three years older, he was finally taller than her by several inches. So when he wrapped his arms around her waist and lifted her from the ground with a laugh, the moment was quite bittersweet. He wasn't little anymore.

"I missed you, too," he said gruffly into her ear. "But you're going to make me look quite soft-hearted." He put her back down on her feet and grinned at her. "You know lawyers cannot be seen to have soft hearts, Jess."

She scoffed and wiped at her eyes with one hand. "You may pretend all you want when you are away from home, but I know you best. You would rather rescue kittens than prepare court arguments."

"That's a pretty picture to paint," a deeper voice said from behind her brother. "Westcote, is this the sister you've been telling me about?"

Tom's quick grin ought to have reassured her, but Jessica stiffened. She'd forgotten in her haste to welcome her brother that he had a guest with him. A colleague he'd written about only briefly.

"Father. Jessica. I would like to introduce Mr. Christopher Holly. Only last week, he received his certificate of fitness from the King's Bench, and he is now a fully-fledged solicitor."

"A pleasure to meet you, Mr. Holly," her father said to the newcomer with a bow. "And congratulations for your achievement."

"Thank you for having me as a guest in your home, Mr. Westcote. And it is a pleasure to meet you at last, Miss Westcote. Your brother speaks of you often."

"Welcome to our home, sir." Jessica made her curtsey as she took in Mr. Holly's neatly tailored attire, the sharp lines of his coat accentuating a trim physique. His meticulously brushed hair, dark and waving, framed a face of strong, refined features. But it was his eyes, deep-set and intense, that hinted at his character. They were the eyes of a man of intellect, a scholar of laws and letters, and they held an undeniable seriousness to them.

They were quite unlike James's brown eyes, dark but full of mischief. James's lips sometimes twitched as if on the verge of a laugh. She much preferred James's open amusement to this stranger's rather stoic appearance. Although why she compared the newcomer to James, she couldn't say.

"Come inside, son. Bring your guest." Her father held his elbow out and Jessica took it. "You both must be tired from your journey."

"Dusty, perhaps, but not tired," Tom said with a laugh. "And relieved to get out of that carriage. Aren't we, Holly?"

Mr. Holly responded with an even, wry tone. "A seat that doesn't bounce along with a horse's gait would be most welcome."

Tom's friend was likely nearer to her age than her brother's, if not a little older, given the number of years he'd had to spend in apprenticeship and clerkship to become a solicitor. Tom's letters had outlined the arduous requirements to pursue that profession to Jessica, and the details came back to her as she entered the house.

"Would you prefer to rest and have refreshment in your rooms, or would you like to take tea with us now?" Her father turned to look over his shoulder. "Either is acceptable, so please do not trouble yourself, Mr. Holly, in doing what suits you best."

"Would a walk in your garden be acceptable prior to refreshment? I think a stretch of the legs is what I need to feel more myself, at least at present."

"Of course."

"Jessica, will you show him the gardens?" Tom asked, sounding far too chipper. "I'd rather have a coffee than take another step."

"It would be my pleasure," she answered in the way they expected, as was polite for the lady of the house. Though she'd counted on Tom as a potential ally in her attempt to stay unattached, it seemed he'd joined their father in trying to marry her off. There was nothing subtle about his push for her to spend a quarter of an hour in company with his friend. "Mr. Holly, this way, if you please."

Her father released her arm, and Mr. Holly stepped forward to offer his. He wasn't so tall as the men in her family, but he still had an inch or two more than she did. And his broad shoulders made her feel quite delicate by comparison. At least that was a welcome change from some of the other men of her acquaintance.

Even if he wasn't quite so tall as James. Who she really must stop thinking about.

"Are you certain you do not mind?" he asked, voice lowered, as they went through to a sitting room with broad doors leading out to a terrace, with steps that would take them down to their modest garden of fountain and flowers. "I am happy to take my walk alone, Miss Westcote."

How thoughtful of him, to not insist upon her attention. Unlike someone else she could name—but wouldn't.

Jessica kept her gaze forward and her smile the picture of contentment. "It is my pleasure to keep you company, Mr. Holly. It is the kindest thing I can do after you were forced to spend so many hours closed up in a carriage with my brother."

"Though I enjoyed his company, I will admit that yours is

more pleasant." He spoke without affectation, as though his words were simple truth rather than an attempt at flirtation. "I haven't been away from London in months. When your brother invited me to the country, I didn't hesitate to accept. It's beautiful here." He waved before him, the gesture encompassing the green hills and trees beyond the garden.

"I am certain the countryside wears on people just as Town does, after a time. Perhaps you will wish to return to the busy streets of London before long." She couldn't even picture what they must be like, full of people and carriages, all scurrying about and trying to move from one busy activity to another. "I have heard it said that the quiet of the country is dull to those used to the city."

Though her closest friends had never said such a thing. Catherine always seemed relieved to return to the castle after spending time in London. James, too. He was happy to return to his library, his books, the familiar. Neither of them had ever made her feel as though she were missing out on something.

Did she know if James preferred the city to the country? She'd never asked him. But her attention belonged to Mr. Holly at present, and she needed to keep it there.

"Perhaps for some. But I was born north of London, in a village that likely isn't on any of the better-known maps." His expression turned thoughtful, and they paused beside the fountain at the center of the formal garden. "I don't plan to return to either the small village or London. A friend of mine in York has offered to lease me an office in that town, instead."

"Really?" Jessica's interest perked. "Have you been to York?" She had, when she was a small child, spent a Christmas there with her uncle's family. They had arrived on Christmas Eve and stayed through Twelfth Night.

"Many times, during boyhood. I spent holidays from school there, with the same friend who offered me the lease." For the first time, Mr. Holly's smile appeared more natural. Comfortable, even. "I find its size suits my idea of convenient living. There are entertainments, a variety of merchants and warehouses, but not so much as to overwhelm a man. You must have visited. It cannot be more than twenty miles from here."

"It is eighteen miles, by the best route," she said, her voice soft. "A few hours' journey in good weather." She had wanted to visit again. Surely, if she journeyed there with her father, or even Catherine, their presence would be enough to keep those uncomfortable fits at bay. Sometimes, all she needed was a hand to hold to still the beating of her heart, or a soft reminder to take a breath.

Still, her father had deemed it too risky.

Funny, because *now* he spoke of marrying her off to someone who would likely take her far from their leased estate. Wouldn't it be better for her to attempt such a journey, and such an environment, before risking everything in marrying a man who might demand more than she was capable of doing?

Her heart raced ahead with her thoughts.

She needed to speak to her father. At once. Show him the fallacy of his plan to wed her to someone without knowing if her condition would allow travel.

"Miss Westcote?" Mr. Holly's voice drew her back to their conversation.

"I beg your pardon, sir. What were you saying? About York?"

His expression remained pleasant, though she caught a

hint of disappointment in his eyes. Merely a flicker. "Perhaps I am more fatigued than I thought. Let us return to the house. A rest before dinner is likely what I need."

She ought to have felt guilty, she knew, neglecting a guest's conversation as she had. Jessica didn't, though. Because she had to speak to Catherine and Lady Retford. They would know precisely how best to approach her father about a possible visit to York. As they were the only two besides her father, and governesses no longer living nearby, who knew her difficulty, they were in the best position to advise her.

After passing Mr. Holly to the care of a footman, Jessica withdrew to her favorite drawing room. There, she settled at the desk and wrote her note to Catherine, her excitement such that her penmanship nearly suffered for it. After folding and sealing the missive, she gave it to a servant and promised herself patience while she waited for a response.

Bessie delivered the response that evening, when she arrived in Jessica's room to prepare her for dinner. Written in Catherine's familiar hand, Jessica read the note with eagerness that soon faded to disappointment.

My Dear Jessica,

I understand your desire to test yourself, to prove that you can manage whatever life might throw at you. I admire your courage in even considering such a journey. But I must ask you to think about the risks. Traveling to a place like York, especially under circumstances that might provoke a fit, could be very dangerous for you without proper support and preparation. You know I would do anything to help you, but I fear that this plan might cause you more harm than good.

You will be disappointed in me. Please know, I want you to succeed. But you must go about your test with caution. Perhaps there's another way to approach this. The fair begins in two days' time. You can practice coping with your illness there, among both strangers and familiar neighbors. It will be challenging but not so potentially overwhelming as a journey to York. We must consider your well-being above all else, even your understandable desire to prove yourself.

I have consulted with my mother, and she agrees. Let us first see how you manage the crowds of the fair. Then we can discuss the possibility of visiting York.

Yours, etc.,

Catherine

Jessica dropped the letter on her dressing table, her stomach churning and her heart falling. Catherine didn't believe her capable of leaving their village. And perhaps her friend was right.

She twisted her fingers in her lap while Bessie arranged her hair, then took in a deep breath and tried to make her fingers remain still. She stared at them, hard.

Ladies didn't fidget. Her first unsympathetic governess taught her that lesson, rapping Jessica's knuckles with a ruler every time her fingers reached for ribbons to tangle between them, or when she twirled the coral beads on her bracelet or fiddled with her gloves.

Other governesses had told her to lock her fingers together in her lap or hide them beneath a table if the impulse persisted, and turn a bracelet or ring round and round. Better to let her hands release some of the built-up energy inside her body than to grow sick. And better her hands and fingers than tapping her heels or toes, which produced noise that made others glance about to see where the tap or rattle came from.

The subtle movements were only symptoms of the greater illness Jessica could not cure. The hysterics. The weakness of character. The reason her father kept her close and among people and places she knew well. Even the familiar could try her from time to time, but not like those years spent preparing for a London Season that never came.

"Are you all right, miss?" Bessie asked, her voice soft. One of her hands left Jessica's hair to rest softly on her shoulder. She met Jessica's eyes in the mirror, concern in her own. "Per'aps we'd better loosen a few of the pins."

Bessie knew. Though they'd never spoken in plain terms, Bessie had witnessed the trembling, the exhaustion, following an episode. And she'd seen the care Jessica took to wear a beaded bracelet she could twist, or a fringed shawl that allowed her to twist the silken strands when she needed a distraction.

And she'd listened when Jessica had once told her, two years or more in the past, "At times the constant brush of fabrics, the pull of my hair, the noise of so many, overwhelms my senses."

Bessie had found creative ways to arrange Jessica's hair that didn't require so many pins. She'd chosen softer fabrics, lighter in weight or feel, for crowded events. And even those little things had done much to ease Jessica's agitation.

"I'm all right." Jessica smiled at her maid. "My hair is perfect. Thank you, Bessie."

"Would you like to wear a bracelet over your glove?" the younger woman asked, tone still gentle. "The one with the blue beads, perhaps? It would match the gown."

And provide her fingers something to do when they were not occupied with knife and fork.

Jessica relaxed and nodded. She would twist the beads, count them, slide them across her wrist. And try to keep her disappointment in herself tucked away.

Planning for the fair, for the arrival of her horrid cousins, for helping James, would take up most of her energy in the coming week. If she could survive that much upheaval, then she could prove to Catherine that a visit to York was within reach, too.

CHAPTER SIXTEEN

James waited half an hour past their usual meeting time before giving up on Jessica. He knew she wasn't ill. Though he hadn't seen her alone since their last meeting at the kissing-gate, as they had agreed, Catherine had been to visit at Fairbrook Lodge several times. She'd returned from each visit to inform the family that all the Westcotes were in good health, and their guest was a perfect gentleman.

Mr. Holly had come with Mr. Westcote to meet the baron, and James had been introduced to the newly certified solicitor, too.

He hadn't been impressed. Though he couldn't say why it mattered, one way or the other. But he hoped the gentleman wasn't proving a bother to Jessica. Up until the moment he'd seen them in church, the day before, seated side-by-side in the Westcote family pew. James had expected Tom's friend to sit on the far end, next to Tom. Instead, Mr. Holly had sat between Jessica and Tom. And shared a prayer book with Jessica.

Though the sight had caused him alarm, James had put aside that feeling. He didn't know what was going on. He would ask Jessica when they met. In private. The next day.

And she hadn't come.

Ottis was as confused as James. The terrier would run to the gate to peer through it, then come back to James and sit, settling in the grass with a huff of displeasure. Or maybe James was giving the dog too much credit.

Perhaps their last meeting had impacted Jessica more than James had guessed. While it had served as a revelation for him in every positive way, she may have had an altogether different reaction. While he had admitted his heart bent toward her, she could have found herself wanting nothing more than to run in the opposite direction.

After waiting until his hope had withered to nothing, James took Ottis back to the kitchens, then made his own way to the library. Unfortunately, Catherine found him before he made it to his safe haven of leather-bound books and comfortable furniture.

"I need you to come with me to the village."

He blinked at her. "The village is literally outside the castle gate. You can be there in thirty paces."

That was the one failing of living in a castle from a more feudal time. The village had been built on the castle's doorstep, the better for merchants and tenants alike to run to the stone walls for protection should any of their neighbors turn threatening. Not that anything of the sort had happened, according to what history James knew of the castle and his ancestry.

"I want you to come with me," she said, amending her previous statement. "I've just been informed that Jessica and

Mr. Holly are taking in the preparations for the fair, and I'd like to see them for myself."

"The preparations or Jessica and Mr. Holly?" he quipped, then winced. He didn't like coupling the two of them together. Not even in conversation with his sister. Misery churned in his stomach. Had Jessica missed her meeting with him to spend time in Mr. Holly's company?

Jealousy wasn't a pleasant emotion in the least. The sooner he could rid himself of it, the better. But the only way to do that would be to reassure himself that Mr. Holly hadn't captured Jessica's interest. And if he was trying to, and Jessica didn't wish him to, then James had a responsibility to sabotage the solicitor's suit just as he had the other men who had visited that summer.

Catherine stared at him as though he'd said something utterly stupid. "Are you going to come with me or not?"

He took in that she already held gloves and reticule in one hand and her bonnet in the other. He could lay claim to his hat and gloves as he left the castle. There was no reason to delay.

"I'm coming, of course. Why would I deny my favorite sister such a small favor?"

"I am your only sister."

"That is beside the point."

She took his arm, and in next to no time they were blinking in the summer sun and crossing the courtyard to the gate, which already stood open. In thirty paces, as James had said, they were in Amoret Village. Though it was far busier than he had seen it in years. Servants from the castle, along with the occupants of the village, were walking to and fro, carrying crates and baskets, tools and lumber.

They followed the traffic flowing down Hollybank Lane,

turning right at the Market Cross just east of All Saints' Church. A statue of a boar, dating back to the founding of the village according to local legend, had been decorated so as to make the boar appear to be wearing a waistcoat and straw hat. They crossed the street in front of the Boars' Head Inn and came at last to the large field where their village held its largest gatherings.

The road along the field was awash with vibrant colors, the sounds of hammers and saws, and the chatter of townsfolk as they prepared for the next day's festivities. Children darted between stalls, their laughter mixing with the calls of merchants arranging their wares, while women gossiped and compared notes on ribbons and fabric to decorate their booths.

Visiting merchants, arriving in creaking wagons filled with their goods, negotiated spots with the Amoret steward, their voices rising above the clatter of excitement.

At the far end of the field, a large wooden stage was under construction, a hive of carpenters and laborers working diligently to erect it. The stage would be the centerpiece of entertainment, adorned with bright banners and garlands, ready to host musicians, dancers, and the visiting theatrical troupe. Long benches had been set up, facing the stage, with space left for people to bring their stools or simply sit on the grass, too.

"Do you see Jessica or Mr. Holly?" Catherine asked, her tone agitated as she stood on her toes, trying to peer over the throng. "Why are so many people here when nothing is to begin until *tomorrow*?"

Though he didn't understand his sister's impatience, he dutifully turned his attention to finding Jessica. He had a clear advantage to finding her, thanks to his height. At last, he spotted her familiar copper-kissed curls beneath a wide-brimmed hat. She was standing in the shade of the inn. Alone.

"I see her." He tugged his sister along behind him as he wove through the crowd. The nearer he came to Jessica, the clearer her expression became. Her face was pale, and her eyes had a distant, glassy look as if her mind were someplace far away from the noise and bustle. She wore a placid smile, though her eyes didn't crinkle at the corners as they would if she meant it. She wrapped and unwrapped the strings of her reticule around her fingers with urgent movements.

Catherine spoke the instant before he did. "Jessica? Are you all right?"

Her shoulders were tense, raised slightly toward her ears, when she blinked and seemed to realize she was no longer alone amid the bustle and noise in the field. Jessica's gaze went first to Catherine, then to James.

The pale gray of her eyes reflected his worry back at him. "Catherine. James." Her voice was somewhat higher pitched than normal, though breathless. "Isn't all of this exciting?"

"Yes. Of course. But, Jess, you are quite pale. Are you well? Do you need to rest?" Catherine's rapid questioning made Jessica's shoulders inch higher and she forced a shaky laugh that made James wince.

"I am perfectly fine." She tried to tug her fingers free of the ribbon, but they were caught. "Merely resting a moment in the shade. Mr. Holly and Tom are about somewhere." Her eyes took on that glassy look again as her lips pressed closed.

Something was wrong. Jessica was ill. Or afraid? He couldn't quite tell. But James didn't like it in the least. Finding her alone and out of sorts, while a whole field of people went about their business as though she didn't exist, made his ire rise.

He lowered his voice, keeping his words soft and even. "Jessica. Will you let me take you inside the inn? Catherine needs cool air and some tea."

Catherine gave him a sharp glance, then nodded her understanding. "Yes. Let's go inside a moment. James, won't you lend Jessica your arm?"

He took the fingers recently freed from the bonnet's ribbon, pressing them gently as he guided her hand through the crook of his elbow. Jessica's breathing, shallow and rapid, worried him. She would swoon if she didn't slow it down. He kept his hand over hers, pressing it gently against his arm, hoping the solid feel of him would help somehow.

Catherine led them along the side of the building to the front, then through the inn's door into the relative quiet of the building closed off from the preparations going on out of doors. James kept his pace steady, drawing Jessica along with him to the back corner of the room, near the warmth of the low fire, to a small round table with two chairs.

Jessica lowered herself into one and Catherine took the other, her eyes wide and taking in her friend with a mix of concern and pity.

He'd never seen Jessica this way. But Catherine seemed more saddened than surprised. His sister looked up at him and raised her eyebrows. "Tea, please, James."

With marching orders clearly given, James went to the counter-top where the innkeeper's wife worked, folding tea towels and speaking with another patron. He slid a coin across the smooth surface. "Tea for the ladies in the corner, if you would, please."

"Of course, Mr. Aldwick." She curtsied, tucked the coin into her apron, and disappeared through a swinging door to the kitchen.

That done, James looked over his shoulder to see Catherine and Jessica in conversation. Jessica's head drooped, reminding him of a wilted bloom, but color had returned to her lips and cheeks. Catherine spoke with an urgent expression, saying something that made Jessica nod gloomily.

His impatience bristled. He wanted to sit at that table, hold her hand, and find out what the devil had happened to leave her in such a state of agitation. Where had her brother gone? What about the solicitor?

He made his way back to the table. The tea would come to them. He snatched up an empty chair along the way and brought it to sit directly across from Jessica. He sat, and when Catherine gave him a reproachful glare, he returned it with added hostility. Let her try to dismiss him. He wouldn't move from that spot until he knew what had happened or until Jessica returned to her usual self.

Gentling his expression to a smile, James turned to Jessica. She had taken her gloves off, laying them across the table, and her hands were tucked out of sight. "There now. Have you ever seen such confusion? A hive of bees has never looked so busy as this town does today. I find it quite overwhelming, especially given the weather."

Jessica's gaze met his, then lowered to the table. "I cannot recall a single time in my life when you wanted to speak to me about the weather, James Aldwick."

He exchanged a quick glance with Catherine, whose eyebrows had raised in surprise. That sounded a little more like Jessica.

"Truly?" He hummed a thoughtful note. "And yet we discuss so many things with such abandon. How have we left such a topic, and a mundane one at that, untouched for this long? Perhaps because we could not possibly turn the weather into a debate. If I say the day is unbearably warm, you wouldn't disagree."

Her lips quirked upward. "I felt quite cold a moment ago, actually."

James resisted the urge to smile, placing his gloves on the table. Their tea would arrive soon. And he had another reason entirely to be free of that layer. "And if there had been a snow-storm, would you now tell me you found the air too hot?"

"Undoubtedly." She pulled in a deep breath and her cheeks turned their usual soft shade of pink. "Though I think we would both wish for an umbrella if it rained."

Every word they said, ridiculous as they were, brought her further away from the trance he'd found her in. He kept one hand atop the table, tapping its surface lightly, while the other he dropped first to his knee. Then stretched out until he found her wrist. Where her hands rested in her lap, they trembled.

Jessica's eyes widened when she felt his touch, but she said nothing, as Catherine spoke. "It's entirely too warm. And I haven't the patience to listen to the two of you debate the merits of umbrellas today."

James circled Jessica's wrist with his fingers, sliding his thumb to the point on her wrist where he felt her pulse beating out a quickened rhythm. Was he the cause of the unusual speed, or was it part of what had overwhelmed her minutes ago? He rubbed the spot gently, his gaze on his sister rather than Jessica.

"Would you prefer we table this debate until tomorrow? Umbrellas are a topic that deserve some focus, I should think, given their usefulness." He addressed himself to Catherine, taking her attention away from her friend. "We could speak on one of your favorite subjects instead. Such as your search for uncommon words. Have you learned any new bits or bobs for your ever-expanding vocabulary?"

Slowly, as his sister expounded on a Latin-based verb she thought society ought to make greater use of, Jessica relaxed beneath his touch. Her pulse slowed. Her smile, when he glanced at her, had softened to something more in keeping with her usual disposition. He made to pull away, but her hand closed around his.

It took a great deal of willpower to *not* look at her, as she grasped his hand. Her skin was warm and soft, her long fingers gentle. And her hand fit so well in his that he wished, for one wistful moment, he didn't have to relinquish it. Ever.

The innkeeper's wife arrived with their tea, and Jessica withdrew from their shared touch. Only then did he dare look at her, to find her eyes glowing and her whole demeanor changed. She wasn't quite relaxed, yet she appeared more like herself than he'd thought possible in such a short amount of time.

Catherine had decided to pour out for all of them when the door to the inn opened again and in came Tom Westcote and Mr. Holly, the two of them wasting no time making their way to the corner.

"Jess, where did you run off to?" Tom asked, a broad grin on his face. "James, I wish you had been with us. The blacksmith is going to give demonstrations tomorrow as to how medieval weaponry was made. He showed us a display of daggers that made me wish I'd lived alongside Robin Hood merely for the pleasure of keeping such things tucked up my sleeves."

Mr. Holly had stepped away to fetch two more chairs to

crowd around the small table, which meant James had to move his chair to Jessica's side. He and his sister, with Jessica tucked between them, exchanged an uncertain glance. Then she gave a slight shake of her head.

They wouldn't tell the men of Jessica's state when they found her. Which meant James couldn't chastise them for leaving her alone. Even though none of it made sense to him. Why would Jessica have been so distressed, in the village where she had grown up, looking as though she would be physically ill at any moment?

Though tempted to take her hand beneath the table again, James didn't reach for her. But he kept one hand resting on his knee, available to her should she need more reassurance. His earlier irritation at her missing their appointment had completely vanished. Now, all he cared about was getting to the bottom of her distress. And doing all he could to ensure she didn't have cause to slip into such a state again.

Jessica walked alongside James as the group made their way from the village back to Fairbrook Lodge. The sun shone brightly overhead, a stark contrast to the storm of emotions still swirling inside her. She stared straight ahead, unwilling to meet James' gaze though she could feel it resting on her profile. Her hands tightened around the ribbons of her reticule.

Embarrassment flooded her cheeks with warmth at the memory of how he had found her, pale and trembling in the throes of panic amidst the bustling crowd. She had hoped to keep her struggles private, especially from James. Their friendship—if she could call it that—was tenuous; this could irreparably damage it. Or worse, give him something to tease her about that he didn't understand. The mere idea of him using her weakness as a weapon made her heart feel bruised.

Yet even through the haze of her oncoming fit, she had recognized the calm reassurance in his voice, the gentle strength of his hand covering hers. He had been her anchor, along with Catherine, keeping her from drifting too far out to sea. Gratitude tempered her shame. Still, uncertainty gnawed at her.

Would James see her as broken and pathetic now that he glimpsed the weakness she battled?

Weariness seeped into her bones. The attacks always left her drained, both mentally and physically. She longed to return to her room and rest, to shut herself away from prying eyes. But she could not escape this walk back with the others, as much as she wished she could.

Drawing in a slow breath, Jessica raised her eyes to glance at James's handsome profile. To her surprise, his expression held no pity or judgment, only patience and understanding.

Something like hope flickered in her chest.

"That was quite the adventure back in the village," James commented lightly as they walked. "Although I confess, I've never been fond of wasps."

Jessica looked at him in surprise. "Wasps?" It felt as though she'd entered into the middle of a conversation rather than the beginning of one. "Whatever do you mean?"

"Why, the buzz of activity and busyness we found. All those merchants and villagers darting about, it reminded me of an aggravated wasps' nest."

Jessica's lips quirked. This sort of thing she could manage

with him. "I would argue they were more like honeybees, each with their own purpose, working hard together."

"Honeybees do sting when bothered though. I'll take my chances with butterflies any day. Surely you agree?" James grinned.

Jessica felt an answering smile touch her face. "On the contrary. Bees are far more useful than butterflies. Where would we be without honey and beeswax?"

"You make fair points." James inclined his head. "I shall have to reconsider my stance on bees. Although I maintain butterflies are less trouble."

Jessica shook her head, a laugh bubbling up. The conversation was inane, yet she delighted in this return to their usual banter. James always matched and challenged her wit.

"I cannot think of many gentlemen who go about expressing an interest or a preference for butterflies," she noted.

"I am unique among my sex, I suppose. Though if we asked every man of our acquaintance if he would rather have a wasp, a bee, or a butterfly trapped beneath his hat, I would lay money on the butterfly being the favorite choice."

As she studied his amused expression, her laughter caught in her throat. When had his smile begun affecting her so? She noticed with startling clarity how his deep brown eyes gleamed with his usual mischief. Her heart stuttered.

That was why she hadn't met him that morning. Despite the time that had passed since their last private interaction, she hadn't forgotten a single sensation that nearness had stirred within her. When she'd foolishly threaded her fingers in his dark hair, coming close enough to breathe in the rich smell of soap on his skin, she'd wanted more from James, more than she had ever wanted from anyone.

She'd thought of little else since, no matter how she'd tried to distract herself.

And now, close to him again, Jessica had to accept that she hadn't imagined any of those strange sensations that had left her feeling bereft without his company for the past week. She was in very real danger of losing her heart to this man. The realization left her torn between longing and regret.

James could never feel the same. They'd fought one another too long. They'd barely found friendship. And she cherished that friendship too much to risk it, no matter how she yearned for more. Her secrets were too heavy for James to willingly bear, too. For *any* man to bear.

He spoke, his voice as gentle as it had been at the inn. "What are you thinking about? One moment, I have you giggling about butterflies in hats, and the next you look as though someone kicked your puppy."

"I don't have a puppy. And if I did, and someone kicked it, I would waste no time in kicking them back."

His low chuckle made her cheeks grow warm, and her stomach fluttered rather pleasantly. The symptoms were kinder echoes of what she felt at the onset of one of her difficult episodes. This feeling of her heart skipping a beat, of her hands and face growing warm, was pleasant rather than alarming. These were things only James had inspired in her.

"If you don't wish to confide in me, I understand. But I hope you know that I'm worried for you. This is the second time I have seen you in a state of distress, Jess." He spoke in a tone the others would not hear, and Jessica looked ahead only to realize they had slowed to a pace that put several yards between them and the other three members of their party.

"At least you weren't the cause this time," she said, trying to keep her voice light.

He winced and looked down at the pebbled path. Immediately, she felt guilty. She stopped and placed her hand on his arm, bringing him to a standstill. He stared at where she touched him, then raised his gaze to hers. His expression was full of regret.

"I am sorry, James. I ought not bring it up again. You apologized, and we let the matter go. Forgive me."

"If I could erase that moment from our history, I would," he admitted. "I regret speaking to you that way. Trying to hurt you. It will never happen again, Jessica."

"I know." She squeezed his arm, then tucked her hand into the folds of her skirt. She started walking again. "I need to apologize for something else. I didn't come to the gate this morning."

He was silent a moment before he said, without reproach, "Ottis missed you."

Before she could respond, the sound of a horse and carriage clattered behind them. James took her hand and pulled her off the road, and ahead of them the others stepped aside, too. The carriage bearing down on them came at a fast clip, with a second carriage following along behind.

Jessica recognized the matched horses and austere uniform of the coachmen at once. "My uncle," she breathed, hand going to her chest as her heart raced unsteadily. "And his family. They've arrived early."

The coach didn't slow, though the window dropped as it passed and one of her cousins, the youngest, appeared.

"Look, it *is* our cousin!" Lady Anne, seventeen years of age, waved as the horses sped along to Fairbrook Lodge. "Jessica, we're here at last!"

"Oh dear," she murmured, raising her hand in a less enthusiastic wave of her own.

"Best hurry, Jess," her brother called as the carriages rumbled past. "You too, James. Now they've seen all of us, you'll have to be on hand to greet them."

Catherine's grumbled, "Must we?" nearly made Jessica laugh, despite the constriction of her lungs.

James led the way back to the road. The concern in his eyes yet remained when he glanced at her. The lack of teasing about her momentary weakness, his understanding and gentle worry on her behalf, lowered her defenses. Especially since she knew she faced more of the same on the morrow, with the fair fully underway and her cousins forcing her into the role of hostess and guide.

"I want to tell you what happened," she blurted, clenching her skirt in her hands as she walked. "But there isn't any time—"

"Meet me tonight. At eleven."

"At night? Alone?" She sucked in a sharp breath, her heart hammered in her ears. "James. We can't."

"You needn't come all the way to the gate. I'll meet you in the garden. At the arch, where we were when it rained." His expression remained serious, his tone urgent. "I want to help, Jess."

She swallowed. The others were laughing ahead, their speed hastened as they turned onto the lane that would take them directly to the Lodge's door. There wasn't time to argue. And there would be no other opportunity to tell him, to ask him for help, before she faced another difficult day of expectation amidst chaos. The weariness in her heart and body made her steps slow and her thoughts muddled, yet she had to decide.

And she knew what she wanted. Even if it wasn't wise.

They were there. Fifty paces from her front door, where

servants unloaded the carriages, and her cousins, uncle, and aunt stood chatting about the conditions of the roads and the heat of the day.

"Will you be there?" James asked once more.

"Yes." The answer came as unexpectedly to her as his suggestion had. She would be there. Most insensibly, she worried the decision would prove more disastrous to her heart than to her reputation.

As they drew even with the carriages, Jessica's steps slowed. Her family's arrival meant the end of this brief interlude with James. She watched him walk ahead, broad shoulders cutting a fine figure, as he bowed to her uncle and aunt.

Her heart twisted.

The comfort she felt in James' presence, the care he showed, his playful banter that never failed to make her smile made it impossible to ignore the truth. She was falling in love with him.

Jessica pressed a hand to her chest, equal parts thrilled and dismayed by the realization. Her head spun, still too near her recent spell. She needed to breathe. And to rest before she let herself think about the consequences of such a thing. Else she could bring on a worse reaction than before.

Resolve steadied her. Tonight, she would unburden herself and share her struggles. James had proven himself worthy of her trust. She would no longer let fear hold her back from accepting the support he could provide. And if he didn't understand after all, she would rather know at that moment then rely on someone who couldn't be counted upon as a friend.

Drawing a deep breath, Jessica joined the throng to greet her cousins. James glanced at her as he made his and

Catherine's excuses to take their leave, his brown eyes warm with understanding. Her heart faltered as she watched him walk away, keenly feeling his absence.

Yet she would see him again quite soon, and that thought bolstered her more than anything else possibly could.

CHAPTER SEVENTEEN

The night air hung heavy, filled with the sounds of night birds and the faint rustling of leaves. Waiting in the darkness of another man's garden felt far too much like something out of a Shakespearean drama. While James had the greatest respect for the Bard and had enjoyed many of his plays, he had no wish to find himself within one. Nothing ever went smoothly for the men in Shakespeare's works. Princes went mad. Lovers far too often fell by the sword. And men like Nick Bottom found themselves a joke rather than the heroes.

Still, he waited like a fool. Whether he played a role in a comedy or tragedy, he'd yet to determine. James paced the length of the garden wall, glancing repeatedly through the archway and down the path that led from the house. Darkness obscured the trees and hedgerows surrounding him. The moon had yet to rise, and the lights in the house had mostly gone out. The family would make an early night of it rather than keep Town hours, anticipating a full day of entertainment at the fair the next day.

Despite the warm night, restless energy kept James moving. He rolled his shoulders, resisting the urge to loosen his cravat. Why had he suggested this clandestine meeting? If they were discovered, it would ruin Jessica. Or at least cause some very uncomfortable conversations with her father and his. And yet, when he had seen her distress that afternoon, the words had spilled out unbidden.

Jessica occupied too many of his waking thoughts as it was. Having a better understanding of what had occurred earlier that day would put his mind at ease on at least that subject. Once she shared what had happened, he would be better equipped to support her. As a friend.

He ignored the rapid beat of his heart whenever she flashed through his mind. Nothing could come of his growing feelings. Not until he knew, with certainty, that she returned them. His father had too many hopes of an advantageous match. James had to know with certainty that he and Jessica felt the same before he dared broach the idea of a courtship with his parents. He'd never had to keep something so important to him hidden, and it irked him that it might take weeks or months to know Jessica's heart.

But he could be patient. He knew her mind was a match for his own. She'd always been quick and clever, and if he could see how well they suited one another, it would not be long before she saw the same.

Or before she realized he had feelings for her that she didn't return, and then she could soundly crush his hopes with a few sharp-tongued words. Perhaps that was the truth of why he had to hide his growing affection for her. Because he was a coward, and he knew she could cut his heart in two with a single sentence.

The crunch of a footstep on gravel made him turn sharply.

Jessica's slim figure took shape in the darkness as she stepped through the archway. Relief crashed over him, though he kept his tone light as he said, "I was beginning to fear you wouldn't appear."

"Did you think I would miss an appointment with you a second time in one day?" Her teasing words held an edge of nervousness.

James clasped his hands behind his back to keep from reaching for her. "I am glad you came."

She stepped closer, features emerging from the shadows. She'd come without any source of light. A wise thing, since anyone looking from the darkened house would see a light on the path at once and wonder who wandered the gardens at night.

But he'd brough a small lantern, the wick low and the light dim enough to not be seen from the other side of the wall. James drank in the sight of her, noting she wore her hair down in a braid along her shoulder. She wore a simple gown, one that likely hadn't required a maid to don, and no gloves. He'd not undressed after his family's dinner, instead dismissing his valet early. Sneaking out of the house as he had, he hadn't donned hat or gloves, either.

There they stood in the silence. Alone, together. A thrill moved through him, partly at their risky behavior, but mostly because she stood before him, a vision of gentle beauty. Her expression still appeared somewhat uncertain, and though the night was warm, she pulled her shawl tighter about her shoulders. He needed to invoke a sense of familiarity, before one of them lost their nerve and did something ridiculous.

He donned a roguish grin. "Now, tell me all your secrets, Jessica Westcote, and I will single-handedly solve all your problems."

Though he longed for more, tonight he would content himself with offering her a patient, listening ear. Her needs were of far greater importance than his.

"That is a tall promise." She paced away from him, the gentle glow from the lamp illuminating her slim figure. The scent of the garden's flowers drifted in the air between them, the setting all too perfect for a romantic scene, though the tremble in her voice told him it would not be that sort of moment between them.

James leaned against the stone wall, watching Jessica pace before him. "You said you wished to confide in me," he prompted gently.

She halted, facing away from him again, arms wrapped around herself. "I do, it's only..." Jessica's words trailed away on a sigh, the sound pained. "I fear you will think less of me. Or that, once I confide in you, your treatment of me will change." She groaned and turned to face him again, her smile stricken rather than warm or confident as he was used to seeing it. "You must think me mad."

"I would never." He kept still, watching her and willing her to feel his sincerity. "That is my answer to any of it, Jessica. How could I? You are my esteemed and honorable enemy." He smiled, though the levity didn't lessen the truth of his words. "Nothing you say will change how I perceive your character or nature."

She tugged mercilessly on the fringe of her shawl, the dismay in her expression escaping with her next words. "But you saw me come undone today, over nothing. There was no reason for it."

James straightened away from the wall, though he did not come closer to her. "I saw that you needed comfort. And I doubt it was nothing. Please, tell me what happened, what you were feeling. I want to understand." He needed to understand.

"Did you ask Catherine?" She searched his eyes, her own faintly reflecting the small flame from the lamp he'd placed on the ground.

He shook his head. "No. My sister has never betrayed the confidence you share with her. Nor would I ask her to. If you were unwilling to explain things to me, it wouldn't be my place to know."

Her lips parted, and her eyes widened in surprise. Then she turned from him again, dropping her gaze to the ground. "Thank you for respecting my friendship with your sister."

"If I didn't, Catherine would throw me in the old stocks in front of the village hall," he said with a lightness he didn't quite feel. When Jessica looked up with a smile, he would have donned the uniform of a jester in that moment if it meant seeing that expression on her face rather than the other, sadder smiles she'd worn that day.

Jessica stared at him, silent and contemplative, before speaking with that tremble still present. "For others, it seems like nothing. What happened today. But for me, it was overwhelming. The noise, all those people. The expectation to talk and laugh, to weave through the crowd as though nothing was wrong. I couldn't breathe, I couldn't focus. I felt..."

"Frightened?" James supplied in a whisper when her words failed her.

Relief filled her eyes. "Yes. Frightened of losing control. It happens sometimes. When I'm around too many people. Strangers, usually. Or in a room that is too full of sound, of bodies, of smells. Everything builds and builds in my mind until I feel I will drown amid the crowd as surely as I would in a sea of water." She swallowed, and he saw her eyes take on a new shine. That of tears. "It's been that way since I was a girl. I don't know why. No one does."

He couldn't bear the heartache in her voice. The shame. He came away from the wall, standing so they were but a step apart. He wanted to take her hand. To hold her. Instead, he urged her gently, "Why have I never seen this in you before now? Are there times when you are not so affected?"

Slowly, she shook her head. "It's been this way for as long as I can remember," Jessica continued, her voice a mere whisper. "Even as a young girl, at social events with my family, I would become overwhelmed."

As Jessica spoke of her childhood, he could vividly imagine her as she had been, a slip of a girl trembling in a corner, pulse racing and breaths coming too fast, invisible to the crowds but so deeply afraid. Yet he'd never seen that side of her. He'd seen the girl who smuggled a flock of chickens into his bedroom. The Jessica who had cleverly used Ottis's training to cause his master trouble. She'd matched him, jest for jest, wit for wit, with her iron gray eyes and quick laughter.

He hadn't known this other side of her existed. Had he not seen her that afternoon, and someone else told him these things about her, he wouldn't believe them.

She wrapped her arms tighter around herself. "I would get heart palpitations and my chest would feel tight. Once, it grew so bad, I nearly fainted during a musicale. I didn't, though. I even played through my piece. You may even remember. It was the summer your mother wanted Catherine and me to start attending events, to ease ourselves into Society before traveling to London." Her voice hitched upward on the last word.

London. The reason she never went, not even as a friend to Catherine, had finally been made clear. His throat tightened.

She hadn't an aversion to Town, and her father hadn't neglected giving her a Season. He'd kept her home to protect her.

Jessica blinked back tears. "I learned to avoid any place busy with people. Father stopped taking me to York. I stayed here, at home, surrounded by familiar people and scenery. While my friends, while your family, went away." She wiped at her tears and a weak laugh escaped her. "And I am grateful for my father's understanding. For his gentle handling of my weakness. But I've spent so much time alone when everyone else goes away."

Had she been lonely? How had she occupied the long winter hours while he and Catherine had navigated London's theaters, ballrooms, and museums? The desire to gather her to him, to hold her against his heart and promise not to leave her again, nearly overtook him. "I'm so sorry, Jessica. I never suspected any of this."

"Why would you?" She took a shaky breath. "We took great pains to hide it. Even here, in the wilds of Yorkshire, people look down on this sort of mental fragility."

"I would never describe your mental abilities as fragile," he said, daring to step closer again. They were nearly shoe-to-slipper. "Nor would anyone who knows you."

She sniffled and smiled up at him, the tear tracks along her cheeks breaking his heart. "The physicians wouldn't agree. There were several, those early years. My father paid for them to come from as far away as Edinburgh. They said it was a form of hysteria, or a lack of strong morals, or a weakness of my mind. The treatments they advised were not gentle. Your mother was such a comfort. She tried, along with my father and Mrs. Vincent—do you remember her? My last governess.

Anyway. They helped me learn strategies to cope with my weakness."

He hated that she believed any part of her weak. But how could he make her see what he did? He reached for her hand, taking it in both of his. Her skin was soft and cool, the tremble in her fingers subtle but unmistakable. He rubbed a gentle circle with his thumb, wishing he could absorb her pain.

"You have such strength, Jess. I cannot imagine the daily struggle you withstand. As I think on it, all I can imagine is a world of crowds. They are daunting to everyone, but not as you describe. I could not face such a thing as you have. I am glad you had help. Please, let me offer myself as another support. I am here for you, in whatever way you need, whenever you have need of me."

James ached at the loneliness she had endured, hidden away while the world went on without her. How frightened she must have felt, unable to make sense of her own mind and body. He longed to wrap her in his embrace and only resisted because he did not wish to startle her.

Anger and protectiveness rose in his chest. She had endured this alone for so long.

"You cannot know how much it means to hear you say that." Jessica glanced down, a few lingering tears glistening on her cheeks. James didn't hesitate this time, pulling his handkerchief from his pocket. With gentle fingers beneath her chin, he tilted her face up.

Her eyes widened at the contact, lips parting in surprise. James's pulse raced at her nearness, but he kept his touch light, dabbing the handkerchief at the tear tracks on her skin. Jessica remained still beneath his ministrations.

When he finished, she did not pull away. His fingers still cradled her chin. An aching tenderness filled his chest.

Without thinking, James brushed his thumb over her cheek. How could someone so soft on the outside be so resilient and carry such strength within?

"You are so very brave," he whispered.

Jessica drew a shaky breath. She leaned into his touch. The world around them faded away until there was only her, the warmth of her skin beneath his fingertips, the soft gleam of lantern-light in her eyes.

This was dangerous, to stand so close. To touch her as he was. And yet James could not bring himself to move away. This connection felt far too right. He let his thumb trail along the line of her jaw before reluctantly letting his hand fall away.

"Thank you," Jessica murmured. "For listening. For understanding."

James managed a nod, not yet trusting his voice. With effort, he steadied his breathing. She gifted him a tremulous smile.

He had hoped to offer her comfort tonight. In the end, somehow, she had soothed his soul. She had granted him her trust, a thing so precious he couldn't quite comprehend it. But he would prove worthy of it.

"Tomorrow will likely prove difficult," Jessica admitted as she stepped aside, bringing them shoulder to shoulder. "The fair will draw a crowd. They said at the inn that all the rooms were full here and in neighboring villages. Lord and Lady Retford advertised the event quite well."

"This fair seems important to you," he noted, looking down at the handkerchief in his hand. He folded it into a small square, wishing he hadn't let her move away, yet relieved he had. Another moment standing so close, he would have succumbed to the desire to kiss her. Already, he wondered what her lips would feel like pressed to his. But this wasn't the time or place, and she didn't need a romantic hero. She needed a friend.

"I am tired of missing what others enjoy," she whispered, this time with a wistful smile on her face. "I don't expect to ever go to London and take the Ton by storm, of course. I would be content enough to go to York, to attend theatricals, to experience new things and meet new people. I want those things, even though they sometimes seem impossible. But no one will let me try. Not unless I can prove I have a greater measure of control than I have displayed thus far."

A sad laugh followed her words, and Jessica twisted her fingers in the fringe of her shawl. "Today was a disaster on that account."

"You were left alone." That was clear enough to him. "Had Tom stayed near, he'd have given you reassurance. Stability. You liken what you feel in those uncertain situations to drowning. When he disappeared, so did the rope that gave you reassurance you could find land again."

Jessica's gaze came to his again, her eyes widening. "Tom doesn't really know. We haven't told him, you see. The difference in our ages, in our paths, didn't make it necessary."

"I'm not blaming him. Well. Not entirely." James tucked the handkerchief away and then took her hand. It was easier this time. "Let me escort you tomorrow. Let me be your line to safety."

"But your father's guests—"

"Arrived yesterday, yes. And your cousins today. What do they matter? I will be at your door before you have finished breakfast." His father wouldn't like James disappearing, but after doing everything his father asked for most of the summer, James saw nothing wrong with taking a day for himself, to do precisely as he wished, with precisely who he wished. "And I will walk with you to the fair. I will be at your beck and call, your disposal, in whatever way you wish or need."

"And if I fail?" she asked, turning away. "If I fall into hysterics, or a swoon, or cry?"

James stopped resisting the urge to take her in his arms. He gave in. Tugging her gently around, guiding her into his embrace with one arm going about her shoulders and the other her waist as he laid his cheek against her forehead. She smelled of vanilla and jasmine, of the summer-softened night around them. She stiffened only a moment before resting her cheek against his chest.

"I'll be there. I'll not let anyone see what you do not wish them to see, sweeping you away, where you can compose yourself in private, give way to tears, rest, or what have you. Then I will give you my arm, when you are ready, and take you out into the world again. As many times as necessary. You will not fail, Jess. Not when you want something. I have years of experience of watching you achieve many things."

Nestled against him, she took in a deep breath and nodded against his chest. "Thank you, James. I'm grateful you're my friend."

His heart fell, but he didn't let the sudden pain of that word dash his hopes. They had been enemies for so long. He could be her friend for a while. Forever, in truth. And perhaps something more, in due time.

"You need your rest," he told her, relaxing his hold and stepping away. "Tomorrow is an important day. Off with you. I'll leave when I know you're safely inside."

"And how will you know that, exactly?" she asked with a grin. "Am I to signal you from my room?"

"Indeed. Light a candle, put it in your window, and then I will creep back through enemy territory to my own rest."

Her soft laughter lingered in the night air and in his heart long after she'd slipped away through the darkness. He waited, watching the windows of the Lodge until a flickering candle appeared in Jessica's window. Then he withdrew, his own lamp quite dim. He doubted he would sleep. And if he did, he would dream of Jessica in his arms.

CHAPTER EIGHTEEN

The day ahead seemed brighter than the one before, knowing, as Jessica did, that she would not face the crowds alone. As she stood at her window, she thought back on what had worked in the past. The ways her governess, her father, and even Catherine had helped her navigate the most difficult moments at assembly balls, Christmas parties, and even sermons on Sundays when her agitation rose for no reason she could understand.

"I must gather my fortitude and present my best self," she murmured to her reflection in the glass. "If I feel faint, it is a small matter to ask to sit for a moment and collect myself. I need not be over-set by the crowds, because I can withdraw to quieter places if necessary."

She twisted the end of her braid, then snatched her fingers away. Wrapping her hands in ribbons and string helped, sometimes, but it also gave away her nervousness. She turned to her dressing table and opened one of the drawers, searching through it until she found a bracelet with beads that spun easily. Then she went in search of a pendant that slid easily on its chain.

A lady could play with her jewelry quite subtly.

"I will not be ruled by my nerves," she said, undoing the necklace's clasp and putting it on. "I will rise above them. And James will help."

She stilled and looked up at herself in the mirror, noting her pink cheeks. Memories from the night before flooded her mind. She couldn't help conjuring James's face, his expression so open and earnest as he listened to her deepest shames. The gentle touch of his fingers on her skin. The way he had pulled her close, one hand tenderly cradling the back of her head as she accepted his comforting embrace.

Jessica's heart quickened at the recollection. She had confessed her most vulnerable self, and he had responded with care, not judgment.

But such acceptance couldn't hint at any romantic intention, could it? James would have been as kind to his sister. Jessica was no more than a friend in distress. Surely, compassion alone had dictated his actions.

And yet, when she allowed her thoughts to linger on the steadiness of his arms around her, the strength and warmth of his embrace, Jessica's breath caught. In that moment, she had felt cherished. Seen not as odd or unstable, but as someone worthy of tenderness and care.

A bittersweet longing filled her heart.

Bessie arrived, and Jessica tried to put James from her mind, engaging her maid in cheerful conversation. All the servants had been given certain hours away from their duties, to better enjoy the festivities in turns. The last day of the fair, many of them would take a half day, too. Everyone, from stable hand to the baron's noblest guest, would have ample opportunity to enjoy the sights and sounds of a summer celebration.

When Bessie left, leaving Jessica dressed and ready but for having breakfast, her thoughts went back to James. His perceived intentions warred in her mind.

She ate breakfast at a full table, the only person missing her aunt who had taken her breakfast in bed. No one noticed that Jessica remained quiet. How could they, when her five cousins kept up a steady stream of chatter about other fairs they had attended and their great enjoyment of "country entertainments." They kept Mr. Holly's attention, and her father was occupied in conversation with her uncle and Tom.

When she rose from the table, a footman came forward and bent to inform her in a quiet voice, "Mr. Aldwick is in the foyer, Miss Westcote. He asked that you be informed after the meal."

Blushing as she thanked the servant, Jessica hurried from the room. As she descended the stairs and saw James waiting, hat in hand as he paced the floor, her lips curved in an involuntary smile. Whatever this day brought, just his presence was comfort enough.

"Good morning, James," she greeted, still leaning over the rail.

His gaze snapped up to hers at once, and a slow grin appeared on his handsome face. "Jessica. Good morning."

For a moment, they only stared at one another. She knew she returned his grin without meaning to, and hoped he didn't think her a simpleton for her unabashed relief. He lifted his hands out to either side when she said nothing, then turned about in a circle. "Will I make a suitable escort, do you think? I couldn't decide between green or blue."

"So, naturally, you chose gray." She descended the steps

slowly, pretending to consider his choice of coat. As her half-boot touched the ground floor, he made a show of tugging at his coat sleeves.

"Naturally. Matching my coat to the color of your eyes." He gestured to the lavender gown she wore. "I chose well. When you wear that color, the gray stands out even more. Complimenting one of your finest features is an admirable reason for fashion choices, I should think."

Jessica laughed, though her heart fluttered at the circumspect route he'd taken to both compliment and reassure her. "I have never heard of a man matching his coat to a woman's eyes."

"Nor have I. I imagine a more fashionable fop would take me to task for committing some cardinal sin of style." His glance took her in again and he came closer, his eyes still merry though his expression grew more serious. "You look lovely today, Jess."

Her heart stuttered and warmth spread across her chest. Had he ever said such a thing to her before? Her lips parted, but she didn't know quite what to say. Then a rather dismal thought came to the forefront of her mind and left via the tip of her tongue. "Are you saying that because of what I told you last evening?"

James slowly shook his head. He stepped forward to take her hand.

"I am only saying aloud what I have previously kept to myself. I can only blame some misguided thought that if I paid you compliments it would give you an advantage in our verbal sparring. A silly, childish notion. It's the truth, Jessica. You look radiant today," James said softly. Despite the gloves they both wore, her fingers tingled beneath the fabric.

Jessica's breath caught, warmth flooding her cheeks.

Before she could respond, Mr. Holly's voice called from above. "Mr. Aldwick. I wasn't aware you were joining us today."

James straightened abruptly, while Jessica stepped away from James and tucked her hands behind her back. As though the mere sight of them might tell others what James's touch had made her feel.

"Miss Westcote and I have often attended village entertainments together. My sister usually accompanies us, but she is preoccupied with assisting our mother today. I decided to continue with tradition as well as I could without her." The bend of the truth didn't bother Jessica in the least if it meant she needn't advertise her weakness and James's kind offer of support.

The other gentleman nodded his understanding as he came down the staircase. "Your family is sponsoring the fair, are they not? I imagine that creates a lot of responsibility for all of you."

"Indeed. It is our duty to make certain everyone is enjoying themselves."

Mr. Holly drew even with them and glanced first at Jessica then at James. "It seems you have already found some success. Miss Westcote is somehow more radiant now than she was a moment ago. I imagine it's the promise of an enjoyable day ahead." Yet the knowing look in Mr. Holly's eyes made her suspect there was much he didn't say that he could have.

Her cheeks, warm before, now felt as if they were on fire. "Of course. I am looking forward to it." And she was. Mostly. Because of James.

"I think it will be some time before Lord Wyndham and his family are ready to walk to the village. Are the two of you making an earlier start of it?"

James gave a firm nod, his tone amicable. “I like to arrive before things grow too crowded. It makes the exploration of the grounds more enjoyable.”

“A splendid idea. I think I’ll linger until Tom is ready. But don’t let me keep the two of you.” He gestured to the door. “I hope we find each other later, Miss Westcote. Mr. Aldwick.”

They took their leave, and the moment the door to Fairbrook Lodge closed behind them, Jessica heaved a sigh of relief. “I thought he would insist on coming with us.”

James raised his eyebrows at her, amusement twinkling in his warm eyes. “Did you? He seemed happy enough to let the two of us leave together. Which is something of a relief to me, if I am honest.”

“Really? Why? Do you think he’d make the day difficult?”

“For one of us, perhaps.” James’s gaze went forward, the corners of his lips turning up slightly. “If he had the interest in you that your brother hoped for.”

Oh. Jessica adjusted the reticule hanging from her wrist. “It was rather underhanded of my brother and father to bring that man into our home, hoping the two of us would form a connection. As pleasant as Mr. Holly is, he isn’t of interest to me in *that* way. Though I am grateful for his friendship with Tom. My brother needs steady gentlemen like that if he is to become a serious man of the law.”

James let her prattle on, that slight and secretive smile lingering on his lips. As though he had some thought that brought him delight, especially as he kept it to himself.

“I hope you slept well, despite the late hour?” he said as they left the lane for the wider road. Already people were walking along the way, all of them going to the fair and market.

“Yes, thank you.” She looked at the clusters of people

walking along, many of them familiar to her. A family with young children, the little ones skipping ahead and then running back when their father called, were just ahead. A gaggle of girls walked together, hands joined, singing a rhyming song. Boys strode in groups, too, some of them walking backward and most of them laughing. There, farther ahead, an elderly couple that seemed to lean on each other for support as much as they used their canes made their way forward. Just beside the couple, a farmer led a mule weighed down by crates of fruit. Behind them, a man drove a wagon while his wife sat beside him with a babe in her lap.

They weren't even at the field yet, or in the crowded streets with vendors' stalls, and Jessica was already surrounded on all sides by people. Her heart beat faster and she stepped closer to James's side.

He glanced down at her and held his arm out, the silent invitation a welcome one as Jessica accepted his escort. "I have a plan," he said, his voice low and audible only to her. "I thought on it most of the evening. I woke up thinking about it, too. You must tell me if you think it a good one."

She nodded silently, her eyes on the crowd ahead of them.

"Firstly, if you begin to feel the least bit uncomfortable, you must let me know. Touch my hand. Take my arm. I do not intend to leave your side." She took in a shaky breath and nodded her thanks. "Arriving early as we are, there will still be crowds. I thought we could begin by walking the perimeter of the field, so you need not feel hemmed in on all sides."

Jessica looked up at him, her eyes widening.

"We can find the quietest places that way, too. And perhaps find which areas to avoid. But if you ever have a moment when you need to step away, to rest or find a moment of quiet, you have but to tell me. Even a glance will be enough, Jess."

"You have given this a lot of thought."

He met her gaze, tilting his head as he did when he was being especially clever. "I haven't the faintest idea what this is like for you, though. I merely tried to think of what I would wish, were I to find myself in a moment of distress. You must tell me if there is more I can do, or if there are things that have proven useful in the past."

The road grew more crowded as they came to the field, and Jessica's lips parted in wonderment. It had been ages since they'd held a fair, and the usual market days were nowhere near so festive as what she saw before her. Ribbons in shades of red, blue, and yellow were artfully woven around the trees, lining the field, lending an air of festivity that seemed to touch every corner of the village ahead, where she glimpsed more bright colors wound through fences and streaming from windows. Large tents were raised to house games of chance, exhibitions of skill, and vendors peddling everything from wooden toys to rare books.

James covered her hand with his and she realized she'd tightened her grasp without meaning to. He kept speaking in that same low, soothing voice. "What else will help you today, Jess? How can we make certain you enjoy yourself?"

She swallowed to loosen the tightness in her throat as excitement warred with fear. What if nothing they did worked? What if the spinning of her thoughts and the vise around her chest overcame her entirely and she swooned?

A gentle tug on her arm kept her following James to stand beneath one of the ribboned trees. He released her arm only to maneuver himself in front of her. Her back touched the tree and a ribbon, lifted by the breeze, stroked her arm. James blocked out the crowd, standing over her like a shield. His deep brown eyes were dark with concern.

"Jess? My dear little ally, talk to me."

She blinked at him. "Dear little ally?" She pursed her lips. "I haven't been anyone's 'little' anything in ages, James."

He stared at her in surprise a moment, then his grin broke through the puzzlement in his expression. "You'll always be littler than me, though."

"Everyone is littler than you," she retorted, finding it easier to breathe. Easier to concentrate on him. "You went from scarecrow to giant overnight."

"And you from a knobbly girl to a Greek statue," he retorted. "And still. Smaller than I am. In almost every way."

"Not in wit," she pointed out.

"No. Never there. We are a match for one another on that account, at least." Was it her imagination, or had his expression turned somewhat wistful? She didn't get long to think on it, as he was speaking again. "Very well. We should return to my original question."

She couldn't recall what that had been.

James's gaze turned gentle once more. "What more can I do for you, dear Jess? What has worked in the past?"

She blushed at the endearment, gentle as it was. Then forced herself to take in a deep breath. "Remind me to breathe," she said on a whisper. "Not to gasp for air, but to take it in slowly. That has helped. Distract me, if you think you can, if my mind seems to wander."

He nodded. "I can do those things. What else?"

"Help me remember where I am," she whispered. "That I'm safe." Why did this feel so shameful to say out loud? James wanted to help her. And she'd discussed these things with her own father, with James's mother, with Catherine. Yet it still felt like defeat, to rely upon him or any of them. Her eyes pricked with tears. "You needn't do this, James. I know I can be difficult, and this burden isn't yours to bear. We can return home, if you wish. Or when Catherine comes, you can leave me in her care. I have no wish to bother you with my shortcomings."

James stared down at her, and his expression softened. Gently, he took her hand in his. "You could never be a burden to me. I want to be here for you, in any way I can."

He brushed his thumb over her knuckles in a soothing caress. "Don't think for a moment that I view this as an obligation. It's a privilege to stand beside you and support you through difficulties. That's what true friends do. And we are that now, are we not? Friends?"

Jessica blinked back tears as she nodded, overcome by his sincerity. James lifted his other hand to brush a loose tendril of hair back from her face.

"Now, shall we try again?" he asked gently. "You mentioned some things that help. I can remind you to breathe deeply and distract you if needed. I'll stay by your side, so you remember you aren't alone. If it all becomes too much, you have but to say the word and we'll find a quiet spot for you to rest. Or I can return you to your home, without judgement. No one can expect you to conquer a life-long challenge in a single day, Jess."

Jessica managed a tremulous smile. "Thank you, James. I don't deserve such kindness, but I'm grateful for it. And for you."

"You are more deserving than most, I think." James shook his head, eyes tender. "It is I who am grateful, for your friendship and your trust." He offered his arm. "Shall we?"

Bolstered by his steadfast support, Jessica nodded and

took his arm. Together, they stepped back into the bustle of the fair. Jessica kept her focus on James's solid presence beside her as they slowly walked the perimeter.

The moment James had laid eyes on Jessica that morning, when she appeared at the top of the stairs with a smile and hope shining in her eyes, he knew he was utterly lost. She was a vision, her coppery-colored waves peeking out from under her bonnet, gray eyes alight with excitement.

He was completely, hopelessly in love.

Walking along the edges of the fair, her trusting touch on his arm, he couldn't deny his good luck to have her as his friend at last. How had his life turned upside-down with such speed? After years of bickering and competitive banter, his feelings for Jessica had deepened into adoration and care over the course of a few weeks.

Or so it seemed. When he thought on the past months, there were signs of his changing perspective. The relief he felt when he saw her for the first time, after his family returned from London, and she appeared as beautiful and happy as ever. He'd immediately accosted her, verbally throwing down the gauntlet in regard to the book she held in her hand that day. They had debated the weaknesses of French novelists for nearly a week.

And he had found her beautiful for ages. But when had her nearness started making his breath catch, his heart race?

"James, look. Candied fruit. We must try some." She gave a gentle tug of his arm and he followed, the realization that he would go wherever she led making him laugh at himself.

Being trusted with her vulnerabilities and her joys felt like the highest honor. To simply be by her side, tending to her needs, made him feel more the gentleman than he ever had in the past.

"You've had nothing but sweets since we arrived," he said, sounding entirely too much like his mother when she took him to task for similar things in his childhood. "Perhaps we should find a game for you to play. There, that one. Tossing rings over glass bottles."

She wrinkled her nose at him. "I haven't the least interest in that. Unless you mean to challenge me. Then I will have to accept, if only to prove my hand steadier than yours. I still wish for the candied fruit, too."

He laughed and obligingly purchased a small pouch of the sweets. Then he led her to the open grass where a farmer's wife collected a penny per couple. She had a basket of flowers for prizes, and Jessica won her own with ease. She twirled a nosegay with sweet peas and daisies, winning the tiny bouquet making her eyes dance with glee.

He didn't mind her winning in the least.

Though crowds and noise didn't bother him, his awareness of how they pressed around them was awakened. He stayed focused on Jessica, alert for any signs of distress. And every time she smiled up at him, displaying a bauble from a vendor or pointing to a juggler or puppet show, the concern he felt turned tender.

When had their endless squabbling turned to real friendship, then buds of romance? Looking back, James regretted not realizing sooner how perfectly matched they were. How had he wasted so much time challenging Jessica when he could have been loving her?

No more. Things had to change. He'd already begun the work of it, too. Savoring each moment they spent together.

She was intelligent, spirited, and kind. His ideal partner in every way. He only hoped Jessica might feel a fraction for him of what he felt for her.

James stood at Jessica's side, watching a Punch and Judy show at the outskirts of the crowd, relishing the way Jessica laughed at the puppets' antics. Until he spotted her cousins Lady Mary and Lady Jane approaching. With sinking spirits, he recalled how the vain, gossiping cousins had fawned over him in London, though neither would ever set their sights so low as a baron's heir.

"Mr. Aldwick," Lady Mary called in pretended delight, and several children watching the show looked over their shoulders with frowns for the loud disturbance. "We are enjoying your family's quaint country affair. Though it is a far cry from London's amusements, is it not?"

Jessica gave him a worried glance, then looked to the puppet stage. The Judy puppet had her hands on her hips, but at Jessica's glance the little wood and fabric figure raised one hand and a harsh voice cackled, "Have you no manners? Shush. We are trying to have an argument!"

Punch shook his wooden fist at them. "Be gone, loud folk. There's a tale we're tryin' to tell!"

Her expression one of absolute mortification, she tugged at James's arm and he took her away from the audience of children and toward her tittering cousins.

Lady Jane latched onto his other arm uninvited. "Mr. Aldwick, we've missed your company. Why did you not call on us in London, during the Season?" She effected a pretty pout and looked over at Jessica. "He usually does, you know. And we nearly always dance together. You know what an excellent dancer Mr. Aldwick is, do you not, cousin?"

"Jessica doesn't care for Mr. Aldwick's company. Or do you

not remember?" Lady Mary smiled at her cousin. "Though perhaps that is past, given the two of you are wandering around arm-in-arm at present. But why didn't we see you more, Mr. Aldwick? Or your charming cousin, Mr. Harrington?" Lady Mary asked, crowding in on Jessica's side as they walked up the middle of a row of tables and tents full of fine wares.

James extracted himself from Lady Jane's grip with a tight smile. "I am certain I saw the both of you at a few events, though it seemed too much trouble to make myself known when you were quite busy with others." In truth, he had actively avoided speaking with any of them. "Perhaps for the best, as I was preoccupied with family matters."

The cousins tittered obliviously at the subtle barb. "And what of Mr. Harrington?" Lady Jane asked again. "Is he here today?"

Unwilling to throw Leo to the wolves, James gave a shrug of his shoulders. "I haven't yet seen him. Though I believe he expressed an interest in spending the majority of his visit with the rector. Something about a new interest in his faith."

"Perhaps we ought to check the church then," Lady Mary said teasingly to her sister. "Mr. Harrington is always so affable."

They had come to the end of the row, and across from them was the paved village square. An old set of stocks were at the center, but otherwise the area was quite empty. For the fair, it had been turned into an outdoor ballroom. Musicians from York, specially hired by his family, played on a temporary stage at one end. Couples filled the area in rows, farmers and gentry alike, laughing as they wove in and out in a reel.

"All this talk of dancing reminds me that it has been some time since we stood up together, Jessica." Sensing Jessica's discomfort in her cousins' company, he asked, "Shall we dance?"

"That would be lovely. Yes, please."

He whisked her away before her cousins could petition for a similar favor. Once out of earshot of the ladies, he bent closer. "Would you rather find a place to rest?" he asked. "It may help take your mind off the crowds."

She glanced at him. "Is that what you would prefer?"

His heart shot forward, and he gave her an honest answer. "I would prefer to dance with you, my first and favorite partner."

Surprise and pleasure crossed her face. "Then I would love to. Dancing always did have a way of freeing me from my own mind. I can forget almost everything else when I'm dancing."

He took her to the new lines forming for another reel. The first time they came close to one another, Jessica whispered, "Thank you for the rescue. They mean well but their conversation can be overwhelming."

James stepped closer than the dance called for, wishing for the intimacy of a waltz but grateful for what he could get. "Think nothing of it. I've been anticipating this dance all day."

With her eyes shining, she gave herself up to the steps, the cousins already forgotten.

If he could declare himself in that instant, he would have. He hadn't seen Jessica so happy, so carefree, in ages. Not since the ball at the beginning of summer, when he'd been dreading a summer of forced pairings with women he had no interest in courting. She'd been dancing that night, but never with him.

For now, he had to remain content simply being near her, caring for her.

Too soon, the music ended. Laughing, Jessica said, "You

always were an excellent dance partner. I've missed our lessons."

"As have I," James admitted. "I've yet to find another partner so perfectly matched to me as you."

Jessica's cheeks colored prettily at the compliment as James escorted her to a quiet bench. "I'll fetch us some refreshments," he said. "Will you be alright on your own briefly?"

She nodded, still glowing from their dance. James hastily made his way to a lemonade stand, eager to return to her side. At the booth selling cider and lemonade, he purchased two cups and turned so quickly with one in each hand that he nearly collided with the person behind him.

"Leo," he said with a laugh. "I was wondering when we would meet today. I apologize that it nearly cost you a soaked waistcoat."

"A small price to pay to introduce you to my charming acquaintance," Leo said, gesturing with his free hand to the woman on his arm. She had black curls, deep brown eyes, and charming features. "Mr. James Aldwick, may I present Miss Roberta Allan, sister-in-law to our rector."

James bowed, holding the cups of lemonade awkwardly to either side. "It is a pleasure to meet you, Miss Allan. I hope you are enjoying your visit with your sister's family."

"Very much so," she returned, her smile bright. "It is such a pleasure to meet you, Mr. Aldwick. Mr. Harrington has told me much about you. Though it seems we caught you in the middle of an errand. Is someone waiting on those cups of lemonade?"

"Indeed. If you would like to come with me, I have someone I think you would like to meet." He cast a meaningful grin at Leo, then led the way back through the crowds and to the bench where he had left Jessica resting happily.

She was still there, though no longer alone. A young boy sat on the bench with her, his arm full of a puppy that Jessica was doting on. James grinned as he approached.

"I see you have found yourself a better partner than me." He winked at the boy, who grinned at him with a gap-toothed smile. The boy was a local farmer's son. "That is a fine dog, Harry." He handed Jessica her refreshment.

"Thank you, Mr. Aldwick. We've six of 'em right now. My father hopes to sell them during the fair, since they're from our best shepherd. You know Dolly, don't you, sir?"

"I do, indeed. I've no doubt she'd produce a fine litter. I hope your father gets fair prices for them."

"You best run along, Harry." Jessica gave the puppy a final scratch behind the ears. "Before I attempt to make off with this one. Thank you for showing her to me."

"You're more'n welcome, Miss Westcote." The boy bobbed his head, cuddled the puppy to his chest, and went away. Jessica's gaze followed him before she noticed James hadn't arrived alone. She stood and curtsied.

"Mr. Harrington, good to see you again. I didn't know you'd returned from your trip to visit your great uncle. Is he well?"

"Entirely too well," Leo answered cheerfully. "Miss Westcote, I'd like to introduce you to someone I met while in Northumbria. Happily, we found we have a connection to Amoret, too. This is Miss Roberta Allan, sister-in-law to the rector."

The ladies curtsied to one another, and James sipped from his cup with his eyebrows raised at his friend.

"It is a pleasure, Miss Allan." Jessica seemed quite at ease, despite the noise and a new person before her. Perhaps a lingering effect from their dance, or the puppy's calming presence, had helped her. Leo withdrew, to make his way back to the lemonade vendor. Miss Allan settled on the bench next to Jessica.

"My sister has asked me to visit a score of times, but it never seemed to work out. I am glad I came at last," Miss Allan said, looking about her with wide-eyed interest. "She made it sound like such a small, sleepy place. I find it hard to believe at the moment."

"It is quiet enough, most of the time," Jessica admitted. "Mr. Aldwick's parents, Lord and Lady Retford, are making the summer a great one for entertainment. We have had more excitement these past two months than in the two years prior."

Miss Allan glanced up at James, her eyebrows raised. "How interesting. Mr. Harrington has told me so much about your family, Mr. Aldwick. It sounds as though you have long been friends."

"Since we were boys," James admitted.

Miss Allan looked at Jessica. "And what about you, Miss Westcote? Mr. Harrington mentioned you, too. Particularly when he acquired a box I painted. He said you looked rather like the lady I depicted, and now that I see you, I must agree."

"Oh? I am afraid to ask what the scene was." Jessica's gaze dropped to her lap, where she turned the now-empty cup in her hands. "I will have to ask Mr. Harrington to show it to me, since he saw a likeness."

"He no longer has it," Miss Allan said with a sly smile in James's direction. "I believe he gave it to another, as a gift. A perfect betrothal gift, he called it."

James's cheeks warmed. He cleared his throat, then drank more lemonade and cleared it again.

"Are you all right, James?" Jessica asked, brows drawn together. "Is the lemonade not to your liking? It was a trifle sour."

"Quite all right." He looked up as Leo approached, glaring at his friend. For his part, Leo only raised his eyebrows as though innocent of any wrongdoing.

"I think we all ought to dance," Leo said, handing lemonade to Miss Allan. "After the ladies have finished their drinks."

"Are you equal to another dance, James?" Jessica raised her eyebrows at James, who grinned back at her.

"So long as my partner is eager, I am, too."

Again, they found themselves at the village square, where the lively notes of a fiddle beckoned them to join in the revelry. First Jessica and Leo danced together, their steps light and graceful, sharing equally in the enjoyment. James and Miss Allan twirled alongside them, their own laughter adding to the merriment. Then James partnered Jessica again, and as their gaze met with each clasp of hands, he wished the moment wouldn't end.

Miss Allan and Leo hadn't seen all of the fair yet, so when the musicians took a break, Jessica offered to act as their guide. She was much happier, much freer, then she had been at the beginning of the day.

They walked through the rows of stalls, Jessica always on James's arm, admiring the myriad of handmade trinkets, baked goods, and fresh produce on display. They found their way back to the games, where Jessica and Miss Allan's cheers filled the air as the gentlemen played both games of skill and games of chance.

Traveling performers had arrived and took their time on the stage, creating a spectacle that captured the attention of many. They juggled daggers, then lit torches, and one man put a sword down his throat while women and children gasped and screamed in shock. Jessica leaned into James's shoulder, her eyes round as saucers, then relaxed when the sword came out and the man bowed to the crowd.

Several times, James steered them away from the crowds to quieter corners and booths. Always when he noticed Jessica's grip on his arm tightening, or the way her fingers would clutch at the pendant on her necklace and slide it hastily back and forth on its chain.

She never seemed to need long to recover, and she gave him a look bright with gratitude when she was ready to face the crowds again.

Hungry from their adventures, they wandered over to a pie vendor, their mouths watering at the delicious aromas wafting through the air. They bought chicken pies, their flavors rich and satisfying, and found a quiet spot to sit and enjoy their treats.

Miss Allan seemed comfortable in their company and teased Leo with ease. Perhaps his friend hadn't been over-eager when he'd told James his hopes for a relationship with the lady.

Perhaps James ought to have more faith in his own feelings for Jessica.

When Jessica's eyes began to droop, and she leaned more into his arm as they walked, James couldn't help the tenderness that stole over his heart. The day filled with the vibrant colors and tantalizing scents of the village fair had left her exhausted.

"Jess?" he asked as the shadows lengthened in the later

afternoon. They stood in the shade of a tree, watching children run a race on the empty side of the field.

"Hm?" She raised her chin to look up at him, the movement languid and soft. "Yes?"

"I think I should take you home now."

"But the fair isn't over," she protested, her voice soft. Then she started to yawn and hastily covered her mouth. "Oh. I beg your pardon."

He chuckled and reached up to tuck a strand of her hair back into her bonnet, behind her ear. He hadn't meant to do such a thing in public, where anyone could see. But he also hadn't been able to help himself.

"The fair goes on for two more days, dear Jess." She didn't even blink at the subtle endearment. "If you exhaust yourself on the first day, how will you make it to the last? And there will be a performance of *A Midsummer Night's Dream*, at least in part, on the last evening."

"And I know how you enjoy Shakespeare." Her eyes widened, then closed while she yawned a second time. "Oh, bother these yawns. I hate it when you're right."

"Do you, though?" he asked, tone thoughtful. "I sometimes think you argue with me even when you know I'm right, just for the sake of the debate."

"James," she said, tone reproachful. "You mustn't try to uncover all my secrets at once. It isn't very gentlemanlike."

The conversation was swiftly turning ridiculous. He brought it back to its start. "May I escort you home now, Jess?"

"I suppose so." She hooked the fingers of her free hand around her pendant again, and her eyes grew distant. "Do you think it went well?"

"The fair? Yes, I am certain my parents will be pleased. Even though I avoided spending any time with our latest guests. Baron Wright will not thank me for ignoring his daughters, but I doubt he truly wants me for a son-in-law anyway. He's the sort of man who thinks books a waste of time, and the mark of a true gentleman is to have as many gambling debts as possible."

"Goodness." Jessica kept pace with him easily as they walked down the road. There were others making their way home, but still some going the opposite way to get to the fair. "Have you not enough debts to please him?"

"I haven't any debts at all."

"Not true." She gave him a rueful smile. "You have owed me sixpence since I was fifteen years old."

He blinked and shook his head. "That cannot be. Whatever for?"

As they strolled away from the village, the noise of the fair growing fainter behind them, their footsteps stayed in sync as they made their way down the familiar path.

"You bet me that I couldn't spit a cherry pit more than six paces," she said with pride. "And, despite the threat to my reputation, I proved you wrong."

That moment came back to him, and he chuckled quietly. "I'd quite forgotten. Leo and I had stolen the cherries from your tea with Catherine. You found us on the ramparts with the whole bowl."

"And you said if I could spit a cherry that distance you would return them and give me sixpence for the show," she finished for him. "You gave me the cherries, but never paid the sixpence."

"I will rectify that tomorrow. Though one could argue that the number of sweets I bought you today ought to settle our debt."

"That wasn't part of the arrangement, and it would never

stand up in court." Her nose wrinkled. "At least I think it wouldn't. I'll have to ask Tom."

Her adorable, sleepy smile made it difficult for him to ignore the urge to sweep her up in his arms and kiss her, right there and then.

They fell into a companionable silence, both lost in thought. As they reached Jessica's home, James took her hand. Beyond them, the front door opened, indicating a footman must have seen them arrive. It made their farewell for the evening less private. But that may have been for the best.

"Thank you, Jess, for a wonderful day."

"You didn't mind being my keeper?" she asked softly, her gaze on his.

"Not even for a moment," he answered truthfully. Then he bowed, and he waited until she walked inside before making his way back to the road, whistling to himself.

Something had shifted between them, that was for sure.

It was a subtle change, but it was one that left him feeling wholly, completely content.

CHAPTER NINETEEN

The door closed behind Jessica, and she stood in the quiet of her home. The memories of the day played in her mind, leaving a smile on her lips and a flutter in her heart. She'd spent the whole of the day in James's company, and she felt the happier for it.

After a nap, she rose to prepare for dinner with her uncle, aunt, cousins, Mr. Holly, and the rest of her family. She had gone to her room before anyone else returned from the fair, and she'd been lucky that Bessie had been present to help her wash from the day's events before slipping beneath the covers.

Once dressed in a gown appropriate for dinner with an earl, Bessie filled the air with gossip about the fair. "Our Mr. Riley was seen escorting Mrs. Turner," she said with obvious relish as she twisted Jessica's hair backward into a soft arrangement. "It seems they have taken their courtship into the open, at last. He even bought her a glass flower at one of the vendor's booths."

Jessica glanced at her own little nosegay laying on her

table, the prize simple but a perfect reminder of her day. She'd lifted it to her nose to inhale the sweet fragrances again and again, finding the flowers as practical to her needs of distraction as they were lovely to look at. "Is that such a certain sign of courtship?"

"Flowers given by a man to a lady in any circumstance ought to be," Bessie answered with a wide smile. "And a glass flower? It will last forever. I'm certain it's a token of love."

If only Jessica could have such assurances. James's attentiveness, the way he had looked at her all day, had distracted her mind and heart. Not completely. But somehow, every time her breath had seized or her head had grown dizzy, he had known. And he'd taken her to the edges of the fair, the shade of trees, the corners of quiet places, until she'd recovered.

As though he were completely aware of her. Completely dedicated to her.

Bessie raised the tongs to give some curl back to a few strands of Jessica's hair when a knock on the door halted her. "Always the most inconvenient interruptions," Bessie muttered with a clack of the iron tongs in her hand. Jessica giggled but pressed her lips together when Bessie gave her an annoyed glance.

"Best answer and see who it could be," she said.

"Yes, miss. But don't you move." Bessie went to the door and opened it only a few inches. Then said aloud, "Miss Aldwick is here, miss."

"Oh. Let her in, of course." Jessica turned in her chair.

Catherine entered the room, still dressed as though she had only just left the fair behind.

Guilt twisted Jessica's stomach. She hadn't looked for her friend at the fair even once, though it was likely Catherine had looked for her. And been quite busy helping her mother organize things in the castle courtyard.

Her friend's eyes were wide and earnest, the soft, quick rustle of her dress betraying her urgency. "Jessica, we must talk," she said, concern in her voice as her hands clutched at her gown.

"Of course." Jessica rose from the table and gave Bessie a nod, dismissing the maid for the moment. "I'll ring for you when I'm ready to continue with my hair, Bessie."

"Yes, miss." Bessie withdrew with a concerned glance at Catherine, the hinges of the door creaking softly as she closed it.

"Catherine, are you all right?" Jessica asked, sitting on the end of her bed. Before she could give herself to worry, she purposefully splayed her hand against the embroidery of her bedspread, the raised threads giving her something to focus on. She exhaled a tight breath and smiled. Then she patted the bedspread to invite her friend to sit, too. "You look as if you've seen a ghost."

Catherine's hesitant step toward the bed, the slight tremble in her hand as she smoothed her skirt, all conveyed a sense of trepidation that made Jessica's heart beat faster.

But this was Catherine. What could be wrong?

"You're starting to scare me, Cate," Jessica murmured, trying to smile but failing.

Shaking her head, Catherine came to stand directly in front of Jessica. "That isn't my intent. Though it is why I am here. I wanted to speak to you all afternoon. Then James returned to the castle, and I found out the two of you had been together all day. I knew I couldn't put it off a moment longer, so I came." She bit her lip. Then a look of agony entered her eyes as she blurted, "I know about you and James, Jessica. I know what you've been doing, discouraging each other's suitors together. It's a terrible plan, and so selfish of you," Catherine said, her voice quivering with emotion.

Jessica's stomach sank unpleasantly, as though someone had dropped a ball of lead into its middle. Her hands and cheeks went suddenly cold. She wouldn't deny it. Not to her best friend. "We're helping each other, Catherine. Neither of us like the idea of our parents' dictating when and who we must wed. I thought you, of all people, would understand our desire not to marry strangers."

Catherine sighed and came forward, taking Jessica's hands in her own. "Oh, Jess. I love you like a sister, and I want to see you happy. But I can't help fearing you're falling in love with James."

Jessica's heart skipped a beat, and she tried to pull away, but Catherine held her firm. "That's ridiculous." The lie made her throat constrict. "James and I are merely working together. We have a common goal."

"No. No, it's more than that. I've seen the way you look at him lately, the way you talk about him. You must think of the consequences of such a thing," Catherine said, her voice softening.

"What do you mean, the way I look at him?" Jessica's heart hammered in her chest, slamming against her ribs and driving her pulse faster and faster. Her hands grew damp, and she clutched the bedspread on either side of her. Had she really given her feelings away? When?

Catherine's expression softened, and pity filled her eyes. "I caught a glimpse of you at the fair. Dancing. You looked so happy. And then when James took your hand to lead you away, you looked at him as though he was the only person in the world. Your whole face was glowing, as though you were lit from within. I've never seen you look that way at anyone or anything else."

Jessica swallowed. She couldn't recall glimpsing Catherine even once. "I'm sorry I didn't find you at the fair," she said softly. "You should have come to speak to me then. James was only helping me. He knows about my...my episodes." She squeezed her eyes shut. "He offered to help me so I could enjoy the fair, and so I could prove that it can be done. I *can* be in crowds without having a fit of hysterics."

"I am glad to hear it," Catherine said softly, but she hadn't moved from where she stood. "That it can be managed, on occasion."

On occasion. Not forever. The way her heart raced in that moment, the number of times James had worked to calm her, attested all too well to the fact that she remained uncured.

"I did it today," she said firmly, more to herself than to her friend. "I will do it again. As many times as necessary. I can go to York."

"Perhaps," Catherine said, her voice gentle. "In the right circumstances, and with the right help, you could manage it."

Why did the doubt in her best friend's voice hurt so much? Catherine said aloud what Jessica had thought privately, but far more hopefully. "I can."

"But not with James," Catherine said. "You mustn't set your heart on my brother, Jessica. Please."

"I haven't," Jessica denied, but she heard it in her voice. The lie was there, in the tremor of her lips and the heat of her chest and cheeks.

Catherine slowly shook her head. "We have been friends, as you said, nearly all our lives. I know you, Jessica. You care for him."

Jessica lowered her eyes to her lap, clutching her hands

together there. Willing them to be still. That urge to stand and run had returned. To get away from her friend, to not listen to what Catherine said. Even though it came from a place of love.

"James is destined to be a politician with his seat in the House of Lords, and his wife will be required to socialize. Can you see yourself in that role, attending balls and parties, always in the public eye? Helping him put forward his party's plans?"

"You don't think I'm good enough for him," Jessica whispered.

"It isn't that." Catherine finally sank onto the bed next to her friend. "If anything, you are far too good for my brother. It's that I'm worried for you, and what such a thing would mean for your peace of mind."

"I was at the fair," Jessica said. "As you said, all day with James. I didn't suffer a single fit. I did well today." She sounded like a child begging to leave the nursery rather than a woman grown. And she hated it.

Catherine's tone gentled, her dark eyes filling with compassion. "But how many times have you *not* made it through an event? You've left assemblies early to cry in the carriage. You've declined invitations because you weren't familiar with enough of the guests. One good day doesn't mean you have it in you to face a lifetime of parties and social events. I've seen my mother working alongside my father. She *thrives* on such things. But you? Could you be happy that way, Jess? Truly?"

Tears welled in Jessica's eyes as Catherine's words sank in. Her friend was right; she had been ignoring the truth, letting her growing feelings for James cloud her judgment. The social obligations that would come with being James's wife made a knot tighten in her stomach. Her throat closed and her lungs squeezed painfully.

It was her childhood all over again. The sick feeling in her stomach when she had to play the pianoforte in front of guests. The spots in her vision when the crowd pushed too close. The damp palms when she curled her hands into fists and wanted to run far, far away from everything and everyone that made her feel trapped. She stared at her friend, desperate for understanding and support.

"I love him," Jessica whispered, the words escaping her lips before she could stop them.

Catherine's lips parted with a gasp, then her whole expression softened. "I'm sorry," she said at last, her own eyes filled with tears. "There is a reason you said you didn't think you would marry. All those things you worried about—I worry about them, too."

A sob escaped Jessica's throat, and her heart shattered like glass. It didn't matter. The way she felt didn't mean she could be what James needed.

Catherine hugged Jessica tightly. "I cannot imagine the hurt you feel, dearest. But you must think of your future, of what will make you truly happy. James's world is not one that will suit you. You *must* think of yourself and what will bring you peace and contentment."

They sat together in silence, the weight of Catherine's words settling over them. Jessica had to face the reality of her situation. But the thought of giving up on her feelings for James, of denying herself the chance to be with the one person who challenged and understood her, was too painful to bear.

Finally, Catherine broke the silence. "Promise me that you'll think this over carefully. You deserve happiness, and I only want what's best for you."

Jessica nodded, her voice barely above a whisper. "I promise. I'll think it over." Already, she knew the easiest path. The best path. It would be to go back to how things were. To pretend her feelings for James hadn't reached the depths of her heart.

With that, Catherine wiped at her tears. "I must go before my mother realizes I left the house before dinner." She forced a wobbly smile. "Everything will work out, Jess. You'll see."

"Don't—" She had to start again, her throat raw with her emotions. Her despair. "Don't tell anyone what I said, please. Don't tell James. He would never let me live it down." She forced a smile but knew it looked as wrong as it felt on her face.

"I won't say a word," Catherine promised, her own expression sorrowful. Understanding. That made it hurt more. Catherine would never hurt Jessica intentionally. Every word she had said had been given in the spirit of friendship and affection. "Time will help. You'll see. Everything will be fine."

She kissed Jessica on the cheek, then left.

Jessica sat alone with her thoughts, her heart heavy with the knowledge that she had to make a decision that would change her life forever. Going to dinner in her current state was out of the question. She would, without a doubt, find herself collapsing beneath her cousins' scrutiny and haughty conversation. Her heart was too tender at present.

She rang for Bessie. "I no longer feel well," she told her maid, who appeared quite surprised by that declaration. "I think a tray with a little soup is all I need. Send my apologies to my father, please."

"Yes, miss." Bessie helped her put her nightclothes back on, not saying a word. Though she certainly looked as though she wished to ask a thousand questions. Then the maid withdrew for the night.

Jessica sat near her hearth and pulled her slippered feet up onto her chair, wrapping her arms around her legs.

She sat there, her feelings numb, her friend's words echoing in her mind. She loved James, but could she find happiness as his wife? Could she withstand a lifetime of social pressures and expectations? Or would she disappoint him?

She hadn't given much thought to what her feelings for him would lead to, too caught up in the moment to consider the consequences of what loving him would mean. Love, if returned, meant marriage. Marriage to James Aldwick meant eventually becoming a baroness, the next Lady Retford.

The current Lady Retford was everything graceful and charming. Her keen brown eyes, which she'd given to both her children, were always assessing. Always watching. Yet her smile never faltered, lighting up her face in a way that had always put Jessica at ease.

The baroness spoke eloquently, yet with purpose. She remembered the smallest details about those she conversed with, making everyone feel remembered and important. And how Jessica had envied the way Lady Retford seemed to float through crowds, conversing with everyone she encountered, never at a loss for words. Comfortable in the world around her.

How did she do it? Had she learned? Had it come naturally?

Even trying to imagine herself in that position, leading conversations, presiding over social affairs and ballrooms, with everyone's eyes on her—it made Jessica feel sick. Her skin went damp with perspiration, and she stood with a sudden need for more air. She went to the window and opened it, then leaned into the darkening sky.

The panic that used to grip her as a child, the terror of public scrutiny that still haunted her at times, hadn't dimmed with time. Not truly. She'd merely stopped exposing herself to situations that made things difficult.

She thought of the day's events, the joy she'd felt with James, the absence of any fits. Was she strong enough now to face a future by his side?

Would he tire of propping up his wife every time the world converged on her? In stories, love was enough to overcome so many things. Yet even his favorite book of late, *Rob Roy*, depicted a loving marriage that existed because the wife had the same inner strength and fortitude as her husband. They were both honorable, loyal, and courageous. Equal in their partnership.

Jessica had lived a spoiled, sheltered life in Amoret's quiet shadows. Protected from discomfort. And still, it came. She wasn't a match for James. Would he see it? Would he grow to despise her weakness? She wouldn't blame him. After all, she felt nothing but hatred for her weakness that no doctor had been able to cure.

She didn't realize she'd started crying until her vision blurred. Tears slipped down her cheeks.

It wasn't fair. It had never been *fair*.

The early evening stars twinkled brightly in the sky above, cold and uncaring of her heartache.

She found the smoke curling from the highest chimney of Amoret Castle. James was likely readying himself for dinner, unaware of the turmoil in her heart. She pictured his smile, the warmth in his eyes when he looked at her.

The choice before her was agonizing.

Should she follow her heart, whatever the consequences? Or heed Catherine's warning and protect herself from future pain? Jessica leaned against the window frame, the darkness of the night matching the uncertainty in her soul. It wasn't really a decision for her to make. All she could do was tell James it was over. She couldn't help him anymore.

Separation would be best. Keeping away from him was the only way to spare herself more pain. She'd been right when she decided never to marry. It would be best, for everyone, if she remained alone with her troubles instead of foisting them on the man she loved.

With so much weighing on her, Jessica wearily closed the window. She crawled into bed, tears dampening her pillow as she drifted off to troubled sleep.

CHAPTER TWENTY

The second day of the fair dawned as bright as the first, and James left his house before breakfast. He took himself into the village, finding the vendors already open, and bought a sausage-stuffed roll from a cheerful butcher's wife. He tried to delay his arrival at Fairbrook Lodge but ultimately found himself at the door earlier than most visitors would be admitted.

He was as eager as Ottis had been as a pup, excited and anticipating the day ahead with every breath he took. He rang the bell, which the servants kept muffled until the family woke, and waited for an answer with full confidence that he'd be asked inside and to breakfast.

But the servant's somber face at the door quickly dampened his spirits. "Mr. Aldwick. I've been asked to make apologies for Miss Westcote, sir. She is not well today and is not accepting visitors."

Confusion and worry etched across James's face. "Not well? What do you mean? Is it serious?" he asked, his voice rising with concern. She'd been perfectly well the evening before. Happy. Content. Beautiful. He'd fully depended on another day in her company.

"I'm not at liberty to say, sir," the servant replied, his face betraying no emotion. "She simply instructed me to give her regrets."

James thanked the servant and retreated, his mind reeling with questions. What could have happened to make Jessica unwell so suddenly? And why couldn't he know what ailed her? Surely, she wasn't embarrassed. He'd been present once when she'd cast up her accounts, due to illness. They'd been in her family's garden, him, Leo, Catherine, and a few other young friends. Jessica had seemed pale, but happy to have them there. Then she'd turned green, practically threw herself into a bush, and made terrible sounds while Catherine sent James running for her father and a servant.

Everyone fell ill from time to time.

Perhaps she was only tired from the day before, and she didn't want to admit that he hadn't helped as much as they hoped. She'd told him her fits could leave her exhausted for hours or days at a time. Had he missed something?

Had he failed her?

Upon his return home, he found Catherine in the breakfast room, along with their father's guests. But when she looked up at him, her eyes held a knowing concern.

He greeted everyone at the table, as required. Then gave his sister a meaningful smile. "Do you have a moment to speak in private, Catherine?"

"Of course. If everyone will excuse me a moment." She rose from the table after their father nodded his permission, though he watched the two of them withdraw from the room with a curious expression.

James took his sister across the hall, opened the door to their father's private study, and closed it behind them again. They didn't ever come in here alone. Usually, his father sat behind the desk, telling them some piece of important news. Or his mother and father had both been in the room, most often in their childhood, to address childhood mischief. It was strange to be in there for a serious discussion without either of his parents present.

He ran his hand through his hair, pacing away from his sister. Then he turned back to her. "Jessica is ill. She isn't attending the fair today."

Catherine's shoulders slumped, but she appeared relieved rather than troubled. "Poor Jess. I'll visit her later."

"The servants said she wasn't taking visitors." Even as he spoke the words, he realized they wouldn't apply to his sister. Catherine was always granted admittance to the house and family. She was closer to Jessica than anyone in the world. For a strange moment, he was jealous of his own sister.

"James," she said slowly, as though choosing her words carefully. "Perhaps it's best not to spend so much time with Jessica. Especially when we have guests, and our parents wish for you to take the matter of finding a wife more seriously." She tucked her hands behind her back, as though she had something to hide.

His brow furrowed, irritation mixing with his worry. "I haven't any idea why you'd suggest that. Jessica and I are friends. *Finally*. Isn't that what you always wanted? For us to stop arguing and get along?"

"Yes. I did want that," she admitted, her brow constricting. "But now might not be the best time. Not when you're trying to get to know other ladies."

"I haven't the slightest desire to get to know anyone else," he said. When her eyes widened, he tried to recover from that admission. "I know what I promised Father. I said I would try to find a wife. I agreed to his scheme of inviting every unmarried woman in the kingdom to our home. But it's been a waste of time."

Catherine huffed and folded her arms across her chest. "Only because you have sabotaged every single one of those ladies thus far. You and Jessica, both."

His jaw dropped open, then he closed it and lowered his gaze to the floor. "Did Jessica tell you?" He wasn't surprised, really. The two told each other everything. They always had.

"No. But as I know you both, and I've had the best seat to this farce you two planned, I saw what was happening. I may have even thought it amusing, at first," she admitted. When he glanced up again, his sister appeared anything but amused.

"And now?" he asked. "Are you going to give the game up to our parents?"

Slowly she shook her head. "No. But you should stop. And you shouldn't see Jessica anymore. Or at least, see her as little as possible."

"Why?" he asked, taking a step closer to his sister. "Don't you want us to be friends?"

He was missing something here. Something his sister wouldn't tell him.

Had he given too much about his feelings away? Had Jessica feigned illness to avoid him, and now Catherine was trying to tell him—? What? That Jessica didn't want a friendship? "Did Jessica tell you to say this?"

"What?" Catherine blinked at him, her surprise genuine. "No. And yes. I mean—I want you both to be friends. Jessica didn't tell me to say anything." She sighed and paced away from him. "Why are you both so stubborn when it comes to one another?"

His thoughts came to a halt as he turned slowly to his sister. "What do you mean by that?"

Catherine turned and walked back to him, then touched his arm, her voice gentle yet firm. "You need to stop meddling with her feelings, James. Because you're my brother, I know you didn't mean to do anything that would hurt her intentionally. But I fear you've not thought about what your actions would mean to Jessica."

He stared at his sister, still not comprehending what she was trying to get at. "I would never hurt her. What are you saying? Stop speaking in such vague terms. It sounds as though I did something wrong, and if that's true, I should like to know what it was so I can correct the mistake."

He'd apologize to Jessica a thousand times, on his knees if need be, to make things right between them. He'd never hesitate to admit wrongdoing again. He'd never make the same mistake twice, either. He loved her too much. The idea that he had caused her pain made him want to run to her that very instant and make reparations.

He wasn't the same man he'd been at the start of summer.

"You haven't hurt her. Yet," his sister said, the last word sharp and full of warning. "But you're being careless with her heart, James. You aren't thinking of what you are doing, leading Jessica along. Flirting with her. Devoting so much time to her. She's bound to get the wrong idea. To form expectations."

James stepped backward, out of his sister's grasp. "You think I'm toying with her. I would never, ever do that to a lady. Not to any woman. That you think so little of me—"

"I don't," Catherine said. She paced away from him again. "You're so stubborn, James, and such a fool sometimes. If you keep spending time with Jessica, if you keep looking at her the way you did at the fair, the way you have nearly all summer, everyone will think you're in love with her. Everyone will expect you to marry her. And that will be a disaster for you both!"

That his sister had divulged his feelings shocked him, but her declaration at the end of her passionate rant made him rear his head back.

"What the devil do you mean? A disaster?"

"You *know* about her hysteria," Catherine said, rounding on him and pointing her finger in accusation. "She told me that you know. And you would still court her? James. You must think of your position and what is expected of you. Jessica cannot be a baroness. London would undo her. The *ton* would eat her alive. She would be miserable as your wife. Why do you think she's said she never intends to marry? She knows how impossible it would be."

Pain sliced through him like a knife. Miserable? The very thing he'd dreamed of, secretly and barely admitting it to himself, would cause the woman he loved misery?

No. Catherine had to be wrong.

"I'll help her," he said. "Or I won't go to London. There are men who never take their seat in the House of Lords."

"You aren't like them, James. You're too responsible," Catherine reminded him, her tone weary and her shoulders slumped. "And you can't be there to hold her hand through everything. Think of all that our mother does for Papa. The parties and events."

He narrowed his eyes at her. "Do you know how many wives of lords *do nothing*? Or only what they wish? Our mother's choice to be a beacon of Society was just that: her choice. No one made her do it. No one expects it of the next baroness, either."

"You have far too rosy a perspective on the situation," Catherine said with a sad shake of her head. "There are too many obstacles for Jessica to overcome."

"And she's strong enough to face as many of them as she wishes," James countered. "With me to support her. And I thought you would be there, too, as her friend." He glared at his sister, confounded by her complete lack of faith in her dearest friend. The person as close to her as a sister. "Don't you believe in her?"

Catherine winced. "I do. But there is a difference between letting her find her way and forcing her into the center of others' attention."

His jaw tightened and he scrubbed a hand through his hair. "Do you really have such a high opinion of our family? Our father is a *baron* in the House of Lords. That is the lowest rung in the peerage. You know that, don't you? I'm not a duke, bringing home a duchess. I'm not even a baron yet. Jessica will have time. She won't be the center of anything unless she wishes it. We are insignificant in more ways than we stand out."

And he preferred it that way, in truth. Catherine was right. He'd go to the House of Lords and take his seat. He'd vote. He'd make arguments. He'd strive to be a man who petitioned for change in all the ways that would help the people who depended on him. But he'd rather be at home every night, with a good book in hand, Ottis at his feet, and Jessica by his side, than at clubs. He'd rather hold Jessica's hand on a walk through Hyde Park than make appearances at balls.

Though he hadn't specifically made those plans, the

future he imagined for himself and Jessica settled deeply in his heart. "Catherine, I intend to court Jessica," he admitted, his voice trembling with the weight of the admission. "And marry her. If she will have me."

Catherine's face softened, but her eyes still held a warning. "I know your heart is in the right place, James. But please, think carefully about this. Consider everything before you proceed. Talk to our father. Our mother. I cannot have you hurting my dearest friend."

"Your heart is in the right place, too," he said. "However, you are terribly wrong about the whole situation. I expected better of you, too, as her closest friend." He left her gaping at him. He strode out of the study, his mind a whirl of thoughts and emotions. Jessica's wellbeing, Catherine's caution, his parents' expectations—all weighed heavily on him. The path before him suddenly seemed fraught with complications, and he knew he needed to tread carefully.

What further weighed on him was not knowing what had kept Jessica at home. Whether it was a true illness, fear, exhaustion, or disgust with him, he hadn't any idea. And wouldn't until he spoke to her.

Perhaps he'd been too cautious. He'd left too many things unsaid. Why was he forever failing with his words? A man who read as much as he did ought to be better with them. He needed to set things right, and quickly. And he would start with his mother.

She had taken breakfast in her room, so he went there first. Outside her door, he took in a deep breath, suddenly having greater sympathy for the anxieties Jessica faced as his stomach churned and his thoughts scattered. He knocked and entered when his mother bid him come in.

She was the only one who knew both Jessica's ailment and everything he would be asking of his future wife.

She would guide him. Tell him the truth.

And then, he'd plan his next steps.

CHAPTER TWENTY-ONE

Though Jessica had managed to avoid seeing anyone through the course of the day, keeping to her room, a note from her father came insisting that she meet with him in the study. Apparently, her uncle had something of great importance to tell them. Immediately, her mind conjured all the worst scenarios.

Perhaps her uncle had lost all the family's money and needed to sell Fairbrook Lodge. Or he wanted the house for another reason and was ending their lease. Perhaps they had done something wrong, or her uncle thought they had, and was cutting them off.

Bessie arrived with her usual cheer subdued, her gaze often meeting Jessica's in the mirror. Though Jessica attempted to maintain a calm smile, her maid's knitted brow told her how pathetic she must look.

None of the things she worried about were likely to happen. Her uncle had always shown them kindness and consideration. Her aunt had some tendencies toward selfishness, which had come out strongly in her daughters' characters, but overall, she had always been pleasant. Yet Jessica still worried. It was difficult not to, given her already vulnerable state of mind and heart.

Jessica sat in front of the mirror, twisting her hands as she examined her reflection. She had chosen a modest gown of pale blue muslin. Comfortable yet appropriate for an important conversation with the men of the family.

Bessie arranged her hair into a simple chignon, a few curled tendrils framing her face. "You look lovely, miss," Bessie said gently.

Jessica managed a weak smile in return.

"Miss?" Bessie tipped her head to the side. "I know it's not my place to say certain things. But I worry for you sometimes. And you seemed so happy, for so many weeks, and then it stopped all at once. I can tell you're worrying about something, fierce-like, and I wish I could help."

Those gentle words soothed Jessica's heart. It always helped to know others cared for her. Her smile came easier this time. "You have a kind heart, Bessie. Thank you. But there isn't anything to be done. I had a lovely summer, but I think I am in need of more quiet for now."

Bessie bit her lip, indecision in her eyes, before she asked, "Is it Mr. Aldwick's fault, miss? I know he used to vex you something terrible, but he seemed so much better of late."

Cheeks burning, Jessica lowered her gaze to the table. Her eyes caught on the nosegay, wilted somewhat now, but the colors were still there. She ought to throw them away. Yet she gathered the little flowers up in her hands.

Did *everyone* know how she felt about James?

"It isn't his fault. It's mine." She smiled at the little flowers, their once-vibrant colors darkened. "Will you dry these for me, please? It may be too late, but I would like to keep them." There wasn't anything wrong with remembering how wonderful things had been when she'd forgotten her future and James's weren't one in the same.

"Of course, miss. If I can't see them to drying out right, we can press them." Bessie took the tiny bouquet with a gentleness that Jessica appreciated. The people who knew her best were always gentle with her.

Except for James. Even after she'd told him the truth. He'd spoken to her the same. Still teased her. Didn't pity her.

Inside, her thoughts churned in turmoil. She couldn't stop thinking about him. If it was her choice, what would she do? Follow her heart and risk a life full of the discomfort and possible embarrassment that would come with marrying the future Baron Aldwick? Or protect herself and walk away from the man she loved?

It didn't matter. There wasn't a choice. James hadn't even told her how he felt, or if he wished to court her. He'd been friendly and flirtatious. An ally in their game to avoid matrimony. But had she seen marks of affection in his actions where he'd likely intended none?

She rose from the dressing table and took hold of the pendant she wore, sliding it back and forth on its chain as she made her way to her father's study.

James had proven himself kind, loyal, and steadfast. He had seen her at her most vulnerable and never turned away. It wasn't his fault she yearned for more.

"I will face this with fortitude," she whispered to herself. "I will carry myself with dignity and grace."

At the study door, she paused, taking a deep breath before entering. The room was all polished wood and leather furnishings, shelves lined with books. Her father sat in a wingback chair, her aunt in another across the rug from him.

Her uncle, Lord Wyndham, stood solemnly by the fireplace. And Tom was there, too, leaning against her father's desk with his arms crossed.

A family meeting of this sort hadn't occurred before. Not in her memory. The seriousness of the moment weighed upon her, but she lifted her chin and dropped her hand to her side as she curtsied. "I hope I didn't keep you waiting long."

"Not at all, Jessica. Here. Have my chair." Her father stood and motioned for her to take the seat across from her aunt.

Sitting would be torture. So she smiled and shook her head, folding her hands in front of her. "I thank you, Papa, but I'd prefer to stand. I've been resting all day and it is good for me to be up, I think."

He gave her a nod but didn't retake the chair for himself. Instead he paced to the edge of the desk and stood next to Tom, giving her brother a reassuring smile. It left the chair open for Jessica, should she decide to take it after all.

"I thank you for agreeing to this conversation tonight," her uncle said, his smile warm and somewhat sad. He went to stand behind his wife, his hand on the back of her chair. The countess looked up at him with a confident gleam in her eyes and nodded for him to continue. Whatever it was he had to say, he and his wife were at an accord on the matter.

Jessica's stomach twisted, and she dug her fingers into the fabric of her gown to keep them still.

"Years ago, when Amelia died," her uncle said, naming Jessica's mother with a softness in his voice, "your aunt and I made a proposition to your father. We offered to take both of you in until he could find a new wife who could be a mother to you. It seemed practical. We had daughters of the same ages as you both. It wouldn't tax the nursery, and we hoped it would give him room to grieve. But he informed us he had no intention to marry again. Instead, he asked for a permanent lease on this house to raise you both. And so he has."

"And I am thankful for having this home all these years, and having you both with me," their father said, his expression full of love for both of them. "I am proud of how you have grown, and I am grateful I have been here for every moment of it."

Jessica had to bite the inside of her cheeks to keep silent. They sounded compassionate and warm, but the seriousness in the air made it difficult for her to breathe. What were they trying to tell her and Tom?

"Then, when it was time for you, Jessica, to enter Society, I offered to sponsor you," her aunt, Lady Wyndham said with a lilt in her voice. "Your father told me of your difficulties then. I assured him we could work around them. But in the end, it was Lady Retford who said it would be best for you to receive your training at home. I deferred to her. I hope that you are not disappointed?"

Slowly, Jessica shook her head. Trying to come out in London, surrounded by her overly eager and tart-tongued cousins, would have been a nightmare. "No, your ladyship. I am not. Though I thank you for your consideration."

"Of course, dear girl." Her aunt's smile changed, turning sad. "I wish you to know, should you ever wish it, I will happily present you into Society in whatever way you think best. You have a place there, if you want it."

Jessica shook her head slightly but stopped when her uncle heaved a sigh, his gaze on Tom rather than on her.

"This conversation cannot really come as a surprise to either of you. I wanted to have it before, but your father said there wasn't any need until you were older, Tom. Because he didn't want you to rely on what I'm about to tell you. Given how well you are doing in your studies to become a barrister, I thought it time. And my brother finally agrees with me." He gave Jessica's father a rueful smile. "I will not have any more children," he said with a finality that made Jessica's heart feel heavy for him.

Her aunt looked down, but the earl put his hand on her shoulder and looked at her with tenderness in his eyes. "I am too old to be a father again. And I am content with my five daughters, who are beautiful and do their parents great credit."

The countess smiled and covered the hand on her shoulder with her own. "Both of us are too old. We have come to terms with it, of course. But then I was so sick a few years ago, I thought it possible Lord Wyndham would find himself in need of a second wife."

She didn't have to say the rest. They all knew what she meant. If his current countess died, he could remarry a younger woman and perhaps father a son.

"And I told Lady Wyndham," he said, eyes on his wife, "that I couldn't possibly be happy with anyone other than her as my countess." He cleared his throat and looked up. "I apologize for speaking of such intimate things so plainly, but I felt it important for you to know, Tom, that there will be no other heir for the title I hold but your father, and then you."

The air stilled as Jessica looked at her brother. Of course, she should have known. Should have suspected such a thing. But they never spoke of it. Never spoke of the fact that their father was next in line for the title, without his brother having had any sons, and that made Tom's place in the succession assured. But her father had never addressed the possibility with them. And no one had dared bring it up to Jessica or Tom, either.

For his part, Tom didn't appear shocked. His expression gave little away, but Jessica knew him quite well. Well enough to see the way his hand clenched at his side, the slight downturn of his mouth, and the way his eyes darkened. He wasn't surprised. He was grim but determined. He gave a slow nod of understanding to their uncle.

"Given how close we are in age," her father continued, "and in health, at present, I doubt I would hold the title for long after my brother has given it up." He looked at the earl in a way that only brothers would look at one another, with understanding born of long acquaintance. "I grew up in an earl's household, and I know what to expect should my time in that position come. But you do not, Tom. And that is why we are all here this evening."

"You have a choice, nephew," their uncle continued. "And Jessica, too, really." He gave her the briefest glance with a sparkle of interest in his eyes, gray like hers and her father's. "Tom, you can continue on in your training to become a barrister, with the knowledge that I hope for another decade or two of good health. Or, you can resign from your apprenticeship with the law and begin one with me. Think of it as an apprenticeship for earldom." He smiled to himself.

"Uncle," Tom said, voice low and rough. "This isn't—I didn't expect for such an opportunity. I'm not certain—"

"Then do not answer me yet," their uncle said, raising his hand to stave off whatever else her brother could say. "Think on it. If I could have your answer before the next session of Parliament begins, I would be appreciative. If you choose to learn from me, know that it means you would come to our home in London and in the country, as often as possible. You would take your place as my heir in every way that matters. Learning about our holdings, our tenancies, our duties, finances, everything. Your education would include meeting political allies, expanding your acquaintances with other important men. You would have a place in my home and an appropriate allowance, as well as accounts with every merchant a man of your age would have need to give custom."

Jessica put a hand over her heart and looked at her brother in awe. She'd been so busy concentrating on her own situation, she'd almost forgotten a world existed in which her choices weren't the only things to face. Her brother's gaze met hers, and that determination wavered a moment. She glimpsed his uncertainty. Perhaps his fear.

"Jessica is invited to be part of this, too," her aunt said, bringing Jessica's attention back to her. "As I said before, you are always welcome. More so, as your rank will eventually match my daughters', we wanted you to know that we have increased your dowry to match theirs. This ensures you can have your choice of husband. Your father told us this morning you've expressed an interest in remaining unmarried, an independent woman. I have a sister who did the same, and she is quite content. You have the means to do that, instead, if you do not wish to marry."

The forced courtships would end. Jessica needn't see another gentleman, or pretend an interest where she felt none, ever again. She listlessly went to the empty chair and lowered herself onto its cushion.

She didn't have to worry about marrying someone who would put her aside, hiding her like a damaged painting, unworthy of a place of pride in heart and home. No one need ever be disappointed in her struggles with crowds, her struggles. Unless...unless a man loved her enough to overlook such things.

"Are you certain?" she asked. "It isn't necessary. My father has assured me I have enough, and I've no wish to—"

"It is already done," her uncle reassured her. He heaved a deep sigh and then a chuckle escaped him. "You have done well, Thomas. How many children would hear such an opportunity as this and not snatch at it with grasping hands?"

"Their restraint does them credit," Lady Wyndham added with a satisfied nod.

Jessica exchanged a glance with her brother as her uncle helped the countess to her feet.

"We will leave you to discuss matters while we prepare for dinner," their uncle said. "And remember. Nothing need be decided right away."

The moment the door closed behind them, Tom sagged all the way down to the floor and dropped his face in his hands. Jessica closed her eyes and leaned back into the chair, and she heard her father chuckle.

"That went better than I expected," he said, sounding quite cheerful. "Some would think such news as the two of you have had would be cause for celebration, a lessening of worry. I am glad you both know it to be otherwise."

Tom's voice, though muffled through his fingers, came through clear enough for Jessica to hear. "It is an exchange of lives. New problems for old. New challenges for those I had already accepted. Is that how you feel, Jess?"

She opened one eye and peered at her brother, seeing he peeped at her from between his fingers. Perhaps she wasn't the only one in the family that found discomfort in unlikely places. Had she ever asked Tom if he faced struggles similar to her own?

"Yes," she said at last. "Though I admit I'm quite relieved I needn't entertain any more suitors." Feeling somewhat bold, she added with relish, "Including Mr. Holly."

Tom dropped his hands and exchanged a sheepish look with his father. "I couldn't help trying. He's a wonderful fellow. Quiet, too. I thought that would suit you."

Strange, but she preferred James's large grins and laughter to Mr. Holly's more subtle smiles.

"Thank you for the thought," she said, relaxing a little more. "But I think he'd suit another better than me."

Their father cleared his throat and they both looked up at him. He went to stand between them, one child on the floor and the other melted into the chair. "Think things through, as they encouraged. Know that whatever you choose, you have my support." His eyes gleamed with that pride again, and what Jessica suspected were unshed tears. "I hope I did the right thing, keeping you both here with me."

Jessica and Tom rose at the same time and went to him, Jessica reaching their father first and wrapping her arms around his waist. Tom's arms came around them both.

"You did perfectly, Father," Tom said.

"We love you so much." Jessica inhaled deeply, the scent of her father as calming as it had been since childhood.

His arms encircled his children and he kissed first Jessica's forehead and then her brother's. "Your mother would be proud of both of you."

For that beautiful moment, Jessica's heart was content. Everything was peaceful. And that allowed her thoughts and her feelings for James to settle in a way they hadn't before.

After dinner, Jessica's mind churned with the revelations of the evening as she bid her father and their guests goodnight.

Her thoughts lingered on James.

She cared for him deeply, loved him, as she had admitted to Catherine. The idea of walking away from him, of losing his smile and laughter from her life, caused an ache in her chest.

Perhaps she had been too cautious. Too swayed by her worries and insecurities. James had seen her at her worst and never judged. He made her want to be braver and more confident in her abilities.

What if she confessed how she felt? Laid her heart bare and asked James to accept her as she was, hysterics and all. She wouldn't know if a life together was possible unless she took that leap.

Jessica went to her window and gazed at the stars twinkling brightly in the night sky.

She knew what she must do. What she wanted to do, deep in her soul. She would tell James she loved him. And if he felt as she did, they would face the future together, come what may.

She closed the window, but before she could latch it, a pebble hit the glass with a loud clatter. She startled and emitted a rather embarrassing squeak. Then she opened the window and leaned out of it, looking down into the dark garden.

"James?" she gasped out. Had her thoughts summoned him? "What are you doing here?"

James grinned up at her, his smile lit from the light still pouring from the dining room windows. "I need to talk to you, Jess," he whispered.

Her heart picked up its speed, making her pulse race and her breath catch. "I'll be right down," she answered, then shut the window. She turned to see Bessie in the doorway, the maid's expression one of surprise. But the surprise turned slowly to a knowing grin.

"Best take a shawl if you're having a walk, miss. The night air can be cool." Bessie looked over her shoulder. "And I'd perhaps take the servants' east staircase."

Snatching a shawl from the end of her bed, Jessica hurried out the door and gave her maid a grateful touch on her hand. "Thank you, Bessie. I won't be long."

"I'll wait," Bessie said, her eyes narrowed slightly. "Remind Mr. Aldwick to behave himself."

Jessica didn't even ask how Bessie knew it was James. She smothered a laugh with her hand and hurried to the servants' stairway. Her courage wouldn't fail her this time. She would tell James everything. And, if he was willing to take a risk on her, she'd follow wherever he led.

CHAPTER TWENTY-TWO

A long day had kept James away from Fairbrook Lodge and Jessica. First, he'd spent an hour in his mother's room, listening and asking dozens of questions. She'd told him to come to his father's study an hour after that, where both his parents listened to him and advised him. He hadn't experienced such an earnest conversation with the two of them in years. At the conclusion of that meeting, James had spent the day with their guests at the fair. He'd even seen Jessica's cousins again, and Mr. Holly, but no sign of Jessica.

Impatience to see her had plagued him, but only because he was so certain of what he had to say. He'd rehearsed it all to himself again and again in his mind. He knew he should wait. Perhaps until the fair was over, or her family left. But he'd lost so much time already. Years and years of it, while he was busy teasing and tormenting her.

When he could have been loving her.

The warm summer air enveloped James as he crept through the moonlit gardens of Fairbrook Lodge. Frogs hidden in the garden sang their nightly songs, a peaceful chorus accompanied only by the soft scraping of his boots on the garden path. Up ahead, the ivy-covered walls of the manor house came into view.

Jessica's bedchamber window was on the third story, overlooking the roses. He and Leo used to toss pebbles at it when they were boys, mischief-makers on a mission to vex her. How different his purpose was tonight.

James paused beneath her window, heart pounding. He picked up a small stone from the ground and steeled his nerves. Perhaps it was too soon, and she'd refuse to see him. Even so, he wouldn't give up on her, on them. He had to know if she felt the same.

With a well-aimed toss, the pebble sailed through the air and tapped the glass pane. James held his breath, peering up. A faint light glowed in her room. Shadows shifted behind the curtains. Then, the window opened. Jessica's face appeared, her eyes wide and expression uncertain.

"James?" she whispered in surprise. "What are you doing here?"

"I need to talk to you, Jess," he replied, voice hushed but earnest. The whole garden went quiet, as though the frogs and the birds all listened for an answer with him.

Jessica didn't even hesitate. "I'll be right down."

He exhaled in relief as she withdrew into her room. His pulse raced in anticipation. The night breeze rustled through trees and flower bushes. Somewhere an owl hooted, deep and lonesome. He tried not to think it an ill omen. It couldn't be.

James paced the garden path, too anxious to stand still as he awaited Jessica's arrival. He rehearsed what he wanted to say again and again in his mind. A confession of love, an assurance he wanted her just as she was, an apology for ever making her doubt.

Pebbles clattered, and he turned to see Jessica slip out a side door into the garden. Moonlight illuminated her face as she approached, highlighting the uncertainty in her eyes. Every word of his carefully planned speech vanished as he stood in awe of her.

"You look beautiful tonight, Jess," he said instead, voice hushed.

She ducked her head, a smile touching her lips. "Good evening to you, too, James."

He came forward, taking her hand without pause. "Come with me? Just behind the wall. Where no one will see."

Her nod was brief, but she didn't take her hand from him. He counted that a good sign as he led her as silently as he could down the path, through the stone archway, and to the other side of the wall. Once there, he put the stone wall against his back and held her hand, staring down at her.

Without a word, she returned his gaze, her eyes searching his in the darkness. He wished there was more than the light of the moon to see every detail of her upturned face. "I should tell you how lovely you are more often," he said without meaning to speak aloud. He'd had a speech prepared, dash it all. But his tongue didn't seem keen to use the prepared words. "Every time I've seen you, for years now, I've thought you beautiful."

She tilted her head to the side. "Even when I called you a scarecrow?" Mischief, familiar and new at the same time, glittered in her eyes.

"Even then," he admitted with an amused huff. "I was all elbows and knees, spindly arms and legs, and you already had that elegant, statuesque look about you."

She raised her eyebrows at him. "That isn't what you used to compare me to."

He sighed and shook his head. "I was a fool. I'm here to make amends for everything. If you'll let me."

Her gaze softened as the night air wrapped them in the scent of her gardens, roses and lavender and warm earth. "I was a silly little thing, too. Forgive me?"

"Always." He pulled her closer and gave a helpless shake of his head. "I have something I must tell you. Indeed, I'd planned out what I would say. But the moment you stepped into the moonlight, I forgot every word of it."

"Perhaps I can help." She took his other hand. "It all started with throwing a rock at my window."

He chuckled. "A pebble. The tiniest of pebbles."

"I had barely closed my window."

"Had you? It seems my timing was perfect." She stood so close. It would be an easy matter to forget words entirely and simply *show* her exactly how he felt. Yet she deserved all of the words he had at his disposal. Too bad they disappeared from his head the moment she stood near him. Best to take what few he had left and make a try for a confession.

"I came to tell you I'm in love with you. You always seem to know what I'm going to say before I say it, though. Besting me so often in our arguments. But in case you didn't realize it, I thought I had better make the matter clear. Even if you don't wish to marry, yet. I'd like to try to talk you into it. Eventually. My heart is yours, completely, if you will have it."

She gazed up at him, lips parted in surprise. Only his name escaped her in a whispered gasp. "James."

He pressed on. "I love you. I have for ages. Even before I loved you, or knew that I did, I thought you beautiful. Intelligent. Witty. Every good thing that you are, I admired it and wanted to tell you. My stupid pride kept me from saying a thing. I couldn't admit that you were wonderful, because I was afraid it meant you had bested me. And if you bested me, why would you ever want to draw swords with me again, my dearest enemy?"

"But you're my *only* enemy," she said, tears glistened in her eyes. Then she winced and laughed. "Oh, that came out all wrong."

He chuckled and drew her hands closer, resting them against his chest. "Then I surrender, Jess. Fully and completely. Everything I am, I surrender it to you. My heart is yours. My future is yours. Everything," he whispered again. "I lay it at your feet. And beg you to give me a chance, to prove I can be the husband you deserve. Someday."

The hard pebbles and soft grass crunched gently under her feet as she drew closer. James was keenly aware of each rustle of fabric and leaves, every quiet sound magnified in the intimate hush of the garden.

Jessica's eyes stayed on his. "What about my weaknesses, James?" she asked in a whisper. "Hysterics. Fits. Whatever you call them. They will not simply stop because you love me." He saw pain in her expression. And yearning.

He squeezed her hands. "If I could take them from you, I would. Only to make you happier and more at ease in the world. Yet they are part of who you are." He saw the hope in her eyes dim and he spoke with greater urgency. "I love you completely, every part of you, with my whole heart. Not in spite of your tender spirit, but because of it. You have a strength in you, a resilience that outshines any social unease. You will never face those trials alone again if you will let me be by your side. I will hold your hand when you need encouragement. I will spirit you away when you need the quiet. I will be a shield, a support, whatever you need. If you will let me."

As James gazed down at Jessica, he noticed how the

moonlight made her skin glow like marble, her eyes luminous dark pools that reflected the glittering stars overhead. He raised a hand to cradle her delicate face, brushing his thumb over the soft curve of her cheek.

Her smile appeared, tremulous but warm. "I cannot bear to be a burden to you, James."

"Burden?" he repeated, incredulously. "I will expect equal support, you know. Your struggles will be mine, and mine will be yours. Who knows my faults better than you do? I have no doubt you could go on and live a full, happy life without me. But I cannot say the same of myself. Let me try, at least give me a chance, to prove myself worthy of your trust and your love."

Jessica leaned into his touch, her rapid breath warm against his palm. He felt her quickened pulse beneath his fingertips. Her lips parted slightly in anticipation, and James's heart raced at her closeness. She hesitated only a moment before whispering, "You have them both. I love you, James."

Joy surged through James at her words. He bent closer, searching her eyes. "You mean it? Even though you've said you didn't want a husband—"

She placed her fingers on his lips, silencing him with the gentle touch. "I was terrified," she whispered. "What man would want me, knowing my faults? Knowing how broken I feel, I couldn't imagine anyone looking past it. And you haven't. You've accepted me instead. Helped me when you didn't have to. I am so relieved." Her eyes glimmered with tears, and he ached to soothe them away.

For the rest of his life, he'd dry her tears, hold her, calm her fears, and—more importantly—rejoice in all her accomplishments and triumphs. He swallowed back his emotion as best he could before speaking.

"I don't want to waste any more time, you know."

"You've always been very impatient," she agreed with a smug smile. "I admit, I feel the same."

"Then you will make me the happiest of men and consent to be my wife?"

Jessica smiled up at him with unconcealed love in her gaze. "Yes."

When their lips met at last, James sighed into the tender kiss, the floral scents and sounds of night enveloping them. He wanted to lose himself forever in this exquisite moment with his beloved. All his doubts vanished, and he would take whatever time she needed—despite his talk of impatience—to reassure her own.

As long as they were together, nothing else mattered.

EPILOGUE

The rest of summer passed pleasantly, each day bringing with it something Jessica looked forward to. The third and final day of the fair came and went in a blur. Jessica came only to sample treats in the morning, rested, and then went back that evening to sit with James and Catherine for the play. She laughed along with them at the antics of the characters and Puck, running about a forest and unable to tell each other how they felt.

A week later, she bid her cousins, uncle, and aunt farewell as they departed for their home north of York, bracing herself for the reactions that were sure to come when news spread of her and James's imminent courtship.

She had confided everything to Catherine the day after the conversation with James, his beautiful promises, her acceptance of his proposal. Though still concerned for them both, Catherine had vowed to stand by Jessica no matter what came.

"All I want is your happiness, dearest one," she'd said,

embracing Jessica tightly. "If James is who you truly want, then I will be there to support you. Both of you."

James had also spoken earnestly to Catherine, assuring her he would care for Jessica and help shield her from anything that distressed her.

"We will only enter society at a pace Jessica is comfortable with," he'd promised. "I will be by her side every step of the way." His parents had reassured her, too, that they would guide her, and she needn't do more than she was comfortable with.

The news that her father and brother would be her uncle's only heirs, thus eventually making Jessica the daughter and sister of future earls, hadn't hurt the baron's acceptance of his son's affections, though James insisted he wouldn't have stopped their courtship even if Jessica's situation hadn't changed.

Jessica's heart swelled thinking back on it all. Doubts still crept in occasionally, but James's unconditional love soothed them. She was ready to take this leap, to fight for the life she wanted with him. And they would begin with a wedding trip to York.

In the days prior to their wedding, James met Jessica at the kissing gate, Ottis usually at his side. But one particular morning, he came alone. His eyes glowed as she came to the kissing gate, but before she could step through, he met her there, with the boards and iron between them.

For a moment, they stood face to face in the intimate space, the gate framing them in that place between their homes. Jessica's heart quickened at their closeness, warmth blooming in her cheeks. She met James's gaze, reading the tender admiration and love shining there as he bent nearer.

The ingenious gate lived up to its name, she thought, as

James's kiss lingered sweetly on her lips. Then he held it open and allowed her through, offering her his arm. "I love you."

He said it so easily, every time he saw her after being apart. Whether it was for the space of a day or only a few hours.

"I love you, too," she responded, feeling both ridiculous and content at the same time. "What is it you wished to show me?"

He gave her a secretive grin and tilted his head. "You have to wait and see. But it's near the lake."

They walked together, arm-in-arm, and Jessica wanted nothing more than to keep moments like this forever in her memory. As they rounded the castle, the lake coming into view, she gave her betrothed a glance.

He caught it and raised his eyebrows. "I know that look. It's the one you wear when you've done something especially clever. Usually something I'll find out later. Like a frog in my pocket at church, or chickens in my bed, or—"

She laughed. "I promise, I haven't done anything like that. Recently." Jessica bit her lip when he gave her a disbelieving look, debating whether to confess her long-held secret to James. "Do you recall several years ago when Sir Hop mysteriously lost part of his leg?"

James chuckled. "Of course. No one ever discovered what happened to it. My mother still thinks I'm somehow to blame."

"Well..." Jessica took a deep breath. "I'm afraid I'm the culprit behind that particular disappearance."

James's eyes widened in surprise. "Really?" He blinked at her. "Why? What did you do with it?"

"It was meant to be a prank," Jessica admitted. "I had decided to borrow the leg and hide it someplace obscure. I thought it would be amusing to see your family search the castle high and low for the missing limb, and then I was going to either hide it in your room *after* it was searched or put it where it would have incriminated you."

"Minx," he said with a wide grin. "Those were your specialties. Doing things that would earn *me* the lecture."

"I know," she said with a laugh. "And I'm sorry."

"You're forgiven. But where did the leg end up?" His eyes glowed with curiosity.

She shook her head ruefully. "Unfortunately, my scheme didn't go as planned. I stayed the night with Catherine while your mother was away. After she fell asleep, I slipped away. I snuck into the armory and removed the leg. I tucked it under my cloak and hurried outside, to put it somewhere I could easily find later. I aimed for the boathouse. But I frightened myself, I suppose. I thought I heard someone following, and I tried to run. It was terribly dark, and I stumbled. The metal leg slipped from my grasp, rolled across the boat dock, into the water, and sank straight to the bottom."

James pressed a hand to his mouth, but his muffled laughter still escaped. "So that's why Sir Hop stands lopsided to this day. Poor old soldier. I always suspected you were behind his injury, but Catherine thought you would have confessed if responsible." His eyes suddenly widened. "Catherine doesn't know either, does she?"

"No. I didn't want her to get in trouble." Jessica sighed theatrically. "A failed prank and a sunken treasure. It seems silly now, but I was quite distraught at the time. Promise you'll keep my shocking confession just between us?"

James's eyes glinted with amusement. "Your secret is safe with me, Lady Thief." He nodded to the boathouse. "And if you will wait here, I'll retrieve the surprise."

She stood still, arms wrapped about herself as he went inside the boathouse. She looked out over the lake, her heart full. Everything would be all right. Lady Retford and her aunt would both help her learn to navigate Society, within the bounds of her personal comfort. Catherine would help, too. Most importantly, James would be there. Loving her through everything, and she would do the same for him.

He emerged from the boathouse with his arms wrapped around something black, white, and fluffy.

She gasped as he came closer and hurried to him, looking down into his arms where two dark eyes in a black and white furry face gazed back at her. A tiny pink tongue stuck out between sharp little teeth. "What do you have there?" she asked, voice soft so as not to startle the puppy.

James grinned at her. "I wanted to give you something special, something you always wanted but never asked for, to begin our adventure together." He passed the wiggly creature to Jessica. "Her mother is the best shepherd in the county, or so I'm told, so she'll certainly be able to keep you safe and sound."

"Oh, she's darling." Jessica cooed to the puppy as it wriggled in her arms, stretching to lick her chin. "She's mine?"

"Completely yours, to follow you about whenever you wish. Ottis likes her, by the by. But I thought she deserved to meet you on her own." He stood back and smiled at her, arms crossed and eyes soft. "You like her?"

"I adore her." Jessica cuddled the pup close. "I always wanted a dog of my own. Thank you." She smiled up at him and found him looking as though he'd never been happier. Overcome with emotion, with gratitude that her once enemy had become her beloved, Jessica went on tiptoes to kiss James soundly.

When their lips parted, she whispered, "Thank you."

James wrapped his arm around her, glancing from the castle to the dock. "Perhaps we ought to try to rescue Sir Hop's missing leg one of these days."

With her sparring partner by her side, she could venture forth, facing whatever came next. Who better to do it with than James? The doubts and fears would likely never fully fade. But with James's steadfast love to anchor her, she had found the courage within herself to follow her heart. Their lives would be richer and fuller together than either could be alone.

Come what may, as long as they had each other, they could conquer anything.

If you enjoyed this story of courtship at Castle Amoret, make certain you pick up the next book in the Castles & Courtship series, *Charming the Recluse* by Mindy Burbidge Strunk.

If you're looking for stories by Sally Britton, you can find more Regency romance in her Castle Clairvoir series.

THE CASTLES & COURTSHIP SERIES

An Amiable Foe by Jennie Goutet

To Know Miss May by Deborah M. Hathaway

A Heart to Keep by Ashtyn Newbold

A Noble Inheritance by Kasey Stockton

The Rules of Matchmaking by Rebecca Connolly

A Suitable Arrangement by Martha Keyes

An Engagement with the Enemy by Sally Britton

Charming the Recluse by Mindy Burbidge Strunk

ALSO BY SALLY BRITTON

Castle Clairvoir Romances:

A Duchess for the Duke | Mr. Gardiner and the Governess

A Companion for the Count | Sir Andrew and the Authoress

Lord Farleigh and Miss Frost

The Inglewood Series:

Rescuing Lord Inglewood | Discovering Grace

Saving Miss Everly | Engaging Sir Isaac

Reforming Lord Neil

The Devoted Hearts Series:

Martha's Patience | The Social Tutor

The Gentleman Physician | His Bluestocking Bride

The Earl and His Lady | Miss Devon's Choice

Courting the Vicar's Daughter | Penny's Yuletide Wish

Stand Alone Regency Romances:

The Captain and Miss Winter | His Unexpected Heiress

A Haunting at Havenwood | Her Unsuitable Match

An Unsuitable Suitor | A Mistletoe Mismatch

Hearts of Arizona Series:

Silver Dollar Duke | Copper for the Countess | A Lady's Heart of Gold

ABOUT THE AUTHOR

I'm Sally Britton, and I live in Oklahoma with my husband and our four incredible children. Our household is complete with two Australian Shepherds, a Queen Tabby Cat, and our Ball Python named Basil.

I began my writing journey in my teenage years, crafting my first story on my mother's electric typewriter at the age of fourteen. Immersing myself in the works of authors like Jane Austen, Louisa May Alcott, and Lucy Maud Montgomery, I felt drawn to create stories set in the elegant and complex worlds of centuries past. Among these tales, my favorite moments were always the declarations of love by the heroines, and it became evident that all of my books would center around these romantic themes.

In 2007, I earned my bachelor's degree in English with a focus on British literature. Not long after, I met and married my husband, and together we've been building our own happily ever after.

The quote, "What is done in love is done well," attributed to Vincent Van Gogh, has become my personal motto. It guides both my life and the stories I write. I believe in crafting narratives where expressing love is an act of bravery, and where kindness consistently emerges as the right choice.

If you'd like to connect with me and stay updated, you can

visit my website at AuthorSallyBritton.com. I also actively engage with readers on Instagram (@authorsallybritton) and have a fan group on Facebook.

Made in United States
North Haven, CT
03 October 2023

42301864R00171